SCAR

A NOVEL BY MICHAEL COLE

SEVERED PRESS
HOBART TASMANIA

SCAR

CHAPTER 1

"I'll say again. If our shareholders like what they see, you will be immediately elevated to Vice President of Skomal Corp. And, I think I can confidently say that they'll love him. So much so, that your department will triple in size, as well as your funding. Not to mention your salary. So, I suppose I should congratulate you in advance, Dr. Zoller."

That conversation replayed in her mind on a loop.

Dr. Olivia Zoller stared at the reflection in her bathroom mirror. She had spent a full day on the state-of-the-art floating laboratory, constructed by Skomal Corp. The living quarters were completely underwater, giving her a mild feeling of entrapment, as though she was in the Mariana Trench. Luckily, she was only seventy-feet deep as opposed to seven miles.

She could hear faint echoes from above. The lab crew were assembling at the dock, ready to greet their new arrival. The boat must've radioed that they were within sight. It was almost time for the transfer. In twenty minutes, Scar would be placed within his pen, where he would live for the remainder of his expected thirty-year lifespan. It was just a matter of getting him in there.

They had gotten this far with no problems. Just a little more to go, then she could shove her success in the faces of those damn professors at the Genetics Research Institute in New York. If she had a penny for every time she was told she couldn't successfully harvest the DNA of extinct species, she wouldn't need to become a VP to be rich.

It was about time to head up to the surface pad.

Olivia brushed her short, dark hair back, then straightened the left shoulder edges of her blouse. This was the moment she wanted her shark tattoo visible. The black, twisting image 'swam' alongside a pinkish-white marking—the scar that started her fascination with sharks. The attack which claimed her brother's life, and nearly hers as well, had only fueled a desire to learn more about these fascinating creatures. It was a long twenty-five year road from that moment until now. No longer was she the helpless twelve-year old. She was the head of the genetics department in Skomal Corp, and she had done the impossible. She had extracted the DNA of the extinct Megalodon shark and combined it with that of the present day great white. So what if it severed her relationship with her parents? So what if two marriages faltered because of her obsession? Like the professors in New York, she'd be laughing in their faces within a few days.

First, it was time to get Scar into his pen.

Olivia gave one last glance at the future Vice President, then exited her private restroom. She gathered her radio and cell phone, and most importantly, her ID badge, then hurried out into the passageway. Halfway between her quarters and the nearest stairwell, a voice blasted through her receiver.

"Dr. Zoller?" It was the head of Operations.

"Go ahead."

"We've got eyes on the Jerimiah. She's about a mile off Pen Four." His voice echoed deep into the series of steel passageways.

"Copy that. Direct him north to Pen Six. We don't want to load the specimen into Four."

"Got it. Pen Six."

Not that she personally cared, but the laboratory was originally built for training dolphins for military applications. Within the next month, the pens would be housing killer whales, dolphins, as well as a few different species of shark. And somewhere through the grapevine, she had heard that her genetic research might come into play. Of course, the shareholders would have to get a look at Scar first, and the research that went into creating him.

Olivia proceeded up the stairwell. Her ears popped as she ascended thirty feet. Of course, she could've taken the elevator, but something about being trapped in that box underwater didn't sit well with her.

The stairway led Olivia up to Delta Platform on the floating laboratory. She swung the door open and took in the salty smell of the ocean. She was on the north side of the laboratory. In front of her was a large pool, extending nearly a hundred-and-fifty feet long and a hundred feet wide, otherwise known as Pen Six. It was one of eight pens circling the massive structure.

When she first arrived by helicopter, she would've described the facility as a flower on the verge of blooming. The 'blossom' of this flower was the center structure, where the engineering and power stations were located, as well as watch towers, helicopter stations, and emergency escape crafts were stored. Directly below were the labs, crew quarters, kitchen, and storage areas. Extending on all sides from the center were eight platforms, acting as the 'sepals' for the flower. Each platform contained a holding pen, designed for different species of marine animal. Already, Dr. Muniz had his bottlenose dolphins delivered to Pen Three, soon to be experimented for Navy research. In one of these pens, he had planned for a killer whale to be housed. The rest of the specimens were just rumors, but she was aware that they were all natural species. The only genetic hybrid was her creation.

And there it was, a half mile in the distance. She could see the *Jerimiah* circling in from the left, directed to line up with Pen Six for transfer as directed by Operations. She saw the flash of lights to her left as the control tower operator began opening the exterior gates.

The section of perimeter fence was as wide as the pool, leaving only three feet of steel between the pen and the ocean. The plan would be for the ship to dock in the open section. Once in place, a crane equipped with a heavy duty harness would transfer the specimen from the holding tank into the pen.

Metal gears whirred loudly as a section of fence separated from its neighbors. Gears on railings beneath the waterline brought the fence back twelve inches, then shifted it to the right, behind the next section. If Dr. Muniz took anything seriously around here, it was security. Nothing was getting in or out as long as those fences were secure.

The *Jerimiah* slowed its approach, with men on the bow deck watching to make sure they were lined up perfectly. She could hear the water swishing in the pool at the center of the ship's deck. Cables were tossed down to help secure the ship to the facility during transfer. Meanwhile, the Captain stepped to the bow rail.

"Good evening, Dr. Zoller," he said. His accent was Belgian, his skin a dark brown and lined with wrinkles.

"What's the status on the specimen?" she replied, not bothering with greetings.

"Alert," he answered. She saw the look in his eyes before he turned away. *Just another self-important bitch on her high horse.* So what if she was? She didn't get to her position by kissing ass and settling for second like others she knew.

"I need more than that," she said. "What are its vitals? Heart rate, blood pressure, movement."

"I know what vitals are," the Captain replied, visibly irritated with her. "You wanna know? It killed two of my crew! It came right out of the water and pulled them back in. We had to shock it into submission."

"Then just sedate the thing and hook a pump to it," she stated. The Captain scoffed. He just told this woman that two of his crew were recently slaughtered, and to her, it was no more than...mere inconvenience? They were just a few sentences into this conversation, and already he had checked out. He just wanted to collect his money, then start writing letters to the spouse of the married crewmember. The other was single with no family, which made it the slightest bit easier.

First, he had to deal with this legend-in-her-own-mind, deliver the shark, and collect his funds.

"We tried sedating it," he said. "It's difficult to penetrate its skin. And no way in hell am I ordering a crewman into the pool to attach a pump to its mouth."

Olivia watched as crewmembers moved along the deck, some of which carried cannisters in their hands.

"We're going to need to sedate it in order to transfer it," she said.

"I'm well aware. We've tried sticking it in the mouth, but it just comes after us. My men have to keep rushing back while others hit it with electrifying rods to keep it from clearing the edge of the pool. So, I'm asking you for your advice."

"Have you tried injecting bait with sedative?"

"No. I didn't know that would work."

"It'll take longer, but it will work. Get one of the tunas you use to feed it, and load it with twenty-two milliliters of xylazine. Hurry up."

The Captain didn't waste time arguing. He directed his crew to collect the supplies. They already had the xylazine on deck, so all they needed was the fish. A couple of minutes later, three crew members dragged a hundred-pound tuna onto the deck. They strapped it to a crane, then loaded it with the sedative.

The creature splashed in its pool. Its eyes were red, like it was born out of some satanic ritual. The Captain had heard that somehow the genetic crossover had screwed with the fish's color and skin texture, but going by how evil it was, he was sure Satan had his hand in it somewhere.

The crane hovered the dead tuna over the pool. The men stayed several yards beyond its edge. Many of them had seen how the fish had breached the water and landed its upper body on the deck. That was when the first victim found himself in its jaws. His screams still echoed in their memories. Hours later, during a feeding, it happened again. The second victim wasn't even standing at the edge. He was at least six feet back, but the shark still got him, then thrashed its body back into the pool. Now, nobody was willing to go withing fifteen feet of the pool.

The crane operator lowered the tuna into the water. Its head generated ripples.

The fish swam in a tight circle, then turned its head toward the meat. It eyed the gift with its red eyes, then turned away. The crane operator swung the fish back and forth, trying to trick the fish into thinking it was alive. But there was no way for him to mimic a heartbeat, and that was what the tuna was lacking.

The fish wanted LIVE prey.

"What's going on, Captain?" Olivia grunted. She stood on the surface pad, arms crossed, eyes narrowed forming an impatient glare. The Captain never wanted to punch a woman in his life, but this Dr. Olivia Zoller was walking that fine line.

"It's not taking the bait," he said.

"Have you tried moving the fish? Is there blood?"

"Believe me, there's been plenty of blood in the ten hours it's been on this ship," he replied. He sucked in a breath, keeping himself from letting loose a hail of profanities. After a sharp exhale, he looked to Olivia again. "It looked right at it. I don't think it's interested."

"Alright," Olivia said. "There's something else we can try. I have a particular sedative that we can put into the pool. The shark will take it in through his gills as he swims about. It shouldn't take too long to take effect." She pulled her radio from her pocket and switched the frequency to support staff below. "Need two containers of 2-phenoxyethanel, stat."

"On our way," the lab assistant said.

Olivia crossed her arms again and waited. Finally, two men in lab coats arrived, carrying heavy white buckets. Olivia pointed to the vessel, directing them to pass the sedatives to the crew. The assistants passed the bucket up to the crew members who had climbed down to the dock. They tied a line around the bucket, then signaled for other crew on top to hoist it up onto the main deck.

The Captain gazed at the clear, oily liquid in the two buckets, then glanced back at Olivia.

"So...just toss it in?"

"Yes," Olivia said, her arms coming partly uncrossed. *Not hard to figure out, you brainless tool.* He read that thought. The woman had a stick up her ass.

He glanced over at two nervous crewmen, who waited with the buckets.

"Go ahead. Be quick, and be careful."

They looked at each other, saw the same nervous expression, then slowly moved for the pool. At six feet, they saw the dorsal fin. It was blue in color. They would've thought of it as beautiful had they not known better—or had seen its hideous face. A large red scar crossed its right eye, a gift from its genetic brethren whom it had slaughtered during infanthood.

They held back while it circled toward them. For a moment, they were ready to drop the buckets and take off running, especially when its nose tilted up at them. The shark turned at the nearest corner, then proceeded to travel along the next wall.

With a sigh of relief, they hurried to the edge and launched the colorless contents into the pool. The circulatory system mixed the sedative in with the rest of the water, ensuring that the shark did not avoid its dose.

"Alright. It's in," the Captain said.

"Keep observing," Olivia said. "It'll slow to a stop. When that happens, you must act quickly."

The crew already had the second crane arm in position. Attached to it were several thick straps designed for carrying over ten thousand pounds. Two divers were in position to get the straps around the fish once it succumbed to the sedation. Neither of them looked eager to approach the edge, let alone dip into that water.

It took just over a minute for the fish to slow to a stop. The divers braved the edge of the pool. It turned over to its left and sank, its pectoral fin pointing skyward.

"Alright, go now!" the Captain ordered. He sympathized with their concerns, but had to keep his tone strict. The longer they waited, the worse it would be. They hit the water simultaneously, followed immediately by the crane cable. They grabbed hold of the straps and guided it down to the fish.

For a moment, they hesitated. Even unconscious, it looked like it would snatch them up at any moment. Its teeth were over two-inches long and serrated. Its belly was grey, contrasting with its blue dorsal side. That scar was blood red, as were those eyes.

Just looking at the beast, it was obvious that nature didn't intend it for this world.

The less they had to see it, the better. They hurried to get the straps around it. They secured the metal clips and tightened the slack. One strap went around its neck and gills, another over its belly, and a third around its tail.

A sudden twitch caused them to back away. The shark's entire body had jolted, as though hit with a spark of electricity. They froze instinctively, not realizing their rapidly beating hearts would've been more than enough to attract it. The shark settled again, completely still.

"Come on! Let's go!" the Captain said. Both divers heard his voice through their earpieces, then quickly went for the surface. The crew cheered for them as they came out of the pool unscathed. The Captain thanked the men for their bravery, then waved to the crane operator. "Alright. Let's get it over there before it suffocates." *Not that it would bother me, personally.*

The crane hoisted the fish from the pool. All hands gazed at its limp, thirty-two foot body. Its jaw hung slack, giving some a view to the back of its throat. One crewmember turned to vomit—he saw an article of clothing in its teeth, worn by one of its victims.

The crane lifted it ten feet over the deck, then extended to the front of the boat. Its hydraulic arm protruded, doubling its length to reach the pool.

Finally, the creature cleared the bow.

"Thank God," the Captain muttered. It was no longer on his ship.

"Did I just see it move?" one crewmember asked.

"I don't think—holy shit, I think it *did* move," another replied. The Captain watched closely. The tail was quivering, and not from the motion of the crane. The jaw was no longer slack. Was the damn thing already coming out of its coma?

He watched it lift its head slightly, then extend its jaws. It needed water, but received nothing but useless air. It was pissed-off and panicking.

"Jesus. Hurry up and get it across!" he shouted.

On the surface platform, Olivia was backing up in shock. Even she had not anticipated that her creation would awaken after just a few minutes. She had instructed her crew to prepare pumps into its mouth upon arrival, which would last at least an hour. But by the looks of it, it wouldn't need them.

She thought of its feeding patterns and its increased metabolism. That had to be the cause. Either way, it wouldn't matter as long as they got it secured in the pen.

Scar awoke with a vengeance. Now, it was thrashing its entire body like a bass on a fishing line. Only, this fish had enough power in a single swing of its tail to cave in a car.

The crane whined, the arm juddering uncontrollably. The operator pressed the levers to get the damn thing in. With a massive twist, the shark threw its body downward. Everyone on board the ship and surface platform heard the metal *cling* of a clip breaking loose. The strap around the shark's neck fell free.

With greater range of motion, it swung its upper body. It bit at the air, its gums as red as its eyes. The arm lowered, the hydraulics squealing under the pressure of combined weight and ferocity.

They heard the snapping of tether and metal, which led to the center strap falling free. It took minimal effort for the third to give way. Scar smashed down onto the pad, its head and tail whipping every which way. Screams filled the air as its caudal fin smacked one of the lab assistants with the report of a gunshot. The impact launched the man right into the hull of the boat, where his skull imploded into red mush.

The shark could taste the mist of nearby saltwater. It needed to swim as urgently as it needed to feed. Luckily, both were in the same direction.

It flapped its body toward the edge, its jaws finding the fallen corpse of the lab tech. Even while suffocating, it didn't hesitate to sink its teeth into his body.

"Shut the gate!" Olivia screamed.

"We can't!" the operator yelled. "The ship is in the way. We won't be able to close it."

"Captain! Back your ship up!"

But it was too late. The shark wiggled its body like a snake, then fell head-first over the side. A tremendous splash swept the platform, turning red as it mixed with the assistant's blood. Olivia never even gave it a glance. She dashed to the edge, just in time to see Scar darting beneath the surface.

For the first time since she entered the bio-tech lab at nineteen, she was flabbergasted. Back then, she had lost her sponsorship due to a disagreement with a fellow student which, due to bad judgement, turned physical. Only with the grace of another sponsor, was she able to get back into the program.

This time, her judgement had failed her on predicting the ease of transferring the fish. She had assured the CEO that it would be a simple process, and that his company would thrive based on the research she would present to the board of directors. Now, she may as well have brought him a tub of minnows. She had nothing.

The crew of both the station and ship stood in stunned silence. All at once, they absorbed the reality of what they had just witnessed.

Scar had escaped, and was free to roam the ocean—and kill at his leisure!

CHAPTER 2

"Dr. Zoller, I don't think I could possibly understate my disappointment," Victor Skomal said.

Olivia's private quarters suddenly felt twenty degrees colder, and ten feet smaller. She didn't know how to respond. She was still reeling from the loss. Everything was going so well, then in the blink of an eye, *snap!* The creature escaped, and was now loose to roam the open sea.

She stared at the floor, too humiliated to look straight into the call monitor.

"Doctor, you're already treading on thin ice for your failure and poor judgement. I'm already out millions of dollars due to your incompetence. At *least* grant me the courtesy of looking me in the eye when I speak to you."

The bastard spoke like the many others who thought they owned her. Her father. Her ex-husband. Her in-laws. The professors in New York, as well as her sponsors. She had heard some say she was entitled. In her mind, they needed *her* more than she needed them. After all, who else had successfully crossed the genes of different species?

But those thoughts meant nothing to Skomal. Only money. Money came from results. And the only results that counted were the ones he could show to his investors. Right now, all he had was a holding pen, which was now as empty as the promises he had made to the people due to arrive.

She turned her head upward and looked into the screen. At its center was Victor Skomal. His face was tense with anger, giving his crooked nose a more sinister appearance. He was a skinny man, not one known for physical strength, but certainly not one to be taken advantage of. He loosened his tie with his finger, then leaned slightly toward the camera.

"Without that shark, I might not have any use for you," he said. Olivia wanted to blast out of her seat and knock the daylights out of him. *Use for you.* Misogynistic prick. She'd seen the way he was at cocktail parties, with a woman on each arm, and another two that followed.

"Its escape had nothing to do with my lab skills," she said. "I can create more hybrids. We have the technology and resources. We can grow a new specimen. I just need a little time."

"Time is something we do not have," Skomal declared. "I have investors coming to inspect within the next three days. I'm no scientist, but I seem to recall it taking weeks before properly generating a new embryo."

"We can show them the footage," she said.

"Footage means nothing without the final result. People like these need to see the specimen in the flesh. And our only product is now swimming out there in the open ocean."

"I had nothing to do with its escape," she replied defensively. "The equipment was that of the contractors. It clearly wasn't rated for the shark's weight."

"The only thing I despise more than a failure who's cost me a lot of money is a *liar* who's cost me a lot of money," Skomal growled. "I've already spoken to head of operations on that facility. He stated that it was not the weight of the shark, but its intense strength and reaction to the sedative that caused it to break free."

Olivia tensed. Head of operations—she wished she knew who he was. Another man who stood in the way of her progress.

"Mr. Skomal, there is good news. I implanted a tracker on Scar. I've been keeping track of his movements. He's heading for the East Coast. If you would let me lead a team, we can catch him and bring him back to the facility. We have the aquatic medical boat at the Virginia facility. I can have it equipped and ready to go within the next couple of hours."

To her dismay, the CEO shook his head.

"But sir?" She hated using that word, especially in that tone. "I can do it!"

"You can do it with your own money and resources. Right now, I need to prepare the other specimens that are coming in. If all else fails, we can rely on our original cover story of using this facility as a large marine animal hospital. We can easily gain public support, and I have *competent* staff who are heading over there right now."

Olivia inhaled deeply and digested his words. After fighting through the bitterness, she asked, "And if I successfully bring Scar back here?"

"Then we proceed with our original deal. I'll even be nice enough to recompensate you for your efforts. But only if you bring that shark back, alive, and within the next seventy-two hours. Until then, I don't know anything about it. No shark was engineered in my labs. No shark was being transported to my facility. *Especially* not a shark that may potentially be responsible for the loss of several civilian lives within the next few days."

Olivia's pulse quickened. That answer was somewhat better than what she feared. Now to brace for the worst…

"And if I fail?"

"Then your chances of being Vice President will be as empty as that pen," Skomal replied. He reached for something behind the camera. The image wobbled slightly. He was about to end the call. "Seventy-two hours. Do what you need to do, but keep my name out of it, unless it's in a phone call stating you're delivering it."

There were no goodbyes or well wishes. The image turned to black.

"You want a shark? I'll give you ten thousand sharks," Olivia muttered, bitterly. There was no time to sulk. She had to get to work fast.

She found the phone and dialed the control room operator. As the line rang, she scrolled down the contact list on her personal phone, settling on the name of *Roark*. Hopefully, he would be available. And willing. She'd worry about that next.

"Operations."

"This is Dr. Zoller. Get me a chopper ready. Stat. I need to go to Smithfield, Virginia, now."

CHAPTER 3

Scar had traveled a hundred miles in just a few short hours. Time and distance had no meaning to him; just the insatiable urge to feed. Instinct spoke to him like a mentor, guiding him west toward shallower waters. Prey was sparse in the open ocean, and his biological design prevented him from traveling into the crushing depths. His liver provided aid to keep him afloat, though the current of life was gifted from the nonstop motions of his caudal fin.

Scar could sense that he was entering populated waters. His lateral line picked up the motions of potential prey moving miles about. The seafloor was now visible where it swam. Before, it was nothing but black abyss, with some dark green and blue colors where the sun's particles scattered.

The effort of carrying his massive bulk compounded his need for sustenance. Scar never questioned why he was so hungry so often, as he didn't have the mental capacity. He didn't care about the 'whys' of the world. He didn't question his existence. He didn't even know he was the only one of his kind. And even if he did, he wouldn't care.

All that mattered was survival, and a violent need to slaughter any living creature that came within reach.

His first victim was a grouper. The fish was adolescent, only measuring at three feet. Still, small fish was better than none. It had recently fed on a few crustaceans along the seabed, and was content with spending the next several hours floating near the surface. It spotted the enormous shark, its presence like a torpedo being fired into enemy waters.

Fish scattered, most of them too slow to avoid the wrath that was entering their ecosystem. Luckily for them, Scar had already settled on a target. With a swing of its tail, the shark jetted for the fleeing grouper. Teeth punched through its back and stomach, expelling thick clouds of blood. Scar shook his head violently, his serrated teeth shredding the flesh of his prey. With one final jerk, he split the dying grouper in two. Guts, intestines, and bits of its previous meal scattered in a red mist, only to be scooped up by the great shark.

He swallowed and pressed on. He needed more. Already, his digestive system was getting to work on the grouper. The human he had consumed earlier had already been dissolved down to its skeleton, which too, was breaking down into a gel. Whatever was left would be expelled within the next hour or so.

Scar swam for another quarter mile. He came across bright reefs, teeming with all kinds of fish, as well as other species of sharks. To him, they were just another item on the menu.

He spotted a whitetip reef shark gliding along the bottom. It was only a few hundred feet deep here, the sun's rays bouncing off the rock and coral. The whitetip was not initially concerned about the presence of the larger fish, until it suddenly started closing in. The whitetip fluttered its tail to run, but like the grouper, it was no match for the great burst of speed demonstrated by Scar.

Mighty jaws clamped down on the whitetip's back. Blood and soot mixed together in an unsightly cloud. Scar tightened his grip, cutting his teeth deeper and deeper, then slammed the much smaller shark into the reef. The whitetip broke away, rolling on the sea bottom like a barrel. Its entire back, including its dorsal fin, was torn away, leaving a perfect oval shape granting access to all the organs inside. Scar swallowed, then bit down on the rest, taking in every last molecule he could.

The vibrations of the struggle traveled through the water like shockwaves. Fish scattered for their lives. Cephalopods and crustaceans scurried for their burrows. What was once a vibrant city of life had now become a vacant landscape, swept by an ambiance of fear.

Scar was partly satisfied. And even if he was fully satisfied, there would still be his desire to kill. No amount of consumption would quell that hunger. He searched the reef for more. A few fish zipped by, one of which accidentally veered too close. It exploded into a red mist, its body shredded by those powerful teeth. Scar continued.

The fish continued to keep their distance, jetting several yards to avoid the giant. The shark would easily outrun them, but each fish was so small, they weren't quite worth the effort, unless he was starving. He wanted larger prey to kill. Something to sink his teeth into. Many of the larger fish and sharks had already vacated, their vibrations blended with the huge collection of motion within the reef.

Ironically, it was one of the most intelligent species that had dared to come within reach.

A common octopus, with a mantle roughly four feet in length, emerged from its cave. It had sensed the motion of a fleeing crab scurrying nearby, and had the confidence that it could snatch it up with its many tentacles and drag it back to its lair. It had successfully outwitted other sharks in their attempts to bite it, and had no reason to suspect it couldn't outwit the grey-bellied creature gliding above.

Even the smartest of beings make mistakes. Even fatal mistakes.

Within a moment, the shark closed the hundred foot distance and impaled the octopus with its teeth. Blue blood and purple ink burst from the soft, leathery tissue. The teeth sawed the cephalopod, ripping away tentacles and chunks of tissue as though it were cotton. All that remained was blood and ink, and a scurrying crab who successfully found its way into a little crevice.

Scar rose to the surface. The floodgates had opened, and he was on a killing spree that would never be satisfied. He didn't feel glee from success or frustration from failure. His brain was like a computer, and it was programmed to kill.

After picking off a few more unfortunate fish, Scar continued west where he sensed several vibrations along the surface. These did not sound like anything created from any sea life he had been exposed to. No, this was mechanical. Artificial, like the machines used by the humans that created it. Scar didn't analyze what these sounds were beyond the fact that they were caused by humans. And humans were food.

Next came distortions. Several objects were gliding across the water in tight circles. They were fast, faster than itself, but such a thing wouldn't stop Scar. He was able to close the distance while the objects circled about, unaware of his presence. His impeccable eyesight, better than any of his natural born cousins, could see the fleshy legs of the human piloting the craft. His instinct to kill surged through his brain, and he ascended.

"Oh yeah!" Troy Beeman shouted. He had one hand on the jet ski handle, with another high up in the air, clutching a half-empty whiskey bottle. It was his second one for the afternoon. Thirty minutes prior, it was unopened. He completed another sharp turn, squinting as ocean mist sprayed his face. "Whoa!"

"You ride that thing like my ol' lady!" Randy shouted. He was several yards in front of Troy, his voice lost in the roar of the engine and spraying of water. Like his buddy, he chugged a bottle as he raced along the water.

Even with his blurred vision, he could see the atoll a few hundred meters to the west. It was basically a big rock sticking out of the water a mile and a half from the northeast corner of Cross Point. It was only a hundred feet or so in diameter, its shores mostly made of rock except for a sandy area on the west side, and a small dock on the south. Two trees grew from its center, giving it a slight cartoonish appearance.

A few other jet skis skidded a few yards from its shores, not too far from the motor yacht docked at the south side.

Both men took great pleasure in tormenting the family that decided to have their picnic on the tiny island. The mother and father set up the blanket under the trees, the former mainly focused on the three-year old. Already, the father was hotheaded from two confrontations with the immature drinkers. They skidded past their yacht repeatedly on their way in.

The husband had prepped one of the skis, his face red with anger. The prick was actually gonna go after them. What he would do if he caught them, they had no idea. But to Troy and Randy, that's what made it so funny.

The two teenage kids were jetting water on the skis. Hard to believe their mother gave birth to them, not to mention had a toddler. Maybe kids from a previous marriage? Troy didn't think so, based on the interactions he witnessed between them. And she was definitely old enough—though that didn't mean she wasn't hot!

The booze rushed to his head and the blood down to his groin, spurring Troy to get another look at the hot mamma in her swimsuit. Randy followed right behind, his mindset the same.

The teenagers turned their heads to the right, then gasped as the two thirty-somethings whipped between them. They spun out of control, their faces splashed by the intense jets of water.

"Haha!" Troy shouted. He saw the parents standing up, the husband now purple with anger. But he wasn't focused on him, but the one beside him. "Great tits, babe!"

"Go freestyle! Take off your top!" Randy shouted. They veered to the right just in time to avoid crashing against the rocks, then zipped around to the north side of the island. The father watched with clenched fists as they ventured off into the distance.

"It's okay," the wife said. This irritated him more. She was actually amused! Hot air blasted from his nostrils. For the next several seconds, he cooled off. He figured he couldn't blame her. They were both in their mid-forties, and compliments on their physical appearance didn't come quite as often. Though, in his eyes, she could've passed for someone in her thirties.

"I'm just getting sick of those pricks," he grumbled.

"Don't pay attention to them," his wife said. She was always the laid back one of the group. She leaned in and whispered, as to not be heard by the toddler. "Pay attention to these." She pressed her chest to his. That worked in settling his mood.

"Oh god, Mom!" their daughter screamed. She and her brother roared their jet skis again, both disgusted at the display of their parents, who laughed hysterically at the misery they caused.

Troy and Randy continued north, chugging their whiskey as they went. After zipping a few hundred meters, they angled back, then lashed the water in tight circles. They cheered and whooped, now almost fully drunk.

Troy wobbled in his seat. He chucked the empty whiskey bottle, then reached into his nylon bag for another. His hand slipped, and he nearly teetered into the thrashing waves.

"Whoa!" he shouted, correcting his posture. He could hear Randy laughing at his near-misfortune, oblivious to the reality that had Troy fallen, he'd have ended up splattered against the front of his jet ski.

Troy held up a middle finger and proceeded to bank again. He thought about making another pass at the hot lady. Then again, he would risk angering her husband beyond the breaking point...

Screw it. Let's do it. Since when did pissing people off worry him?

He let go of the handlebars, and raised his hands high. After making a sexual gesture with his fingers, he pointed at the atoll, then grabbed the controls and turned south.

"Woohoo!" Randy whooped. They were closing in, though still a bit wide to the left side. They started to circle, lining up with the side of the dock. It was a thousand feet off and closing.

Troy was so focused on trying to spot the woman, that he never noticed the torpedo shape rising in front of him. The resulting eruption of water, however, was impossible to miss, as was the gaping mouthful of razor-shape teeth that engulfed him.

Scar broke the surface, his chin smashing the front of the jet ski. His jaws snapped shut over the human's trunk. Arms and legs thrashed as the teeth plunged along his center. Scar tasted the blood. It was warmer than fish and squid. As quickly as he appeared, he disappeared under the waves, along with the battered jet ski.

Randy screamed in horror after seeing the enormous jaws and fin, and the dying body of his friend flaying about. The crescent-shaped tail had barely missed him as the thing plunged back down.

"Oh god!" he shouted. "Oh god! Oh fuck! Jesus! God!" He looked back to see if the thing was after him. His vision was blurred by booze and sea water. There was nothing but ocean and froth. No Troy and no jet ski.

He heard new screams, then other motors. He whipped back around. The kids! They barely zipped out of the way of the insane drunkard as he sped toward the island at ninety-two miles per hour. Up ahead was a bunch of rocks, and two panicking parents.

He banked to the right, avoiding the shore, and putting himself into the side of the yacht. The jet ski hit the bow, flinging its operator overhead. It had catapulted him high, the momentum causing him to summersault in midair. Upside down, the back of his head and shoulders struck the gunwale.

"Jesus!" the husband shouted, watching the man plummet into the water on the other side of the boat. He ripped off his shirt and raced across the shore, ready to save the man whom he was about to strangle minutes ago.

The drunkard sank below the water. He leapt in, already waist deep. Luckily, the water was clear. He grabbed the man by the tank top and dragged him onto the shore.

"Kids, bring it in, please," the wife said, barely keeping herself from hysterics. The two teenagers slowly brought their jet skis around the stern of the yacht. As they approached, they gazed in awe at the huge crease in the hull, and the water that was now seeping inside.

"Holy shit," the boy said.

"Watch your language," their mother said. She checked on the three-year old, who had hardly noticed any of the chaos. He was just busy playing with his Legos.

She rushed to help drag the man on shore. "Is he alive?" Her husband checked for a pulse.

"Yes, but he's bleeding badly." He looked up and saw the damage to his yacht. The hull was badly breached, and there was no way to tell how much water was getting in. "We're never getting back to the island. Call the Sheriff." She rushed for the blanket and found her purse. Her hand dug around until it found the smartphone.

As she dialed 9-1-1, she noticed the kids watching the water.

"Where's the other one?" one of them asked. She glanced out into the ocean. There was no other jet skier to be seen.

"I—I have no idea," she said.

"9-1-1, what's your emergency?"

"Uh, hi! Please send help. We're on the atoll. We have an injured man here. He crashed his jet ski into our boat…"

CHAPTER 4

Located right in-between Smith Island and Virginia Beach was Cross Point, accurately named for its geological location. A seven-mile in diameter mass, housing roughly one-thousand residents, the island was thirty miles east of the Chesapeake Bay Bridge. Like much of the East Coast, the island proved to be a major attraction, home to some of the best fishing in the state. Two years in a row, record-sized Atlantic Marlin were measured at the south harbor. Charting season was at its peak, with local fishermen taking eager mainlanders out to bag the big one. Some knew what they were doing, others had no clue, and it was easy to tell the difference. But as long as they had the coin, the locals paid no mind to it.

It was Mid-July, and the population had ballooned to five thousand. The north and west beaches were crammed with vacationers ecstatic to swim, surf, fish, and sunbathe. A few thousand feet beyond, paddleboats, skis, and parasailers filled the horizon. After eight in the morning, one could not look out to the ocean without seeing some kind of activity.

For Sheriff Nick Piatt, that was one of the best parts of the summer. In his three years as Sheriff, and the eight he served as a Deputy, it never failed to amuse him how clumsy people could be. He had witnessed enough falls, flips, malfunctions, and just plain dumb moments to write a television show. And it was hilarious, as long as it didn't end in serious injury. Luckily, that rarely happened, at least nothing more serious than a few broken bones. And usually, judging by the clumsy and ridiculous behavior leading up to it, those injuries were karma at its finest.

Nick drove in his police issue Ford F-250. On its side were the words *Cross Point Island Sheriff's Department.* He cruised along North Beach, watching the vast activity taking place along the two-mile stretch. People were moving about like ants. The air was abounding with the aroma of delicious food. It was lunchtime, and like a chemical reaction, those aromas triggered a gurgling in his stomach. There was too much to choose from: hot dogs; burgers; chili…bad idea on that one. He'd done that before, which triggered another bodily need—right as an All-Units call came in.

The one time some idiot tried barbequing with a propane grill on his boat, while his companion was reeling in an eight-hundred foot marlin that spent more time in the air than the water. That last leap ended up onto the deck. Needless to say, that fish…and the boat, got barbequed before the hook even came out.

That was a long two hours.

"No, no—gotta eat light," he told himself. Just the thought of it seemed depressing. He had a salad and a fillet of salmon in the fridge back in the office. But it was summer, damn it! He wanted real meat! A quarter-pounder was what the heart, and stomach, desired. And the temptation was winning him over.

He continued west, and started gazing at the various bar & grills. He passed Master Chef Joel's restaurant. Good food, but WAY overpriced. Next, was Abby Alverez's Fish Fry. Nick liked fish, but he'd been eating a lot of it for his diet, and was starting to grow sick of it.

He noticed something as he passed the restaurant. There was a small lot a few dozen yards down for the lifeguards to park. There were two parking spaces marked off for the police. He had assigned Officer Matt Roper and the rookie, David Hummer to be on foot patrol in this area. Yet, there was only one vehicle. He heard them radio their beginning mileage to Dispatch at the start of the shift, so he knew they were in separate cars. So, why only one?

Nick scanned the beach with his eyes. No blue and white uniforms to be seen.

"Roper, why do I have a feeling I know what you're up to?" he said aloud. Looks like lunch would have to wait. *Time to be the boss.*

****

"Yee-hah!" David Hummer exclaimed. The twenty-one-year-old redhead jolted as the fish on the end of his line tried to pull him off the pier.

"You got him, baby! Just wear him out," Roper said. There were over twenty vacationers gathered around them, whooping with beer bottles in hand.

"Come on, boy!" one said.

"He's used to catching baby bluegills around the lily pads!" another said, leading to a wave of cackling.

The rod bent nearly to a ninety-degree angle.

"Come on, you little bastard!" the young officer said. He pulled the rod back then reeled in the slack.

"I can see him," Roper said, pointing thirty feet out. "He came up. He's going down again!"

"I can feel that," David groaned, his pole bending yet again. The fish was determined to get away from him. He let it tire itself out, then pulled back and reeled it closer. The cheering resumed, drawing others to the pier. David's brow was glistening with sweat, but he didn't care. This was great! In the past ten minutes, he had practically become a celebrity. Some of the folks even had their smartphones out and were filming the event.

As he brought the fish within ten feet of the pier, he noticed that the cheering had died out. For a split-second, he worried that he lost the fish, and was the only one to not know it. But then he saw its brown body approach the surface.

"Almost got it!" He reeled it in, then lifted it up over the pier. Surprisingly, Roper wasn't there to help. Finally, David looked over his shoulder. Immediately, he noticed Roper looking toward the lot behind him. The crowd parted, making way for a very stern-looking Sheriff.

Nick Piatt would not normally be described as intimidating in appearance. He was only five-eight in height, had a couple of nicks on his chin from shaving, and despite being in his mid-thirties, he still had something of a baby-face. But he was the Sheriff, and the few times his temper burned, it got red hot.

Roper scratched his balding scalp nervously, then smiled.

"Hey, Sheriff!"

The crowd waited with varying emotions. Some were nervous, thinking they were about to watch a verbal volcanic eruption. Others grinned, for the very same reason. Afterall, there was no joy like watching someone else's misfortune.

"What the hell is this?" Nick said, pointing at the pier.

"Well uh," Roper stopped to clear his throat, "We were patrolling. All was going well. The tourists were enjoying themselves. And, uh…"

"So, you decided to pursue some runaway flounder?" Nick said. David smiled nervously, his fishing rod tilting toward the ocean as the fish attempted one last time to escape.

"Well, Sheriff, he was very suspicious looking," he said. "As you can see, he's trying very VERY hard to get away."

"Ha!" Nick exclaimed. "A smartass. I should've known that's what I hired. You've been working here for two months, and already you think the Cross Point Sheriff's Department is a place for clowns."

"Well no, but…"

"Finish reeling that sucker in," Nick demanded. David swallowed, unsure if this was somehow a test. Somehow, the realization that the iPhones were still recording was enough to spur him from staring like an idiot and follow his instruction. He turned around and cranked the reel, then swung the ten-pound fish over the pier.

Several tourists cheered and clapped their hands. Roper took the fish and presented it to the Sheriff, who stepped forward to look at it.

"Look at you," Nick said. "Pathetic on all counts. Clearly, you don't take your duties seriously. You know how I know that?"

David scratched his eyebrow, stalling for an answer.

"Because I'm not walking the beach?"

"No! Jesus, boy, you have a lot to learn." He pointed at the fish. "Because you catch a measly twelve-inch long flounder! A real Deputy shoots for the stars! Give me that thing! I'm gonna show you how it's done!"

The crowd erupted with a mix of cheering, laughter, and applause as Nick snatched the pole from the Deputy's hand. He dug his hand into the bait bucket and snatched a minnow, then impaled a j-hook through its back. David, relieved that he wasn't in trouble, stepped to the side as Nick made his cast. The crowd erupted again as the lure struck down about seventy-five feet off the pier. He let the weight drag the bait down to the bottom, then slowly started reeling it in.

After a dozen cranks, he felt a sharp tug. He had a bite. He gave the flounder roughly thirty seconds to get a hold of the bait, then yanked up on the rod.

"Fish on!" he shouted. The pole bent into a wide arch. "Ah, I love it when she bends like that!"

The crowd cheered and laughed, while Roper got ready with the net.

"Damn, Sheriff!" he said, catching a glimpse of the fish nearing the surface. "I think you've got a twenty-incher!"

"Someone's gotta show the rookie how to do it!" Nick replied. He reeled the fish closer to the pier. The fish dove low again, its entire body waving like a flag. "Oh no you don't!"

Beer bottles rose to the sky as the crowd applauded the sheriff. More people gathered to see the spectacle.

"Look, Sheriff! I think he's bigger than twenty inches!" one tourist shouted.

"Damn right!" Nick glanced over to David. "As I said, if you want to make the department proud, don't settle for dinky little sardines like that."

Right then, their radios crackled.

"Dispatch to Sheriff. Come in, please."

"Awe, COME ON!" Nick exclaimed. Both David and Roper burst into laughter as Nick tried to get the fish in before answering the call.

"Sheriff? Please respond."

Roper took the initiative. "Sheriff's wrestling with an insanely important case, Dispatch. Anything I can relay to him?"

The crowd chuckled.

"We have a report of an injury out at the atoll. Jet ski crashed into a family's yacht. Caller reports injured person smells of alcohol."

"Ah, damn it," Nick replied. He turned to the left and thrust the rod into the hands of a twelve-year old standing nearby. "Here kid, it's yours. Let's go, guys."

"Consider that message relayed, Dispatch," Roper said.

"You ride with me, kid. Roper, follow us to the dock." Nick hurried into the driver's seat of his truck and turned on the flashers. "Always at lunchtime!"

He turned the wheel and followed the road south to the dock, the sirens echoing across the whole side of the island.

CHAPTER 5

Lisa Robinson opened the transom doors and knelt at the back deck of her yacht. In her hand was a bucketful of salmon, which she had purchased directly from some of the local fishermen.

She smiled as she did every day when she met the pod of orcas at this same exact location. They always gathered a mile east of the atoll, the pod eager to see the human who had personally saved one of their young from a fisherman's net. Lisa remembered the frantic displays of flukes and flippers, along with the expelling of fins. It was like they were trying to get their attention that day. By God's grace, they had found the right person.

Lisa had been monitoring the pod in the year since the incident. The calf had grown at least eighteen-inches since their first encounter. He had the energy of a human toddler, darting in-between the adults, but always racing back to his mother, who approached their human friend. Normally, pods of orcas would typically let nobody near their young, but in a rare display, they showed no resistance when she successfully implanted a tracking device on his dorsal fin.

It was one of the most remarkable things she had ever experienced since beginning her studies on marine biology. She had tracked sharks across the Atlantic, dove along coral reefs, rode on the backfins of bottlenose dolphins, and even experienced a sixteen-foot great white take a tuna from her hand with the gentleness of a toddler. But interacting with this pod dwarfed all of those amazing experiences.

Killer whales sometimes took an interest in humans, but not to this extent. It seemed that the rescuing of the infant had triggered a personal bond. Now, she encountered them regularly while they were in the area. And to her amazement, they took the tuna from her hands as though individually trained by professionals.

"Alright. I'm here," she said to them. Several of the pod members splashed in circles further back, while the pack leaders edged to the front for their daily snack. "You guys are gonna make me go broke!" She chuckled, then tossed a fish into the biggest one's mouth.

"There you go, Charlie," she said. The orca swallowed the fish and raised his head up, revealing the C-shaped scar on his chin. He moved out of the way to allow his mate to take a turn. Lisa smiled again. "Yes, Daisy. I missed you too. No, I haven't forgotten your fish." She tossed one into the female's mouth. She turned, revealing the tracker on the side of her dorsal fin. Remarkably, several of the pod members had allowed Lisa to implant a tag, allowing her to study their patterns. In the past year, she was able to trace their migration to the Arctic waters along the northern coast of Greenland, then back.

The mother moved to the side, allowing the runt to look up at Lisa. He had a full mouthful of teeth now, and his mother had just recently cut him off from nursing. Lisa had named him Cutlass, as the curve of his dorsal fin had reminded her of that of a pirate's blade.

"Here you go," Lisa said. She tossed a tuna into the runt's mouth. He closed his jaws over it and dove beneath his pod with the excitement of a kid with a new toy. Lisa watched his little black body darting everywhere, getting more courageous each day.

As Lisa leaned down for another tuna, she noticed faint sparkles of red and blue along the west. They were police lights. From the looks of it, they were heading toward the atoll.

"Huh? I wonder what's going on over there," she said to the pod. The next one in line bumped the dive board, sparking laughter from the marine biologist. The orca wanted his fish, and was essentially saying "What's the holdup, woman?!"

"Alright! Alright," she said. As she tossed the fish into its mouth, she glanced back at the lights, her curiosity getting the better of her. Not regarding the incident itself, but whether the Sheriff himself was responding to the call. There was no way to tell from this distance. Hell, had it not been for the flashers, the police boats would've looked like any other vessel in the vicinity.

She thought of sending him a text, but knew better than to interrupt him while he was working. At least, she had a joke in store for him—that for once, he had work that didn't involve fishing, socializing, and boating. But, that's why the island community loved him. He won them over with his outgoing and fun personality, rather than strict militant enforcement of the law. Occasionally, when people got rough, he'd resort to that, but in general, he helped keep the atmosphere light and friendly. Thus, most people didn't want to be the asshole that caused problems.

She had seen him around numerous times in her sixteen months on Cross Point. A month ago, he asked her out. She accepted, and he picked her up that evening. What she thought would be an evening with dinner and roses began completely different than what she expected. He took her to the gun range!

So, there she stood in her shift dress, with a nine-millimeter clutched between her palms, and ear protection squeezing her skull. It was her first time firing a weapon of any kind. He had shown her how to hold it, and loaded it for her. Her first five rounds fell low, hitting the paper target where it would *really* hurt.

"Center mass, Doc. Center mass."

"I figured that'd slow him down a little more."

"Well, absolutely. But, you know, some guy's equipment is smaller than others."

That got a laugh out of her, even now as she reflected on it. She did better with the next magazine full of bullets. She couldn't deny she was having fun, even if she didn't want to admit it. She'd been working late in the night since, leaving no chance for a second date. Not for lack of trying on Nick's part. She'd gotten a few calls and texts from him since, offering to take her out. She didn't want to say no, but she was hesitant to say yes. There was no telling how much longer the Virginia Institute of Marine Science would want to keep her here studying migration patterns and reef populations. The hammerhead populations had doubled, which indicated they might want to keep her here to monitor them, but they could change their minds any day.

The choice was simple; don't get attached to anything you couldn't leave behind that same day. Unfortunately, that rule was already broken with Cross Point. She just loved the place. Weather wasn't as cold as the northern islands, but not excruciatingly hot either. She had to deal with hurricanes in the fall, but that was inevitable anywhere she traveled on the coast. The people were nice. The fishermen were always helping her with samples, with some giving her fish tales of seeing a rare species—though one of those actually proved to be true, which led to her finding and tagging a goblin shark. And there was the abundance of life on the reefs, which provided hundreds of different species to examine.

The bump of an orca against her hull brought Lisa back to reality.

"Sorry, sorry," she said, tossing a fish into its mouth. The orcas clicked, then brushed water with their flippers. "Yeah, I know. I'm taking too long. Little entitled leeches, you guys!" She chuckled and finished working her way through the group.

The sound of an approaching motor drew her attention to the north. Only one idiot on the island had a motor that loud.

"Oh, for fuck's sake," she groaned as Barney Grey approached. The ONE part of Cross Point she could live without.

Forty-eight years old, with thirty-eight of those years on the water, Barney Grey only had two specialties: fish and chew tobacco. Many of the other fishermen on Cross Point would suggest he had a third specialty, which was being a thorn in the side of virtually everyone he ever came across.

Of course, Barney never knew what people didn't like about him. They must've been too dumb to like him. It couldn't possibly have anything to do with his use of explosives to catch fish, or illegal use of drift nets, which led to various encounters with that pesky researcher.

More than once, they'd gotten into it. She had the gall to present him his fishing net, sliced up with scissors to save her precious fish. In his mind, there was plenty of fish in the sea to study.

But today, he was especially pissed. She had been hanging out with those damn whales for the past month, and he KNEW that they were getting into his nets. He couldn't make complaints about the drift nets, as he might as well have gone to Sheriff Piatt and said, 'arrest me!' But what happened to him ten minutes ago, he wasn't going to stand for.

He had made a glorious pass, scoring hundreds of mackerel in his net. He brought the nets halfway up when he saw the enormous shape rushing under his boat. The lines went taut, and before he realized what was happening, his boat was going backward!

The transom had started to dip, the bow raising high. Whatever had him was big and strong, and had started to dive. Only with the grace of his nets tearing, did he and his boat break away clean. While catching his breath, and arming himself with a shotgun, Barney watched as the shape picked off his catch one by one, before swimming off.

He had been on the water long enough to know that no sharks were that big, or hungry. The only creatures he'd seen that could do that were those damn killer whales. They had taken his catch, damaged his equipment, and nearly sunk his boat. And now, that annoying woman was there feeding them! *Yeah, great. Entice them to stay around here.* Well, he'll show her. And those damn whales!

The orcas branched out a bit, annoyed by the rattling vibrations from Barney's motor. Lisa leaned on the transom, then felt her back pockets for her phone. Perhaps it would be a good idea to text Nick.

CHAPTER 6

Nick could feel his phone vibrating against his belt as he stepped up onto the island.

"Only *now* does someone want to chitchat," he muttered. The paramedics had beaten him to the island and were already checking the victim's vitals.

"He's breathing," one said. "Definitely smell the whiskey in his breath."

"He's had a few bottles worth, judging by what we've seen," Mr. McCluskey said. His kids and wife stood on the north side of the island to make room for the first responders.

"He must've had a lot of booze to go right smack into the boat," David Hummer said.

"Probably thought he was in a race and that this was the finish line ribbon," Nick said. He turned toward Mr. Henderson. "I suppose you guys are the ones who called it in?"

"That's us," Mr. Henderson replied.

"That your boat he crashed into?" David asked. Nick resisted the urge to smack his palm into his forehead.

"No. I'm sure they swam over here," he said. David bit his lip. *Yeah, that was a dumb question.*

"We'll have to swim to get back, though," Henderson said. "The idiot put the front of his jet ski through our hull. There's saltwater getting in. God knows what it's doing to the engine."

Nick stepped onto the dock and took a look. The starboard bow appeared as though a Japanese submarine had fired a torpedo into it.

"Yeah, you've got issues," he said. "Tell you what, I'll have you catch a ride with my Deputy over there, once the paramedics have this man lifted out. If you would, give Deputy Hummer here your information so we can do a report. I think the insurance company should cover the damage based on the circumstances."

"Still puts a kink in our rope!" Henderson said, clearly irritated.

"Was this guy alone?" Nick asked.

"No. There was one other being equally stupid," Mrs. Henderson replied. Her husband grimaced, knowing she was actually flattered by their compliments.

"They almost ran us over twice," their daughter said.

"Really? Any idea where the other one went?" Nick asked. They all shook their heads.

"They were zipping all over the place, splashing water, drinking, and shouting," Mr. Henderson said. He handed his license to David, who started recording the data he needed. "They came by, made some lude remarks, drove off over there—" he pointed north, "then we just stopped paying attention to them. Thought maybe they'd go away. Heard some splashing, then a big splash, then five seconds later, that guy comes flying toward the island. He nearly hits my kids, then banks left, then smacks into my boat."

"No sign of the other after that?" Nick asked.

"No. It was like he just vanished," Mrs. Henderson said.

"Probably didn't want to be caught with *this?*" the paramedic supervisor suggested. He was on the east shore, leaning over some of the rocks. He stood straight and turned around, revealing the whiskey bottle discarded by the thrill-seekers.

"Got another one in his bag here," one of the others said.

"Probably," Mr. Henderson said. "They did race off that way before this one came back. Maybe he just kept going."

"Well, once this numbskull is in a condition to talk, maybe we'll learn a thing or two," Nick said. "David, you have his info?"

"Yes, Sheriff."

"Alright." He got on his radio. "Dispatch, can you get in touch with Corey Burch and get him to bring his tugboat out here?"

"Will do, Sheriff."

"Sheriff, what about our jet skis?" Mr. Henderson asked. "We were keeping them on our yacht, but if the boat's gonna get worked on, it's probably best to keep them out. And we have nowhere else to store them."

Nick thought for a moment. "I know a guy who can hang on to them for you. I'll have him come out tomorrow and get them. I'd do it today, but he's on the mainland and won't be back until tomorrow, and the boat storage guys won't take jet skis. Apparently, they're too easy to steal, even though it's never happened since I've lived here. But that's the policy. What we'll do is, we'll shackle them to the dock, and I'll have my deputies come get them tomorrow."

"I'm fine with that," Mr. Henderson said.

"Great. If you don't mind, just hand the keys to Deputy Hummer, and we'll get you squared away," Nick said. He started walking to his patrol boat, which was tied at the end of the dock behind the paramedics. His phone started buzzing again. "Okay, who the hell is so eager to—" He recognized Lisa's number. Once again, his voice was as giddy as a schoolboy. "Hey! Sheriff Nick here."

28

"Hi, Nick. It's—"

"Oh, Lisa, you know you don't need any introduction."

"You're sweet," she replied. *"Unfortunately, I could use your help. Is that you over there at the atoll?"*

Nick started glancing around. "Spying on me now, are you?"

"You wish."

Nick chuckled. *Maybe.*

"I've got an angry fisherman harassing me. More specifically, Barney Grey."

"Angry fisherman would've worked," Nick replied. "Where you at?"

"East of your position. A little less than a mile, roughly."

Nick turned and gazed at the horizon. He could see a couple of boats far out, looking like little grains of pepper in the distance.

"I see you. Give me a minute. I'll be right over." He hung up then boarded his patrol boat. He noticed David right behind him. He took his wallet out and jammed the two keys inside it. The rookie looked up and saw his boss' questioning stare.

"Oh! Sometimes things fall out of my pockets," David said. "I just feel better keeping the keys in my wallet."

Nick frowned. "Alright, kid. But don't forget to put them in storage at the station. Those keys get lost…"

"Don't worry, Sheriff. I'm very responsible. And organized!" David said with a smile.

"Responsible and organized, huh? Is that why you still have Mr. Henderson's license?"

David glanced down, saw the card, then muttered, "shit!" before running back.

Nick shook his head. "Oh, David. Thank God you're not working in L.A." After the rookie returned, they steered away from the dock and proceeded east.

CHAPTER 7

Nick could smell the stale fumes from Barney's engine as he approached. Good thing they'd be conversing from a distance because Barney's breath was the only thing that stank worse than his exhaust—the ones from his boat.

There was nothing new about Barney Grey being irate. Nick described it as short-man syndrome. The bastard was five-foot-two and had to weigh a hundred-and-twenty pounds soaking wet. His appearance and personality contrasted sharply with virtually every other resident in Cross Point. He looked twenty years older than he was, and he was only forty-five. When Nick first saw him, he assumed he was a chain smoker, only to discover that was not, in fact, the case. Poor diet though, and no exercise, and a general bad attitude. Then there was the bad hygiene.

Over to the left was Lisa's boat. Nick could see her leaning on the gunwale, arms crossed, passively enduring Barney's rant. He was pointing a finger down at the water. That's when Nick realized there was a pod of killer whales nearby. He remembered Lisa mentioning that she encountered them every day around this time. Considering that they were in the vicinity, Nick suspected that Barney's beef had something to do with them.

Then again, he might've simply been pissed that the sky was blue that day.

As he steered closer, he could hear the idiot's voice. He even sounded like a chain smoker.

"You're interfering with people's livelihoods, lady! I've lost a day's catch, and now have to spend twelve-grand on a brand new net thanks to these little bastards that you hang around with!"

Barney paused, only to look at the Sheriff. Nick brought the boat to a stop, then grinned at the fisherman. This was going to be fun.

"Hey, Barney. What's wrong? Not one happy family today?"

"He is turning purple," Lisa quipped. Nick snickered, barely keeping a full laugh from blasting out.

"Oh, you're funny!" Barney retorted, spit shooting from his lips. Nick stepped around the cockpit, then narrowed his gaze. Now, he wasn't joking.

"Not as funny as you'll look behind bars if you even imply to threaten Dr. Robinson," he said.

"I'm not threatening—"

"Barney, I see the shotgun, you dummy! The barrel's sticking up over the coaming, over by that pile of rust you call a wheelhouse."

"It's these damn whales," Barney said. "They stole my catch! They tore my net out from under me!"

"Hmm, I should put them on the payroll," Nick said. "Have them help me find some of the illegal drifts you've got floating out there."

"I don't have any—"

"Oh, don't bullshit me, Barney. One of these days, I'm gonna catch you in the act, dude. And that's gonna be a good day."

Barney shook his head. Best not to respond to that statement. Didn't want to provide any evidence, or even allude to his use of drift nets.

"No! I was trawling! I had a net full of tuna, then one or more of these bastards swam underneath me and nearly dragged me under!"

"I doubt that," Lisa said. "They won't go near most boats, especially nets. They're more than a little sensitive about nets, considering they almost lost one of their offspring in one...which I highly suspect was yours, Mr. Grey."

"Nothing else in these waters as big as what I saw! It was definitely them whales!" Barney said.

"Considering how many fish you've killed, I'm not too concerned about it," Nick said. Barney whipped his gaze back at him, puzzled and angry. Nick scoffed at the reaction. "Oh, don't play dumb. I know about your use of explosives. Kill twice as many fish as you bring in."

"And God knows what else," Lisa added.

"You know, with that in mind, I should probably take a look in that boat of yours. Probably got some dynamite in that cargo hold right now. What do you think, Rookie?"

David did his best not to look nervous. He leaned toward the Sheriff and whispered, "Don't we need a warrant?"

"Shut up and agree with me."

David cleared his throat. "Hell yes, Sheriff!" he said, loudly.

"Brandishing a shotgun like that, I say we have probable cause," Nick added. Barney's face soured even more. He kicked something on the deck, then marched to his wheelhouse. Before entering, he turned around and pointed a finger at Lisa.

"Those damn whales better stay clear of me and my boat!"

"Barney, nothing on this earth would want to come within fifty yards of you," she retorted.

"Make that a hundred," Nick said.

"Fuck the police!" Barney growled, flipping him the bird. Like the coward he was, he didn't wait for a reaction. He hurried to his helm and sped north, hooking wide to head back to the mainland.

"And he wonders why he can't get any chartering business," David muttered.

Nick blew a sigh of relief, then leaned over to talk to Lisa.

"Glad that's over," he said.

"Not as glad as I," she remarked. "Thanks for coming. It was nothing I wouldn't have been able to handle normally, but he seemed dead set on clearing these orcas from the area. I didn't want to risk it escalating."

"Good call," Nick said. "You can never tell what that moron's gonna do. You did good to call me. Hate to see anything bad happen to your friends."

"Well, it was actually *him* I was concerned about," she replied. "The bond I've formed with this pod is absolutely amazing. I was diving with them one time, and a group of hammerheads lingered too closely. I don't think they were even interested in eating me, but the pod didn't see it that way. Tore those hammerheads up, and didn't even eat them!"

"You think they were protecting you?" Nick asked.

"I really do think so. The calf and his mother were a few hundred feet away at that moment, so it wasn't them they were concerned about."

"Would they do anything like Barney described?" David asked.

"Hell no," Lisa said. "They shy away from most running motors. And nets are like the devil to them." She started to chuckle. "You know? This is a scientist thing, I suppose, but the most annoying part of the whole interaction was him calling them 'whales.' They're dolphins, technically. At least he didn't refer to them as fish."

"Oh, right. What a dummy. Unlike me! *I* totally knew killer *whales* were not whales."

"Why are they called that?" David asked.

"Just an old misconception," Lisa said. "Ancient sailors called them *asesina ballenas*, which means 'whale killer' because they've witnessed them killing larger species. Over time, it somehow got flipped around to 'killer whales' and people just got used to it. But no, they're dolphins. BIG dolphins."

Nick watched the pod start to group around her boat again like a bunch of puppies around their master. She leaned over the water and whistled. A few of them stopped and pointed their heads up at her.

"Wow! They must *really* like you!" he exclaimed.

"We're friends," Lisa said with a smile. She opened another bucket of fish and tossed one into a set of jaws. "Alright, Charlie. Let someone else have a turn."

She made a shooing motion, then whistled at another orca.

"Charlie?" David asked. "You name all of these whales—orcas?"

Lisa chuckled. "Easier than numbering them. Plus, they all have their own personalities. Charlie's the leader. Daisy's his mate. The youngster is their offspring. Then there's Ralf, Freddy, Maureen, Holly…"

David lost track after Charlie.

Lisa continued, "We've seen studies of orcas interacting with humans, but I can't think of many cases where it's gotten to this extent. I think their intelligence is even higher than what we've anticipated."

"Very fascinating," Nick said. He gazed down at the orcas. "Hey guys, since you're all so smart, maybe you can help me convince Dr. Robinson to go to dinner with me tonight!"

Lisa looked back over at him.

"You could try asking me first," she said.

"You keep saying you're busy! Now I've met the culprits who are monopolizing your time! I'm negotiating."

"Oh, is that right, Sheriff?" she said. Nick focused on the orcas again.

"You know, she won't listen to me, but she might listen to you guys," he said. "Nod your heads if you think she should go. Come on! Do it!" He nodded his head, hoping to get one of them to imitate.

To his surprise, the one Lisa called Charlie did. Nick laughed, both from genuine astonishment, and personal triumph. He threw his hands up in the air as though scoring the extra point in a football game.

"Yes!"

To his right, David Hummer stood, completely astounded by the actions of the orcas. Was that a coincidence, or did the thing actually imitate him? Unbeknownst to him, Lisa was wondering the same thing.

Amazing, she thought. Her eyes went back to Nick.

"Well, Charlie didn't say I couldn't make conditions," she said.

Nick felt slightly nervous. "What would those be?"

"One, really. No gun range this time," she said.

"I guess I can live with that," Nick said. "Even though it could save your life one day."

"Probably would've needed it against Barney, had we not shown up," David added. Nick nodded. *I knew this kid had some smarts.*

Lisa chuckled. There was a part of her that enjoyed the shooting range. *Maybe another time.*

"You busy at five?"

"FIVE!?!" Nick said, pretending to be offended. "You think I get off at any decent time?! I'm a Sheriff of a very busy island. I have responsibilities. I run a department, for crying out loud…Just kidding. Five's great!"

"Sounds great. You know where to pick me up. Until then, I have to get back to my previous dates!" She tossed a fish to another orca. "Thanks for your help, Sheriff!"

"No problem!" Nick said. He returned to the helm and began taking the vessel back to port. David couldn't help but notice a little extra energy to the already energetic Sheriff.

"Got about three and a half hours to kill," he said.

"I already have the answer," Nick replied. "First, we're going to finish that report and get everything set up for the Henderson family. After that, I need a small something-to-eat to tide me over. THEN, I'm going back to the pier with a fishing pole to regain my title of Lord of the Quayside!"

The men laughed and bumped fists.

Five o'clock couldn't come soon enough for Nick Piatt.

CHAPTER 8

Pete Drier could smell the sweet vanilla scent of his cigar before he even pulled it out of the box. God, he loved charter season, especially when the client was Jane Warner. She actually remembered what he liked!

It was her third year vacationing at Cross Point. Both previous years, she had chartered his boat three times for some lobster diving. She always came alone, and he swore that lowcut top was meant for his eyes. To his amazement, she asked if he could dive with her. Thank God he had his diving gear handy. He never forgot how thirty minutes of her charter was spent in the water, the rest in his personal cabin. Turns out, that lowcut top probably was meant for him.

Up until then, he had never experienced such instant mutual attraction. It seemed like something out of a movie or book, but never real life. Yet, it happened, and he enjoyed the hell out of it. He was the ruff-and-gruff type she liked, with just the right amount of growth around the jaw, and a physique reminiscent of his active lifestyle. She had a country accent that was distinct without being too thick, and legs that should've landed her in a *Georgia Florida Line* music video.

After she left that first year, Pete figured he'd never see her again. It was a one week fling, nothing more. Then, mid-July the following year, she returned. It didn't take long for her to make a reservation aboard his vessel. There was one problem, however: he was engaged.

"What? You too good for me?" Jane had asked.

"No. It's just…I can't do that anymore."

"Nobody has to know…"

"I'm sorry…I can't…" He remembered the guilt he felt for initially even considering being unfaithful. Yet, he couldn't withdraw himself from her kiss. And when the hands undid his belt, he didn't resist.

"You were saying?"

Pete didn't think he was the cheating type until that moment. Yet, there was a sexual magnetism that drew the two of them together. It wasn't love, just lust. Neither could describe it—there was just something they had that the other craved. With this in mind, Pete never bothered to call off his wedding. He loved his soon-to-be wife, but justified in his mind that he deserved a little side romp. And besides, Jane would leave town at the end of the week, and probably never return again. She knew he'd be married the next time they met, right? She wouldn't cheat with a married guy, certainly. On top of that, there were other places to vacation.

Certainly, she'd go to Florida, or Hawaii, or any other resort on either coast. It's not like she had been coming around every year her entire life. She only just recently started. He couldn't be the only person she wanted to have a wild fling with.

Yet, this year, she returned. The first thing she did upon arrival was check into her rented beach home. The second thing was make her 'appointments' with Pete Drier's Charter.

This time, he was a married man. *Happily* married.

Pete shuddered when he saw Jane step out of her rental car and approach his booth, which was located on his property. Instinctively, he looked back to see if his wife was nearby, although he knew she had gone off to work for the day. His mind swirled with his physical desires and moral standing. He couldn't cheat on his wife! He wasn't that kind. A girlfriend, yes. A fiancé? Not proud of it, but hey! It wasn't marriage as far as he was concerned, so he justified it. But now, he was tied. There was no way around it; this would be adultery. Something he often spoke against. He remembered discovering his friend cheating on his wife with a an out of town woman, and verbally tore him apart. And now, he was doing the exact same thing.

No...he wouldn't do it. Yet, he couldn't bring himself to turn her away. He made the slightest effort possible to deter her with the "No, I'm married," approach. His tone failed to sell it, as did his eyes, which went immediately to her cleavage and legs. She smiled, knowing he couldn't resist the bait.

"I don't know what you're getting at sir. I'm just hoping to do a little marlin fishing. Catch the big one, as they say."

Then, she presented to him a gift. It was another vice that marriage, specifically his marriage, forbade him of. Cigars. His wife hated the smell of tobacco, no matter the flavor. Naturally, he let his gripes slip through during one of last year's 'arrangements'. The offer added to the enticement in many ways. It was nice to have a woman who enjoyed the smell of cigars; it was another thing he couldn't get at home; and the fact that she was trying this hard to lure him into her arms made him feel desirable.

Pete marked the schedule, still convincing himself it'd be just a fishing trip. Just another day at the office, so to speak.

Who the hell am I kidding?

Pete stepped out of the wheelhouse and gazed down at the aft deck. Jane leaned back in the chair, her golden skin warmed by the sun's touch. She wore a blue bikini top and cutoff jean shorts that were so small they might as well have been bikini bottoms. Her legs were crossed, her fishing pole in hand. To her credit, she actually paid for the whole day, as marlin fishing was not usually something that could be completed in a short trip.

She must've heard him step out, because she glanced up and smiled. His eyes went to her neckline, and everything below. His heart was racing. Beads of sweat were starting to form at his brow, and it wasn't because of the heat.

He climbed down and took a seat beside her, cigar in mouth.

"Any luck?" he asked.

"Depends on what you mean," Jane said. She reached back with both arms and straightened her hair behind her neck. Her body arched slightly, the way it did when they embraced. She was daring him to come over and take her.

For the tenth time, he glanced out at their surroundings. There were no boats nearby. Thank goodness, because if someone saw the tan beauty on his deck, with no other companions other than himself, they would raise some serious questions. Word traveled fast on Cross Point. It wouldn't matter if he somehow managed to resist temptation. If they were seen, it would all be known to the community. There'd be no hiding it from his wife, and some of his friends would threaten to beat his ass.

Still, he couldn't stop staring.

"You enjoying your cigar?" Jane asked.

"Very much so," he said, then took a long draw. Might as well smell like smoke to cover up the smell of buttercream lotion. Amanda Drier would be mad, but not 'I'm divorcing you' mad.

"I love the smell," she replied. She cracked open a beer and handed it to him. He usually had a policy of no drinking while touring, but apparently this was the day for breaking rules. They drank together and passed some time with some small talk.

"Enjoying married life?" she asked.

"Yes." He sounded unconvinced. It was the truth, except for this very moment. The worst part was he knew she was toying with him, and he was letting her do it. Verbal foreplay, he had heard someone describe it as.

"What a shame," Jane said. "I guess that means we can't relive our good memories together." She leaned back in her chair, her bikini top daring to slip low. She stretched one of her legs. Her muscular tone was one of a marathon runner, and she was flaunting it. There was a joy in her eyes. There was no greater power she felt than when she tortured a man with simply her physique. "Worst part is, I'm not sure if I'll be coming here again. I think my parents and brother want to do a big family trip in Cancun next year. Who knows where I'll be the year after that. I guess I'll have to settle for the memories of the good times we've had in the past."

Son of a bitch! Pete couldn't even sit still now. How was he to respond to this?! Not only was she trying to get him to cheat, but she was trying to get him to initiate it! At least if she made the moves on him, he felt he could justify it as getting lost in the moment. A mistake! But being the one to make the first move made it worse, somehow, like he was just some unfaithful prick who didn't appreciate his wife and wanted to sleep around.

"Don't you have anyone?" he asked, hoping to steer the conversation away. Every attempt at diversion made him feel dumber. He let this happen. He *knew* what he was in for when he put her on the boat. It was like a drug. He knew it would destroy him, but he just had to be near it!

"I thought I did, but I guess not," she replied. Yet, there was no disappointment in her voice. Her fingertips were brushing her thigh as she watched the fishing line.

Pete sucked in a deep breath. She really knew how to play this game!

"You really not coming back next year?" Pete asked.

"Not looking like it. Maybe if I had more money and vacation time, I would, but I don't. And there's talk of taking a trip out of the country the following year. So, this'll probably be my last visit for at least a few years. Hopefully I'll catch myself a trophy and make a lasting memory."

Pete glanced about again. It was getting later in the afternoon. Most of the other charters were heading in for the day. The speedboaters and parasailers didn't normally come this far out, and even if they did, they were mostly tourists and wouldn't recognize his yacht. The fishermen usually did their fishing further east, as this area was unofficially reserved for tourist activities.

Aside from a few boats in the horizon, this section of ocean was theirs.

Pete couldn't take it any longer. Maybe she was lying about next year, but he didn't care. As far as he was concerned, this would be the last time he could have Jane Warner.

You only live once, he thought.

She fluttered her eyelashes at him, seeing the shifting of his bodyweight. She turned her chair to face him, then uncrossed her legs. At the same time, she cocked her head slightly toward the cabin. *Shall we— get some shade?*

Finally, Pete made the move. He crossed over in a single, long step, and pressed his lips to hers. Her hands found his and pulled them to her body. The feel of her soft, silky skin put him into overdrive. His fingers slipped under her shorts, ready to lift her out of the seat and carry her into the cabin.

He had accepted his fate as a dirtbag husband who screwed around behind his wife's back.

As he lifted her up to carry out the deed, the fishing rod suddenly bent into a perfect semicircle. The reel cranked, the taut line lashing a few inches side to side. Jane dug her tongue once more into Pete's mouth, then returned to her seat.

"Guess you'll have to wait, sailor. Got a bigger pole to grab at the moment."

Pete chuckled, then stepped to the transom. He watched, forcing himself to be interested on whatever was at the edge of her line. Of course, it had to bite NOW! If it was a marlin, it could be hours before she got it in.

Jane pulled the rod back and cranked the handle.

"Whoa! Got myself a biggun!" she exclaimed. The line moved to the right, then straightened until the fish was nearly at the surface. Pete could see the yellow markings and blue scales of a yellowfin tuna.

"Not a marlin, but still a damn good fish! I'd say it's about four hundred pounds!"

"Must be my lucky day!" Jane said. "I'll have to celebrate." Pete saw the wink.

God, I'm a piece of shit. Worst part is...I don't really care right now.

With this victory, Jane was guaranteed to be extra fiery, and he was the one who got to benefit from it.

The tuna's upper body breached, its lower jaw hyperextended. With a heavy splash, it dove deep again, bending Jane's pole and nearly dragging her off the seat. Pete moved around her and fastened her harness...which gave him an excuse to caress her chest and abdomen for a moment.

"Oh yeah, baby," she said in a low voice. She pulled back on the rod, then cranked in the slack. Forty meters to go. Her skin was glistening with sweat, her muscles flexing from the strain.

Pete grinned and watched the line, ready to grab the tuna and haul it aboard. At this rate, it wouldn't take too long.

Shockwaves of distress swept across Scar's lateral line like ripples in a pond. There was a struggling lifeform in his proximity. He fluttered his caudal fin to close in on the signals. Whatever it was, it wasn't very deep. So, he ascended to the sunlit surface.

His red eye found the silhouette of the tuna. It was twisting and turning, fighting against some strange invisible force. There was another shape behind it. A vessel! A smaller version of the kind that he had recently escaped from. These vessels carried land-dwelling prey, similar to those that imprisoned him. Humans.

Hunger stirred within him. Scar would take the fish first, then engage with the humans.

The tuna was trying to escape, but was going nowhere. Easier prey was hard to come by, even for Scar. The fish pulled against the invisible force and tried to plunge into the dark abyss. Then, it sensed Scar's menacing presence.

The tuna saw the red eyes, blue skin, and torpedo shape of its most feared enemy coming from the depths. It was no longer the abyss that offered sanctuary, but the surface. The tuna spun and jetted for the surface. It did not care about the strange shape that drifted nearby, nor was it concerned with the vocalizations from the creatures aboard it. It just needed to get away from the predator behind it.

It only took a few swift swings of Scar's tail to close the distance. His eyes rolled back and his jaws extended, baring rows of white teeth.

"Whoa!" Pete screamed. For a split-second, he saw the tuna about to breach. Then a cone-shaped shadow swept in from behind. The water erupted as though a bomb had been detonated. Through the waves, they could see huge pectoral fins, a crescent-shaped caudal fin flapping about, and white teeth closing down.

Jane screamed as the carnivore struck down. Blood and water swept the deck, hitting her bare feet. The fishing line was no longer tight. She stared, flabbergasted.

That was a shark. But she had never seen one so huge.

"My god! Did you see that?!" she said.

"Yeah..." he said, near the point of hyperventilating. Jane reeled in her line, and lifted the severed head of her tuna on board the deck. The teeth had sliced right through the eyes, leaving only part of the head and its mouth, which remained gaped as though the fish had screamed in its final moments.

"Jesus, I wish we got that on film," Jane said.

"Uh, no," Pete said. He was just starting to settle down from the adrenaline rush.

"Would've gotten a lot of hits on *YouTube,*" she said.

"Exactly. And it would be all over the internet what we're doing out here," Pete replied. He moved to the transom and looked into the water. "Where the hell did it go?"

"Probably full after that big tuna," Jane said. She took a breath and smiled, exhilarated by what she had just witnessed. "Whoa! That was amazing!" Pete looked at her like she was crazy, but then allowed himself to grin. It wasn't every day you got to see a huge shark leap out of the water, unless it was on the *Discovery Channel.*

"It was kinda cool," he admitted. "Got my heart racing a bit."

"You sure it was the shark? Or could it have been…" Jane tugged on the shoulder strap of her bikini, slowly pulling it down. Pete could feel his energy returning.

That's right. I'm a piece of shit. And I'm gonna enjoy the hell out of it.

He swooped in toward her like the shark had done with its prey. His hands grabbed at her clothes, ready to tear them off and take her into his cabin.

An explosive force hit the yacht from underneath, teetering it to starboard, and launching the lovers to the deck. Jane screamed, frantically trying to fix her clothes, while looking out past the guardrail. The yacht had not even begun to settle when it got hit again, this time somewhere near the front.

Pete was on his feet, now under the influence of another adrenaline rush that shook his hands and legs.

"Let's get out of here," he said, pulling Jane to her feet and leading her to the walkaround deck. They found a ladder and started climbing for the fly deck.

"Is it the shark?"

"I don't know," he replied. "I don't see—oh God." He looked over his shoulder and saw the shape moving beneath the surface. The water exploded, and he saw the red eyes glowing red, and the huge jaws opening wide as it catapulted itself onto the boat…right where Jane stood. She didn't see it until those jaws closed around her. Her scream was as brief as the pop of a balloon. The shark's head crashed through the cabin, rolling the yacht to starboard.

Jane was finally inside Pete's cabin, her shoulder even brushing by the soft fabric of his bed, while the rest of her was munched by the jaws of the fish. She gagged and kicked, then drowned in her own blood before her mulched body was slurped into the shark's throat.

After swallowing, Scar was now acutely aware of the fact that he was out of water. He was now trapped inside the hole he had punched into the boat, and did not have the capacity to move backward. With only a few minutes before suffocation drained his senses, the shark did the only thing he could do: thrash and bite.

Scar whipped his whole body, his tail assaulting the air outside the vessel. The shifting of his bulk wreaked havoc on the damaged vessel. The structure beneath the pilothouse cracked heavily. A series of *cracks* resounded from within the ship.

On the side deck, Pete was crawling on his hands and knees, shifting side to side from the rocking of his vessel. Against his better judgement, he looked over his shoulder. The shark's lower half was slashing back and forth, shifting its weight. More huge *cracks* filled his ears, until finally, the pilothouse collapsed. The structure came down as though hit with demolition, spilling its ruins into the ocean and freeing the intruder.

The shark thrashed once more, flinging itself off the ship and landing in the water with a titanic splash.

Huge swells hit the vessel, pushing Pete along the foredeck. Hyperventilating, he watched the water settle, then looked back at his boat. The pilothouse was completely gone, rendering the boat inoperable. With the structure gone, it almost resembled a giant canoe. His radio and phone were somewhere inside that wreckage, leaving him with nothing but a life raft. And after seeing what that shark had done to his boat, no way was he going to take that measly raft onto the water. Pete Drier was trapped.

He looked at the water. There was currently no movement...none that he could see.

"Where is it?!" he said. He heard no answer. "Watch the starboard side and I'll take the—" He stopped abruptly. In the state of fright, he had momentarily forgotten that Jane was no longer with him. The realization that she was dead nearly broke his psyche. What completely broke it was the emergence of that silhouette, rapidly ascending to the surface. The ocean unveiled into a series of waves, and the shark breached.

Scar opened his mouth and seized the panicking human. His upper body crashed down on the bow of the vessel, cracking it all the way to the bottom. He balanced on its edge for a moment, thrashing the human side to side. Kicking and screaming served no purpose except to help the serrated teeth do their work. Warm blood splashed his throat, and by the time Scar returned to the water, he had ripped the man in two. The upper half hit the water and drifted a few feet, a look of terror frozen on the dead face before Scar circled back and snatched it up.

CHAPTER 9

"I don't care how much she's offering. I'm not taking her assignment."

"It's a large sum, Boss."

"How many times do I have to tell you, Dorn? I'm not speaking to that bitch."

"It's your call. All I'll say is that she's very persistent."

Roark Fender scowled at the thought of speaking to Dr. Olivia Zoller. The woman was a control freak with a chip on her shoulder. A large chip, which may as well have been a boulder. In fact, he would've preferred it was a boulder, because it would've crushed her into the ground.

His associate, Dorn, waited by the door for an answer. The former legionnaire had almost successfully hidden that smirk on his face. He loved hunting, whether it was man or beast, and the last job they pulled for Dr. Zoller was by far one of their most interesting ones. Though, it left Roark permanently scarred.

"I don't care that she flew all the way over here from God-knows-where. She can't seem to manage her pets. Let her deal with it," Roark said. Dorn didn't move. It seemed his boss was talking to himself rather than him.

"You want me to go downstairs and tell her that?"

Roark groaned. He hated that she was even in his house, let alone attempting to recruit him for another job. He loved working and shooting guns, and in his profession, they were often one of the same. Like Dorn, he usually felt that the more dangerous the target, the better. Usually. But he also wanted to come out alive, and, knowing Olivia, this was a target that she wanted captured alive. Unfortunately, the last asset he was sent to capture, he had no choice but to kill it. It was either him or it, and he chose it. Besides, he was not in the business of capturing animals. Blowing them up, no problem. But capturing them?

His face throbbed where the last one had made its mark.

Of course, there was more to it than that, and that prick Dorn knew it.

"Get that shit-eating grin off your face."

Dorn shrugged. "Hey. Maybe something good will come of this meeting. Maybe you two will...rekindle." He made a few crude motions with his fingers. Roark glared, pretending to be angered. Again, Dorn saw right through it.

"Bring her in," he groaned, immediately turning his back. Dorn chuckled and found the stairway. Roark waited, already hating himself for letting this go further.

A few seconds later, he heard feet against the stairway.

Olivia Zoller stepped onto the atrium. On the other side, three rooms across, was the mercenary Roark, reaching into a cabinet and pulling out a cigar. The scar from the last time he worked for her was now a pink mark that ran from his left eyebrow, all the way down his face and neck, ending somewhere along his chest.

He wore black. It was always black, as though he felt he needed to be stealthy wherever he went. Even his hair was jet black, as was the pupil in that left eye where the last experiment slashed him.

Roark groaned, seeing the geneticist in those stupid slacks and tank top, which she only wore to show off that tattoo of hers. Like anyone cared about sharks. It was as if she was trying to come off as attractive and unattractive at the same time. Whatever message it was supposed to convey, he'd never understand.

But hey, smash that patriarchy, right?!

It had been a few years since they'd seen each other…which was one of the reasons Olivia was bitter to hire him. The company had used Roark in the past, and often kept him near their main facility to help enhance security, as well as perform a few under-the-table jobs that were never specified.

Then came a heightened time of security. A foreign company, specializing in research similar to Olivia's, had hacked a company computer and learned of the progress being made at Skomal Corp. As this company had been suspected of hiring hitmen to take out competitors' assets, Skomal hired Roark to be her bodyguard. Being around each other twenty-four-seven allowed them to get to know each other a little better. During that time, he introduced her to whiskey and barbeque—something she always avoided since childhood. To her amazement, she actually enjoyed them. The bodyguard duty lasted a month, during which they were forced to spend literally every minute with each other.

Of course, it wasn't all pleasant. She seemed to harbor a resentment toward him for reasons he couldn't quite figure out at first. Then, he learned about that chip on her shoulder. Every person she took issue with had a common factor…something that half the world, including himself, shared.

Didn't stop him from screwing her though. Enough whiskey would drown out most annoyances. For him, the best part was that she pretended not to like it.

Yeah, sure you didn't.
The memory softened his grimacing expression.

"Nice place you got here," she said.

"Spit it out," he said, dry tobacco flakes shooting from his lips. "You want something. Probably won't get it. And I'd rather tell you 'no' sooner rather than later, but I know you won't accept the answer until you've pleaded your case."

"Good. I'm glad you're not in the mood to wait," she said. She found a chair near the corner and helped herself to it, then immediately eyed the coffee machine that was on the table. Roark chuckled, then lit the cigar. The broad was already acting like she owned the place. "Whatever happened to the whiskey?"

"Pssh!" Roark opened another cabinet, revealing all sorts of whiskey bottles and glasses. He pulled out a bottle of Elijah Craig and filled a shot glass. He was gonna need it.

"I could use one," Olivia said.

"Not coarse enough for you," he said, throwing the shot into his throat. Despite his reply, he pulled another glass and filled it, then slapped it onto the table. A few drops hit her wrist, as well as the papers she pulled out of the suitcase. She quelled her irritation, then proceeded to place the files on the table.

Roark downed his second shot, then gazed down at a photo of a huge shark inside of a pool. She flipped to the next photo, showing the fish going for a dead seal being lowered by a pulley.

"So, that's the next fish you lost?" he said.

"It was twenty-feet long at the time this photo was taken," Olivia said.

"At the time? How big is it now?"

"Thirty-two feet," Olivia answered. Roark burst out into a fit of laughter.

"You lost a shark that size?!"

"We were transferring it to our floating laboratory and it woke up from sedation," she said. "I need to catch it soon, or else the company will bury the project."

"Sounds like you have quite the problem," Roark said. He drew on the cigar, filling the atrium with smoke.

"I'm willing to double the payment from the last job..."

"Funny, I didn't get anything from the last job except *this*." Roark ran his finger along his scar.

The genetically modified sawfish had lived up to its name. Though, unlike the shark in the photo, that specimen was actually being stolen by people hired by a rival company, along with some data files. That was when Olivia first recruited Roark, offering him a substantial sum to bring the specimen back alive after eliminating the bastards who stole it.

The people were the easy part. He was able to track them down to Florida, where they were going to ship the fish overseas on a cargo plane retrofitted for transporting sea creatures. The bastards didn't even know they weren't alone in the docks. Roark and his team didn't have to fire a single shot. With a little patience, all it took was a knife to the throat here, a crack of a neck there, and before long, the whole area was Roark's for the taking.

The cargo plane was docked like a boat. Its cargo ramp was open, the specimen inside. All they had to do was get it out. Except, the creature was already in the process of doing that itself. With amazing strength, it had cracked the container it was trapped in—right as the team had infiltrated the cargo hold. The fish broke free, flooding the plane, and lashing out with its razor-sharp snout.

Suddenly, the nerves along his scar began to pulse. He remembered vividly the sensation of the slash. To his surprise, it was dull, as though he was being cut with the back of a knife. It would've finished the job had he not unloaded his rifle into it. A hundred-and-twenty stitches later, as well as two liters of blood, and yet, the woman had the gall to ramrod him for his failure. She even withheld her payment, stating she didn't hire his team to kill her specimen.

Olivia threw back her shot of whiskey. Thankfully, Roark had placed the bottle on the table. She helped herself to a refill.

"I'll be going with you on this one," she said.

"Good. Then I'll have bait," he said.

"You're an ass."

"You're a bitch. And I think you enjoy it," Roark said. He smiled, watching her face tense. She certainly didn't enjoy being *called* one.

"You want the job or not?"

"No."

She shuttered, which widened his smile. It was clear she needed him far more than he needed her. And her reaction confirmed his suspicion that she didn't have time to go mercenary shopping. It wasn't a line of business she was too familiar with.

He watched her fill another shot. Her hand was trembling as it raised the glass. The stakes were high with this one.

"Listen…I know things might be awkward between us—"

"Not for me," he chuckled. Olivia resisted the urge to snap at him. There was too much at stake to let her personal feelings get in the way.

She waited a moment and let the booze go to her head. Oh, how she was going to need it. She began filling her fourth.

"Roark, I really need your help. You're the only person who can pull this off."

"No, I'm just the only one you know," he retorted.

"No, it's the truth. I believe you and your crew are the only ones who can do this."

"Yeah? What are you offering?"

"Two-mil," she said. The drink entered her mouth immediately following the answer. She had a feeling she wouldn't like his response.

"Two million...hmmm..." He hesitated just long enough to make her go for the bottle again. *Might as well drink from the neck, the way you're going.* "Not a bad pay rate. And this is from you? Not Skomal?"

"I'll be reimbursed if the mission goes well," she said.

"Ahh. Reimbursed. *If* it goes well. Something tells me Skomal's not happy with you. Is your position as Vice President in jeopardy?"

And there it was. She grabbed the bottle and filled the shot glass. She winced this time, then rested her head on her hand.

"I really need this favor."

"Not a favor. It's a job."

"Fine. I'm offering two million. I have the supplies in order. There's a boat that Skomal Corp had manufactured at our secondary floating laboratory, still under construction a hundred miles off Wassaw. It has all the supplies we need, including a tank to store the shark in. We can restrain it, while pumping water over its gills until we deliver it to the lab. I have the sedatives and cables. I just need somebody that can handle a boat, and help me capture a shark." Roark didn't answer. Olivia was leaning forward, the booze softening her sensibilities, thus allowing her to beg him. "Please. It won't be like the last time. You'll be better prepared, and not trapped in an enclosed area with it."

"Hmm." Olivia hated that sound. It always meant he had something up his sleeve. "Two million is a good payment."

"So, you'll do it?"

"Unfortunately, my policy is that I need a little something up front."

Olivia stood up. "That kind of money takes time to move. I don't have the funds to get it to you now!"

"Oh," he said, glancing down at her neckline. He ran his finger over her shoulder, and to her shark tattoo. "What a shame you have nothing to offer. Well, nice seeing you again, Dr. Zoller." He turned and disappeared into the door at the end. She saw the bed and private bathroom inside before the door swung shut.

She sank back into the chair, landing harder than she intended. That bastard! She wanted to knock over the table and scream like an adolescent. He was still pissed at her. Why? Because he failed at his last mission? Because he didn't like taking orders from a woman? What was his deal? She was offering him two million, yet he wouldn't take it.

Her eyes went back to the bottle.

There was only one other method of persuasion that she hadn't tried yet. She remembered their times while he served as a bodyguard. She knew what pleased him. And she could use a little something other than the booze to alleviate some of the stress.

Still, a bitterness crept up. He had a power over her, and she couldn't stand it. And he was smart enough not to demand what he wanted outright, meaning she would have to make the initiation.

She didn't have time to ponder her options. Besides, there were none. She thought of her coveted position as VP, and the power she would wield within the company. In time, Skomal would retire and she would be able to reform the company's image to her liking. It was a lifetime of ambition that rested at her fingertips. All of that warranted a little sacrifice of her principles.

Olivia grabbed the bottle and downed a couple of gulps of whiskey. She brushed her hands through her hair, took a breath, moistened her neck with a few drops, then went for the door.

Roark wasn't surprised to see it open. He was in his private bathroom, shirtless, running a razor over the bristles on his chin. With a few strokes, all of the short black hairs were eliminated. During this time, the cigar was still clenched in his mouth.

He watched Olivia in the mirror as she approached. She licked her lips, her eyes narrowed at his muscular back. He let her approach, then put her hands around his waist, the fingertips pushing under his waistline.

"You don't think I've forgotten our times together, do you?"

"Only the attitude that came after," he said. She reached around and plucked the cigar from his mouth, then forcibly turned him around. She pressed her mouth to his, her tongue digging deep.

She pulled away, but only to ask, "How's that for attitude?" Roark initiated the next kiss. Right away, her hands went for his belt buckle, while his hands started working under her tank top. Somewhere in the process, they moved further down to her thighs, then lifted her up. She moaned pleasurably as he slammed her onto the bed then put his weight on her.

Olivia closed her eyes and let the mercenary do his will. The part she hated most was that she was actually enjoying it.

CHAPTER 10

The time read 5:03.

Of course, he was running late. Just like last time. Probably planning some new extravaganza to precede dinner.

Lisa smiled. Nick was a character alright. It was one of the reasons the island community loved him. Like many girls thought when being eyed by a man, she wondered what was so special about her that he liked. Certainly, there were several single ladies on this island, most of them so gorgeous that they ought to be in Hollywood. The only thing that she thought he may have found intriguing was her PhD.

Or maybe because they had personalities that somehow clicked. Whatever the case, she was happy he made the initiative. She went for a simple white linen shirt and straight legged jeans. Knowing Nick, he'd probably be dressed in something equally casual.

Right then, she heard the knock on her door.

"Guess who?" his voice came through.

"Had I not known any better, I'd say a creep," she retorted, opening the door. She was mostly right in her prediction; his white button shirt was actually very sharp.

"No creeps here! I've run them all out of town," he said. Lisa smiled and leaned against the door frame.

"So, what's your scheme?" she said. Nick pretended to look offended.

"Scheme?! You know me! I've got nothing but a romantic dinner at the Verne Bar and Grill!'

"Yeah, uh-huh. Something tells me I'm in for some gunpowder before that happens," Lisa said.

"Nahhhh," Nick said. "Remember? You said no shooting range."

"I see right through you," she said.

"Trust me!" he replied. Grinning at his mischievous deeds, Lisa shut the door behind her and followed him to his truck.

****

Ferris wheels spun, merry-go-rounds rotated, and a thousand balloons popped as the Cross Point Carnival opened up for the late afternoon.

"Oh yeah, this town ain't big enough for the two of us," Nick mimicked a country accent. Lisa laughed as he fired the toy gun at the

49

little figures with the bullseye at their center. They wobbled around on horses, some moving on mechanical levers, then fell over when the pellet struck the bullseye.

Carnival music rang out as Nick successfully eliminated all of the targets.

He glanced at his date, as victorious as a five-year old would be in this situation.

"You're safe now, ma'am!" He pretended to tilt an invisible cowboy hat.

"I'm starting to see why you're still single," she joked.

"Some ladies say I'm charming," he said. "Besides, I'm the Sheriff of these parts." He slung the rifle over his shoulder.

"Eh-hem," the shooting gallery clerk leaned forward. "That'll be another five dollars, Sheriff."

Nick paid the money, then handed the rifle to Lisa. "Your turn."

Lisa grinned as she took the rifle. She glanced over at the clerk. "What was his score?"

"Uh…twelve targets in thirty-nine seconds," he replied. Lisa cocked the rifle lever.

"Then I've got thirty-eight seconds."

The timer buzzed and all twelve targets sprang up. Right away, Lisa dropped two 'thugs' riding on horseback. They went down with a sharp *ping* and a whirly sound effect. She dropped a third and a fourth.

Nick's eyes went to the timer. Ten seconds in, with eight bullseyes to go. Seven.

Lisa took down another hiding behind a cardboard bush. Another *ping* signified a direct hit on one peeking out from a rock further up the 'hill'.

Twenty seconds in. The remaining five were the tricky ones. There was another on horseback. Lisa took a moment to line up her shot. A single miss would mean she lost the competition.

She placed the shot perfectly, dropping the 'gunman', then moved on to eliminate one popping out under a rock. *Ping!* It went down. With rapid fire, she took down the last two, then moved to the final one: a thug hiding behind a hostage. There was a sensor in the hostage that would indicate if she hit the wrong target. Eight seconds to go.

The target was moving too, which made it trickier.

Five seconds. Four. Three. Two.

She squeezed the trigger and heard the desired *ping*.

"Yes!"

"Thirty-eight seconds. We have a winner," the clerk said.

"Well..." Nick shrugged his shoulder. "I taught her everything she knows."

"Yeah, sure," the clerk said. "Ma'am, which prize would you like?" Lisa glanced up at the display of prizes. Most of them were stuffed items that she had far outgrown. However, one item did catch her eye: a squishy jellyfish toy that lit up into a series of colors. She thought of her nephew back in Michigan who was turning three around now. She could mail it and have it there in time for his birthday.

"I'll take that, please."

"You got it." The clerk handed her the prize.

"Hey, what about me?" Nick said. "I still dropped all twelve targets."

"There's a pink pony that might suit you, Sheriff," the clerk retorted.

Nick glanced at it. "It is pretty."

Lisa laughed and took him by the arm. "Let's go."

"But I want my pony," Nick joked. He turned around and walked through the carnival with her. "So, what would you like to do next? Dinner? They make a kickass burger at Verne's."

"I love the idea," Lisa said. "But there's one thing I decided I want to do first." She stopped, squeezed his hand, then winked. Nick's eyebrows raised. He was reading her mind.

"Wait? *That?!*"

She nodded, her grin widening.

"Really? You want to?"

"Mmhmm," she nodded. "Right now. Let's go."

****

The gunshot echoed through the indoor range. Lisa grinned ear to ear, seeing the paper target shiver from the hit. She fired again, putting another round through the torso of the human shape.

"I knew this would grow on you," Nick said.

"Yeah-yeah," she said. She squeezed off another shot, popping a hole through the neck. She finished working through the magazine, then set the empty weapon on the table. "Alright, fine. You've got me hooked."

"Imagine what it's like to be me," he replied. "I'm surrounded by guns I always want to shoot."

"But you're the Sheriff, meaning you're in charge. I have a feeling you can shoot as much as you want to."

"Well, we *do* have room in the budget for training supplies...which includes ammo. It might be just a coincidence that we're constantly making orders for additional ammo. Gotta keep our officers trained!

Right?"

"What's that you carry?" Lisa asked. Nick looked at his waist.

"Oh, that? That's a Colt Trooper. Was actually my grandfather's. Then my dad's. Now to me."

"Oh, wow! All cops?"

"Yep. Though, none ever worked in such a sweet place as this," Nick said.

"You like it here, huh?"

"I LOVE it here," Nick said. His stomach growled, causing his date to laugh. "I'll tell you all about my life...once I get some appetizers in my stomach."

****

The smell of simmering food invaded Nick's senses as they walked into the Verne Bar and Grill. Classic rock played in the background, though not so loud that it made conversation impossible. Fifteen feet straight ahead was the bar, and to the left were an array of tables. At the back of the building were a set of double doors leading to the back patio. Most of the people seated were locals, which created a more casual atmosphere that contrasted that of high-energy tourists that wanted to drink and dance all night.

"Whoa. Finally," he said. He glanced at Lisa, who was almost as hungry as him now. Almost. "I'm surprised you've never been here."

"I've been working nonstop," she replied. "Besides, I'm by myself. I'm not in the habit of going to restaurants and eating alone. And I don't drink, so going to the bar feels kind of pointless."

"Well, damn. I should've asked you out sooner just to make you feel more at home!"

"Yep. You'll have to make it up to me by ordering a big plate of mozzarella sticks with a side of marinara."

Nick glanced to the hostess. "You heard her!"

"I'll get right on that, Sheriff. First, let me show you to your table. Inside or out?"

Nick and Lisa picked an outdoor table, which gave them a view of the south pier and the ocean beyond.

"Here's your menus, and your waiter will be right with you," the hostess said.

"Thanks," Nick said, immediately flipping through his menu. He noticed Lisa's grin. "Yeah, sorry, right now, food is where my heart's at."

"Don't worry. Me too," she replied.

After a glass of Coke and a plate of mozzarella sticks and tortilla chips, Lisa had proceeded to ask him about his previous life in law enforcement, which led to a long monologue about his father's career, then his time in the academy.

"First job was in Washtenaw County, Michigan. Just bad. Not even just the crime, but the department. Very poorly run. And Ann Arbor, blech! Too much red tape. I got to bounce around a couple of departments until I found this place online. Figured it would be a nice change of pace. As it turns out, I was right!"

"Same with me. Started working in Maine, then all the way in Seattle, then did a few months research in Alaska. Nice places, but too chilly for my taste. This is my favorite post so far."

"You get a say in how long you can stay?"

"If I produce enough results, I can plead my case," she answered.

"What exactly do you research?" Nick asked.

"Migration patterns. Reef populations. Feeding habits. We have a few specimens tagged around here. I got word from the Institution a few days ago asking me to tag a great white, so I'll be busy once I get the shark cage in order."

"Yeah? What happens if he tries to bust through the cage and eat you?" Nick said. Lisa snorted, then shook her head.

"Someone's been watching a certain *Spielberg* movie," she said. "First of all, great whites don't typically get big enough to do that kind of damage. I've had a few rock the cage, but nothing too major. Once you give them a tuna, they calm down a bit."

"Ah. I figured you'd have a few near death experiences to boast about," Nick said.

"You're the cop. I figured *you'd* be full of heroic stories," Lisa retorted.

"Just one," Nick said.

"Yeah? What happened?" Lisa asked.

Nick shrugged. "In my early years, I had my share of domestic stuff. Some DUIs. People overdosing on drugs. A few shootings that led to arrests, but nothing like you saw in *Heat*. But there was one bank robbery that went bad. Three assholes decided to rob a bank. Shot a bank guard on the way out. My pals and I chased them for fifteen miles before we were able to force them over a spike belt. Apparently, they didn't want to be taken. We found out afterward that their leader was wanted for two murder cases. My guess is that he was trying to leave the country, but needed the funds to do it. They hit the belt. Tires went poof! Their getaway car fishtails until it overturns. The driver was ready to give up, which pissed off the leader. He put a round through the guy's head, then aimed at me and my partner. I fired first."

Lisa's eyes went wide.

"He was dead before hitting the ground. It was like blowing out a match. Too bad his associate didn't take the hint. Bad boy opened up on us. He was still inside the car. Without clear line of sight, we had to go nuts on the vehicle, blasting holes until we were certain it was safe enough to move in."

"Oh my goodness, Nick. I'm sorry. I didn't actually think…"

"No, no, it's fine," he said, waving his hand. "You always hear of these people who need counseling, and I'm not talking bad about them, but I never had issues with it. The guy was a killer, and judging by his track record, probably would've murdered again had he gotten away. Hopefully, that doesn't make me seem like a weirdo."

"Not at all," Lisa said. "Just didn't realize you'd experienced such a thing. Did they ever determine for sure that he was guilty of those murder charges?"

Nick nodded. "Both single women, living alone. I guess it's one of the reasons I encourage gun ownership." He took a sip of his coke, then smiled nervously. "I'm sorry. I'm so used to speaking freely, that I realize this probably isn't a good date topic."

"Oh, no, it's fine," Lisa said. "It's not like we've just met." It was true; they'd chatted casually quite a bit in the last sixteen months. "Besides, it sounds like he got what he deserved. I've studied what it costs to keep a single criminal behind bars for life, and frankly, I'm glad my dollars aren't going to that guy."

"Same here. Besides, he was wearing a Cleveland Browns jersey, and that *really* pissed me off."

The joke successfully alleviated the mood. Lisa smiled.

"Yeah, he deserved what he got just for that."

"Steelers fan?"

"Yes, sir," she replied. "Used to be Detroit, but, well, I guess I'm done having my heart broken."

"Don't blame you there," Nick said. "Those whales—I mean, those orcas you were feeding could probably play better than those idiots."

"They're intelligent enough," Lisa said. "Don't open the floodgates. I'll rant all night long about them."

"Go ahead. I'm gonna be stuffing my face with a burger shortly," Nick said. The waitress arrived with her notepad in hand. "Right on time. I'll take the classic. Well done, with everything."

"You got it, Sheriff. Oh, while I take the lady's order, I think there's someone at the bar asking about you."

"Tourist?"

"No. I think it's Mrs. Drier. I guess she saw your truck. I know you're off duty, and didn't want to disturb you."

"No, it's fine," Nick said. He stood up. "Please excuse me, Lisa."

"Good. Means the rest of these sticks are mine," she joked.

"Save some for the orcas," he replied. He stepped through the double doors and saw Amanda Drier standing by the bar. She was leaning over the counter, her face wet, and hands trembling slightly. There appeared to be relief in her eyes when she saw Nick.

"Sheriff!" she said.

"Amanda. What can I do for you?" he answered.

"It's that bastard, Pete," she said. Suddenly, her face was red with anger.

Nick swallowed. *Oh, boy.* He remembered the same look in her eyes precisely a year ago when someone told her they spotted her then-fiancé alone on his yacht with a tan beauty. Amanda had come to the Sheriff, ready to report the yacht missing, since Pete was overdue to return. The two co-owned the vessel together, despite not being married at the time. He remembered how mad she was, and spent the next few days worrying about having to respond to an argument between them. But to his surprise, nothing came of it. Perhaps Amanda didn't press the issue, or was somehow convinced the idiot wasn't fooling around. All he knew was that she married him regardless.

With that in mind, he saw regret in her eyes along with the anger.

"What'd he do?" he asked.

"He was due to be back by five o'clock. It's six-thirty now, and that idiot's still gone. With my boat."

"It's his boat too," Nick said calmly. "By law, he isn't required to have a curfew on that boat."

"I knew he was fooling around," Amanda said. "I never should've married that jerk to begin with."

"Amanda, you don't know he's..."

"He's never run behind in his life," she said. "Except for last year. Mid-July, when he went out, alone with that skank."

"Alright, alright, keep your voice down please. We're in a public space." He led her to the end of the bar where it was a little more secluded. "Do you know for sure he's out messing around?"

"I found buttercream on our pier," she said. "The bitch must've dropped it on her way in."

"That doesn't mean anything. He probably took out a young couple, or a whole family..."

"The calendar had only one name," she retorted. Nick squeezed his eyes shut and prayed for a quick means out of this scenario.

"Okay. Even so, the yacht's not stolen. I can't order him in, even if I found him with a hot babe in his lap." Amanda's face soured further. "Okay, bad image. Sorry. Tell you what, if he's not back by morning, I'll go out looking for him. Okay?"

Amanda took a long, drawn-out breath before finally nodding.

Oh, thank God. Nick patted her on the shoulder. "Go get some rest, will you?"

"Thanks, Sheriff."

"No problem." Nick waited long enough to make sure she was actually leaving, then finally returned to the patio.

"Heard you were out there with another woman," Lisa said, glaring at him. Nick's eyes went wide.

"Wha—no! Not, I mean..."

Lisa laughed. "Oh, man, the look on your face! That was so worth it."

"Oh, man!" Nick said. He relaxed and smiled. Some of the other patrons turned and chuckled at him.

"Man, Sheriff! I don't think I've seen you nervous EVER!" one of them said. Nick looked to the left and saw Hank the fisherman, sitting alone with a burger, a bowl of hot chili, a beer, and a smile on his face.

"After spending eight years with all of you freaks of nature, nothing scares me anymore," the Sheriff retorted. As he sat back down, the waitress returned for the refills.

"Your food will be right out."

"Excellent. I'm so hungry, I'm practically an orca," Nick said.

"I *have* fed them burgers as an experiment," Lisa laughed.

"Yeah? Mutual interest in burgers, Dr. Robinson...I'm starting to think that pod and I have too much in common."

"Maybe that's why I went out with you," she joked.

"As long as you don't feed me tuna." Nick started sipping his coke and listened to Lisa explain her fascination with the pod and marine biology.

CHAPTER 11

The night grew dark and the waters calm. Aside from a few scattered yachts, the only motion on the surface were the swells made by the slumbering pod of orcas. They moved their flukes slowly, keeping a gradual pace as they rested along the surface. In their unihemispheric sleep, they were able to maintain awareness of their surroundings. After a few hours, their brains would switch hemispheres, allowing the other half to rest. The group rested in a right formation, keeping the youngster protected in the middle.

Only two of their members had moved beyond the pack: Charlie and Freddy, nicknamed for a few scrapes on the tip of his right flipper that resembled a claw. Their human companion, Dr. Robinson, had theorized that Freddy had inspected a fish trap made with wire mesh, which scraped him as he steered away. The two brothers traveled side by side, leaving their mates and siblings to slumber a half mile beside them.

They were night hunters. They preferred the total darkness. Seals and porpoises, with their great hearing, were difficult to hunt during the day. But under cover of night, and their use of echolocation, Charlie and Freddy learned they could track down their prey and move in closer before being detected. And by the time they were detected, it was usually too late for the hunted.

The duo located a pack of seals that were feeding on sea urchins and small fish near the atoll. It was a large pack, which almost guaranteed success. Even if they all fled at once, they were slower and less agile than the orcas. Their only safe haven was land, and the only land in the immediate proximity was the atoll, and the seals would be hard pressed to fit all of their members on the tiny dot of land. The orcas took a breath and swam low, keeping themselves concealed in the depths. With the aid of night, they were nearly invisible. They moved into the shallows, then separated. Sooner or later, one of the seals would dive deep to grab itself another sea urchin, which were overpopulating the East Coast shoreline.

Several minutes passed, then one of the furry creatures splashed down. Charlie lashed first, grabbing the prey by the head before it realized the trap it swam into. As Charlie ravaged the seal, Freddy made his move on another that had attempted a dive. Flapping his tail, he launched himself toward the surface and snatched its prey. The whale went airborne, the bleeding seal writhing in its mouth. The circle of life completed its spin for the critter as the orca crushed it in its jaws and swallowed it.

Neither Freddy nor Charlie were ready to quit. There were more seals nearby. Like a flock of birds, they raced for the tight stretch of land, bumping into each other as they took refuge from the predators. A group of five that swam further out started making their way for the atoll, only to realize that the orcas were now turning toward them. There was no chance of reaching the land, let alone cramming themselves with the rest of their group. With no other choice, the five seals darted to the west in a desperate attempt to reach the larger island.

The two killer whales increased speed. Their dorsal fins sliced the water like black knives, looking more and more menacing to any seal that dared to look back.

One of them took a chance and turned left, hoping that the predators would ignore it in favor of the larger group. The plan only half-worked. Charlie banked left to pursue, while Freddy proceeded to follow the other four.

Charlie lunged. The lone seal dove, then banked right. The orca's jaws clenched over nothing but water. For him, it was nothing more than a minor convenience. The seal wouldn't be able to keep this up for much longer. Charlie turned to the right. The seal was thirty feet ahead of him, his brown fur glistening in the moonlight as he raced for the surface. Charlie followed. He could make out the target's form directly above. There was no escape this time. All Charlie needed to do was wave his tail.

Before he made the move, another form entered his vision. It was torpedo-shaped, eyes glowing red in the dark night. White teeth reflected the moonlight. They were triangular, the mouth revealing a horrible tunnel. It was a shark.

The seal tried to dive, but was too slow. The fish bit down on it and thrashed it about. The teeth worked through the meat like buzz saws. With one final flay, the seal was torn in two.

Scar consumed the dead seal, then turned his attention on the killer whale. Like them, it was intending to stalk the seals and devour as many as possible. But now, it had a new target.

Charlie unleashed a cry, alerting Freddy to the threat. The companion abandoned his chase in favor of meeting the new threat. Like Charlie, Freddy was alarmed by the horrible red eyes. Even the scar over the right eye seemed to glow. The fish was far larger than any other carnivorous shark they had ever encountered. Most great whites were ten feet smaller than them, but this one was significantly larger. It even surpassed them in length.

Now, they were on a new mission. A predator like this was a direct threat to the pod and the youngster. There was only one plan of action: destroy the threat.

The killer whales separated, with Charlie circling around the back.

Scar moved slowly, watching the orca in front, while using his lateral line and Ampellae of Lorenzini to gauge the other's movements. Freddy swam aggressively, trying to keep the fish from noticing its companion. Suddenly, like a bolt of lightning, the shark shot right for him.

Charlie lashed for the caudal fin, but was too late.

Scar rammed directly into Freddy's snout, resulting in a thunderclap echo that traveled far and wide. The orca was knocked upward, his jaws biting high above the shark's snout. Scar moved in for the exposed underside.

The orca thrashed in agony as the jaws of death sank into his underside, right below his left flipper. He tried to pull away, but Scar pressed inward to follow. His head jerked violently, sawing his teeth against his opponent's flesh.

Charlie rushed in for the rescue, mouth agape. He bit down on the shark's tail right behind the caudal fin. He felt a couple of his teeth chip. The shark's skin was like rock! He let go and bit again, unable to penetrate.

A smack of the caudal fin against his face sent Charlie tumbling downward, while Scar proceeded to rip apart his companion. There was no more moonlight illuminating these waters, as it was blacked out by a cloud of blood.

The killer whale squealed, then spun into a corkscrew, prying himself from those horrible teeth. Flesh ripped and blood spurted, but he came free. Freddy knew he would not outrun the fish with his injury. His best bet would be to meet the enemy head on. He dove briefly, then circled underneath. The shark aimed down to follow him, only to turn around.

Charlie slowed, his sneak attack subverted. All of a sudden, he was on the defensive. Scar came in at full speed, jaws hyperextended. The orca realized the danger he was in, and banked right. After barely avoiding the bite, he rushed past the shark, who missed a second attempt, this time aimed at the fluke.

Scar turned around, ready to pursue the mammal, only to be struck from underneath. Freddy had charged with full force, resulting in an impact powerful enough to launch the larger predator out of the surface.

Scar's red eyes glowed in the night air, drawing the attention of the seals that gathered on the atoll. He struck down in a violent splash, then immediately followed the blood trail. The orca that struck him was circling back for another try. And the unwounded one was coming in from the right.

Charlie closed in and bit on the left pectoral fin. The skin was softer here, but still strong. He dove, dragging the beast with him. Freddy swam in from up top, still gushing huge clouds of blood from his wound. The orca was sluggish now, but still determined to see the fight through. He clamped his jaws over the dorsal fin, then together, the duo dragged the shark into the depths, intending to pin it against the seabed and drown it.

However, neither were prepared for Scar's brute force. The fish twisted back and forth, lashing with his head and tail. His caudal fin struck Freddy's injury, sparking pain and weakening his grip. The tip of that tail was like a tooth. It sliced again and again. The orcas were almost at the bottom when the weaker member lost his grip. With half of the driving force gone, Scar turned sharply to the right, yanking his pectoral fin free from Charlie's mouth. As he completed his turn, his caudal fin slapped the orca, the tip of it lacerating his right eye.

Scar completed his circle, as well as his decision to attack the wounded orca or the other.

Charlie, his right eye now blind, never saw the attack coming. The fish bit his right flipper and tore it away with ease. Charlie twisted in agony, then tried to take flight. He only managed two flaps of his fluke before the shark closed in again and bit. The serrated edges, like teeth in and of themselves, shredded Charlie's tail. With the fluke still in his mouth, Scar turned. Now it was *he* who was dragging the orca to the depths.

He thrashed his head, turning the flesh into ribbons. He then let go, but only to turn his attention on Freddy, who was coming in from above. Scar hooked to the side, dodging the orca's attack altogether. Freddy attempted to turn, but was too slow and weak. The shark moved in again and rammed his jaws into Freddy's already gaping wound.

Down below, Charlie could do nothing but watch as the fish tore apart his companion. Freddy was twitching, barely alive, forced to endure the horrible torture of having his stomach and entrails removed. Rib bones broke away, with pieces of meat trailing from them.

Charlie flapped his tail gently. Each movement was excruciating, but he couldn't stay here and wait for death. He had to warn the other pod members. The youngster would have no chance against this shark. Unfortunately, he had to use his dying companion as a diversion to grant him a head start.

The orca accelerated, plowing through a thick cloud of blood and guts. He heard one final dying cry from his hunting companion. The orca clicked, telling him goodbye.

Red eyes glowed through the death cloud. Scar bit repeatedly, tearing large chunks of flesh from his dead opponent. The struggling motions of the remaining orca caused ripples that tingled his lateral line. Scar's hunger had been satiated...for the moment. Now, all he wanted to do was kill.

He pushed the dead orca with his snout, then sped through the murky water, following the vibrations.

The pod awoke suddenly to a series of alarming pulsed calls. Immediately, they circled the young one. Charlie continued his clicks, relaying emotions of grief, anger, as well as warning.

This was no normal adversary that was approaching. Several orcas clicked back, as though questioning the matter. Charlie's mate, Daisy, stayed close to their young. She whistled, sensing the approach of the large creature that Charlie was warning them about.

Charlie called to his mate one final time, then circled back to confront the fish.

Scar's mouth was open slightly, with bits of Freddy's flesh dangling from his teeth. Charlie sped right at him, then clamped his jaws over his snout. He flapped his wounded tail, driving the shark backward.

Several other pod members joined in, only to be caught off guard by the shark's thick, pebbly skin. The fish shook his head loose from Charlie's grasp, then lashed to the right at a whale that was gnawing at his pectoral fin. His teeth shredded flesh and blubber, forcing the orca away. In that same attack, Scar swatted his razor tail, lacerating another below the jaw.

It was all out war now. Scar didn't need to choose any target. The orcas were everywhere. All he needed to do was bite, and he'd find a target. He weaved back and forth, biting at the swarm of orcas. Echoes of painful calls sparked horror to the youngster and his mother, and the others that remained to protect him.

Scar swam in a tight loop, dodging one attack while simultaneously initiating one of his own. He clamped his jaws shut over the dorsal fin of another orca, and ripped it clean off its back. The orca cried out and raced to the surface, trailing blood. Scar ascended with it. As he did, another rushed in from the side, only to be knocked away by a swing of his snout. The orca spun and sank like a corpse. By the time it got its bearing, the shark had caught up with the wounded member.

Scar ripped into the bleeding orca's belly. The victim lifted its head into the air and echoed its screams into the night sky. Blood bubbled all around it. Scar took in a mouthful of flesh, then pulled away, extending intestines from the dying orca's now sinking body.

Finally, the pod broke off. Their leader's warnings were correct. This beast was not like any other creature in the sea. It was invulnerable to their attacks. In addition, it wasn't killing for food. It was just killing.

Coordinated by whistles from Charlie, the pod returned to the others, then began racing north. Charlie remained in the back, exchanging clicks with Daisy and the youngster. His injuries were getting the better of him, and the fish was closing in on the pod. There was no other choice.

He spun back and engaged the fish. Jaws snapped and tails whipped as the two beasts wrestled. Charlie bit at Scar's throat, growling in frustration, as he was unable to pierce that flesh.

As the pod continued onward, only Daisy held back, unable to assist her mate without leaving her young.

Charlie and Scar were rolling over each other, appearing as though they were trying to wrap around the other like snakes. There was blood in the water. The shark had grabbed the pod leader by the tail, and was pulling him toward the island. Charlie swung to the left and nipped at the shark's tail, but only succeeded in chipping his teeth. Scar released in favor of a better grip…which was Charlie's other flipper.

He tore it clean off, then bit at his face, ravaging Charlie's other eye. Now completely blind, the orca thrashed blindly, listening to the cries of his mate who watched from a distance. He managed one final call before the fish bit the top of his head, ripping open his blowhole.

Water flooded his airways. Charlie twisted and turned, then jolted as the jaws closed over his belly, ripping him wide open. He was drowning and bleeding to death at the same time. Either method would've killed him in the same amount of time. Scar swallowed mouthfuls of flesh, then proceeded to swim off. The rest of the pod had moved far off, and were not worth the energy pursuing at the moment.

Daisy mourned the loss of her mate as she reunited with her young. The pod swam north in unison. Those with bite wounds would heal. Others carried scars that ran deep.

Daisy's wound would never truly heal. The death of her mate was horrific and sudden, and would always remain in her memory. The only thing that would overpower such a ghost would be revenge. Sooner or later, she would meet that shark again. She would not let her mate's death go unavenged. Nor would the pod that faithfully followed him.

They would bide their time. Before long, they would return.

CHAPTER 12

Olivia downed half her water bottle in one sitting, stopping only to swallow before finishing the rest. Her head throbbed from the excessive intake of alcohol that assisted in her 'down payment' to the mercenary leader. The bastard was seated next to her, his cigar smoke filling the fuselage of the helicopter they rode in.

During the two-hour flight, she had to endure the endless banter between the six mercenaries sharing the fuselage with her. Sitting directly across was Dorn. The bastard couldn't keep that shit-eating smile off his face every time his eyes went her way. It was as though he was taunting her. *Yeah, I know what you two did.*

To his left was Jacques. Olivia preferred him most out of the entire group, because he spoke the least. He clung to his M4 Carbine like a Viking with an axe, his glare equally as menacing. She knew he was a scarred man, both physically and mentally. His ballcap was as battered as his rugged face. She never asked why, and frankly, she never cared. As long as the bastard got the job done.

A stark contrast to his persona was the man sitting left of him. Heitmeyer could not seem to go two minutes without telling some kind of pornographic joke. And his companions were finding each one hilarious, though there were a couple that made even this vulgar bunch cringe. But for the most part, Heitmeyer was the team comedian, and his stupid jokes and the teammates' dumb reactions were like fingernails on a chalkboard for her.

"You have any idea how to make your girlfriend scream during sex?" He grinned, enjoying the anticipation as his teammates shook their heads. "Call and tell her about it!"

The fuselage filled with laughter. Already, Heitmeyer was starting his next joke.

"Why does Dr. Pepper come in a bottle?" Again, he paused. "Because his wife died!"

Olivia shut her eyes and rubbed her temples. The laughter echoed in the confined space. At the start of the trip, she had fooled herself into thinking the most annoying part of this trip would be the drone of the rotors. Now, she would pay most of her finances to shut this group up.

Her blood pressure rose further at the sound of Lowery's voice. Even without looking to her right, she knew that the mercenary seated on the other side of Roark was leaning over to gaze at her.

"I think the good doctor's getting airsick," he said.

"Fuck off," Olivia muttered.

"I think she is!" Mason said.

Olivia's scowl could've been etched on her face, as it never seemed to waiver during the whole trip. Even the sixty-year old merc was getting in on this.

Why am I surprised? The guy looks more like a has-been in a biker gang than a trained mercenary with that grey, overgrown goatee, sunglasses, sleeve tattoos, and shaved head.

"Probably just pissed," Dorn said.

"Not as pissed as this girl I once knew," Heitmeyer said. "She kept yelling at me, 'give it to me! Give it to me! I'm so wet, give it to me now!' I told her 'no'. She could scream at me all she wanted, but I wasn't gonna give her the damn umbrella."

Again, everyone but Jacques filled the fuselage with laughter. That, combined with the vibrations from the chopper, stirred her stomach. She could feel herself getting pale.

"Almost there," the pilot said.

Oh, finally! Olivia was just starting to feel the seat pocket for the barf bag, but something about knowing the flight was ending calmed her.

"So, Doc?" Heitmeyer asked. Begrudgingly, she looked his way, expecting another joke. "We've been in the air for two hours, and you haven't really given us a briefing."

"We're hunting a shark. We're capturing it alive for transport back to a lab my company has in the Atlantic," she answered. A few of the men chuckled at her annoyed tone. "Hasn't Roark explained that to you?"

"He told us exactly what you just said," Heitmeyer replied. "But how the hell are we gonna capture it alive?"

"We're going to lure it with bait, which will be loaded with a sedative," she replied. "The boat you're about to see has a holding tank that'll be secure enough to transport him."

"Him?" Dorn laughed. Even Jacques smirked at the use of the word.

"Force of habit," Olivia replied. "I call him Scar."

"Funny, we call *him* Scar too!" Heitmeyer said, pointing at Roark.

"Yeah?" Roark leaned in. "Want to share the nickname?" Heitmeyer's grin shrank, and he sat straight in his chair. It was one of those awkward moments when he couldn't tell whether his boss was joking or serious.

The chopper set down on a cement landing pad a few dozen yards from a large industrial-looking building. To the east was a small harbor. Several workmen were at the dock, loading supplies into what appeared to be a medium-sized yacht.

The fuselage door opened up. Olivia breathed a sigh of relief after stepping on solid ground. Roark walked to her left. The prick had had a smirk on his face since they both awoke that morning after many hours of vigorous activity. Knowing him, he'd try for seconds once the mission was over.

Olivia glanced back at the team of mercenaries, each walking with shotguns and assault rifles.

"Don't forget you guys are here to capture my shark *alive*."

"Oh, that's not a problem, ma'am," Dorn explained. "These are only to ensure payment."

Olivia's glare intensified, then was directed at Roark. He glanced at her, then back forward.

"There a problem with that?"

"You don't trust me?!"

"I don't trust anyone until I'm paid in full," he replied. Olivia wanted to lambast him, but held back. Now wasn't the time. She just needed to get through the next day or so. Afterwards, this would be nothing but a memory.

They stepped onto the dock. It was at this point when the mercenaries noticed the *Skomal Corp* logos on the workers' shirts.

"I didn't know you had a facility here," Roark said.

"Skomal's expanding," Olivia said. "We're hoping to have labs across the country. We have one in Africa, and two in the Middle East."

"Yeah? What are you developing for them over there?"

It was Jacques that spoke. His voice was growly, almost lizard-like. She didn't look back at him, as it just dawned that the scars on his face might be the result of chemical weapons, similar to the ones that Skomal may or may not have been selling to governments and private groups across the Atlantic. She went with the usual lie.

"Medical research. There's lots of diseases in those regions that don't currently have a cure." She left it at that.

The vessel was about a hundred feet in length. It had a main forward deck in front of the pilothouse, and a large fly deck that extended over the aft deck. A metal guardrail lined the gunwale on each deck. On the transom railing were two battery powered spotlights pointing outward. Similar spotlights had been attached to both sides of the forward, aft, and fly decks. Beneath the transom was a tight lining, barely visible, where a ramp separated to provide entry into the cargo hold.

"We have everything set and ready to go," one of the workers said.

"Good," Olivia said, stepping by him. "Is someone in the pilothouse?"

"Yes."

"Have them open the ramp."

The worker barked the commands through a radio. A moment later, the door opened with a dull groan. It lowered all the way into the water, revealing the holding chamber inside. There were huge body restraints made with stainless steel on the starboard side, looking like giant handcuffs, that would close down and latch into slots on the port side. At the end were two pumps, one for water, the other for a steady supply of sedative to circulate over Scar's gills.

"Should I have to explain the use of any of this to you men?" she asked the mercenaries.

"Only how you expect us to get the fish in there," Mason said.

"As I've said, we're going to lure it with chum and bait, which will be loaded with a high dose of tranquilizer. It's a fast-acting drug. Plus, Scar's metabolism should break it down quickly. It'll take a number of minutes for it to kick in. When it does, we'll use a drone to fasten a cable around his neck and reel him into the tank."

"I'm glad she mentioned drone, because no way in hell am I going in that water," Heitmeyer said.

"Shark's glad too. Seeing your sore ass skinny dipping would drive anything away," Dorn replied.

"You sure we have enough supplies?" Roark said.

"Yes," Olivia said. "We have enough chum to fill the entire ocean. If we were to run out, I'm sure you wouldn't mind sacrificing him." She pointed at Heitmeyer.

Roark smirked. "That idea is a bit tempting. What about repair supplies?"

"Got that too. We have everything," Olivia said.

"Beer too?" Mason said. Olivia groaned. Being around these guys while sober was bad enough.

"No," she stated bluntly. "Now, can we get started? It's a few hours journey to Scar's location."

"And that is?"

"He's been moving steadily around a location called Cross Point," Olivia answered.

"Oh, perfect!" Roark said. "Grand place for feasting on tourists! You realize how busy that location is?"

"Discretion is one of the reasons this boat was designed to look like a typical luxury yacht," Olivia said. "As long as you don't wear your stupid tactical vests out in the open like you are right now, we'll go unnoticed."

"You better hope so," Roark said, "because I don't believe in loose ends."

"Neither do I," Olivia said. Roark scoffed.

"You sure about that? Seems a little low, even for you," he said. Olivia shook her head.

"This shark is to be delivered to the lab within two days. I don't care who you have to shoot to get it done," she said.

"Wow. You really are a bitch," he said.

"Says the guy who does the shooting," she replied.

"Only because you're paying me." That smirk returned. "You really will do anything to get ahead, won't you?"

Olivia gave no response. "Get on the boat."

Roark glanced back at his team. "You heard her, boys. Heitmeyer, you're the helmsman."

"Aye-aye, sir! Arrr, I'm on it!" the merc said, mimicking a pirate voice. He rushed in-between Roark and Olivia and climbed aboard.

"And change your outfits," she demanded. "I told you before to look casual, and you all had to dress like you're invading a foreign country."

"Better than looking like we're about to waitress at a vegan restaurant," Dorn retorted. The mercs laughed, then proceeded to board the vessel, leaving a steaming mad Olivia Zoller on the dock.

Three or four hours travel time to the destination, with no telling how long it would take to capture the shark, followed by ten hours travel time to the lab. She should've packed some of Roark's whiskey.

CHAPTER 13

Nick and Lisa embraced in the golden tint of the candlelight. Their arms wrapped around each other, fingertips brushing bare skin. Passion elevated blood pressure. He pressed his lips to hers and felt her body writhe against him.

Then, right as he rolled on top of her, a new light entered the room. It was bright as the morning sunrise. It overpowered his senses, and suddenly, he felt himself lifting away as though floating on a cloud. As he lifted, an obnoxious ringing filled his ears.

Nick leaned up in bed, then slammed a fist into that prick of an alarm clock that stirred him from one of the best dreams he'd had in years. The sun was just starting to peek over the horizon, its rays beaming right through his window. He glanced back and forth, gradually coming back from the bliss of the dream, then finally accepted the reality that he was alone.

He fell back against his pillow and groaned.

"Ugh, I hate being a nice, respectful guy," he said. His mind immediately went to last night's date. It had gone well. They talked more about Lisa's fascinating career, as well as things she hoped to accomplish in the future, and a little about Nick's mundane routine here on the island. He liked mundane; it was simple, low stress, and easy. As he got older, he began to appreciate those things more and more. But he was starting to worry she wouldn't like mundane, so he did his best to avoid it for the most part. It was good conversational manners anyway to focus on her life instead. After their dinner, he drove her home, but was lucky enough to steal a kiss from her. She probably would've let him in if he made the move.

But... he was a nice, respectful guy.

His alarm rang again.

"Alright, alright! I'm getting up," he told it. The next stop was the shower, then the closet to get ready for work.

****

By eight a.m., Lisa Robinson was on her research yacht, going over the invoices sent by the Institution. It contained the usual requests; numbers of crab populations, collect coral samples, provide updates on hammerhead migrations, as well as a confirmation for the list of supplies she had recently ordered.

It was hard to keep a straight thought, as her mind was on the date with Nick. She felt something last night, and she really hoped he would take her out again. The idea of getting attached brought back the usual anxieties pertaining to her job and what the future held in store for her, but they weren't as bad. Perhaps it was just the dopamine hit from the flood of endorphins blocking her concerns. Or perhaps it was confidence that things would somehow work out.

Eh, it's way too early to think about long term stuff. We've only been on two dates.

The sight of her smartphone lying on the work desk brought the temptation to text Nick. Knowing him, he'd probably be ecstatic, even more so if she mentioned going to the gun range to shoot off a couple AR-15s.

Her thought was interrupted by an orange blinking light on her computer. One of the window tabs had updated information for her to review. She clicked on the tab and expanded it. It was the tracking markers for the orca pods. The reader flashed an alert that one was no longer sending off a signal.

Lisa clicked a few keys to bring up the satellite. Most of the pod had moved a few miles to the northeast, while two others remained not too far from the atoll.

"What's going on here? Out hunting?"

She knew from her observations that Freddy and Charlie often separated from the group to hunt seals. However, that was usually during the night. At this time in the day, the pod often stuck close together. She checked the time again. Usually, the pod would start gathering in their normal spot by now.

Eh, maybe they found a new feeding ground. There's time still. They might regroup. Still, she found it odd for the pod to be that far separated from their leader. It was inconsistent with all of the previous behaviors of this particular group.

She checked her bank account to make sure the expense fund had been replenished by the Institution. It had.

Perfect! The next stop for the day would be the docks to see if she could pick up some fish for the pod. Then, she would stop by a temperature buoy on the north side of the island. By the time she was done with all of that, it would be time to meet with the pod, assuming they would return from whatever it was they were doing.

****

There wasn't much activity for the Sheriff's department. A few parking tickets, a few dine and dashes, but nothing major.

At 9:30, Nick was in his office, going over the reports regarding the jet ski incident near the atoll, as well as a few incident reports that came in during the night shift. One report involved damage to a pier on the east side of the island. One of the legs had been broken away, as if something had grabbed it and snapped it like a twig.

Another report was regarding a complaint from a fisherman, suggesting that something had ripped through a trawl net. At first, he figured it was Barney Grey trying to stir up trouble again, until he realized it was Jesse Black who made the call.

"Okay, what's going on here? We have some sort of net-shredding fiend on the loose?" he asked himself. He heard a knock on the door. "Come in."

Patty, the front desk secretary, poked her head through the doorway.

"Hi, Sheriff. Hate to bother you, but I've got someone wanting to report a missing person. The deputies are out on post, so I thought I'd direct her to you."

"Oh, *her*," Nick said. "Let me guess. It's Amanda Drier again, wanting me to track down Pete for effing around."

"No, actually," Patty said. "This is Mika Kusmer. Though, Amanda Drier did call Dispatch to follow up on Pete."

"He never came home?"

"No, sir."

Nick stood up from his desk. "Alright, this week officially sucks. Is Mika in the front lobby?"

"She is. If you want, I'll radio one of the deputies to take the report."

"No, I'll take care of it. Sounds like she wants to talk to me directly." Nick walked with Patty to the front lobby, where the twenty-eight-year-old Green Eel Bar and Grill waitress was seated. She was dressed in her work clothes, having worked a double shift yesterday with an eight hour turnaround before going back in this morning. Being a frequent visitor there, Nick knew how the shifts worked. She should've started an hour ago.

"Mika. What's the trouble?" Nick asked. Her dark skin was pale, her brow moist from sweat. Her braids were unkempt, as was her uniform.

"Sheriff. I've been trying to call Rosco all morning. He never came back from fishing. He's been out late before, but never all night. He still hasn't come back."

"Okay. Keep calm. I'm sure he's fine. There's not much out there to give him trouble. When was the last time you saw him?"

"Six-thirty, yesterday morning," she answered. "We spoke on the phone around nine. He said he was having a good trip and would probably be back early. He usually comes in at six p.m."

"Do you know of anyone else who might've seen him during this time that I can talk to?"

"I asked his fishing buddies. There's Barry and Esteban, but neither of them have seen him. He's not answering his phone. I can't even get a GPS signal on it."

"Alright. Don't worry. I'll start looking for him right away. Do you know where he tends to fish?"

"Uh, usually the northeast side. He's been having a lot of luck out there lately. I think he goes about five miles out, but it varies."

At least that was something, though not much. Five miles was a lot of space to cover. If he didn't turn up with anything by the end of the day, he'd have to alert the Coast Guard. It wasn't too uncommon for fishermen to be out all night, even without telling their spouses. They often got caught up in the work. However, Rosco didn't strike him as the type to not call. Perhaps he didn't have a signal? That was possible, since cell reception sucked anywhere further than a half mile from the island.

This is what I get for bragging this job gives me peace and quiet.

"I'm gonna go out and look for him," Nick told her. "I'll get my deputies on it. We'll make sure he comes home safe and sound. And if it turns out he stayed out all night without calling, I'll slap him for you."

Mika chuckled. "Thanks, Sheriff."

"No problem. Do whatever you need to do to relax. Take a sick day. Watch Netflix." He guided Mika out the door. She thanked him, then went out into the parking lot. Nick waited until she was in her car, then approached the secretary's desk. His easy-going, optimistic expression shed away to make room for a grim, serious one. "Patty? What time did Amanda call?"

"Ten minutes ago. Wanted to inform you that Pete had not returned. No sign of their yacht, either."

Nick felt a tinge of anxiety creeping into his stomach.

"Alright, two reports like this is not a coincidence. Get word to the dispatch office and make sure they're aware of the missing persons' names and listen for any mention of them in future calls. If we're lucky, someone might report that they've found them."

"Do you want us to put an APB on them?"

"At this point, yeah. Neither of these cases are looking too good. I'm gonna be out on a boat to see if I can find clues. If I don't find anything, we'll have to notify the Coast Guard."

He grabbed the keys to his truck and hurried out the door. As he started the engine, he clicked the radio transmitter.

"Unit One to Three and Eight. Meet me over by the west harbor. Right now."

CHAPTER 14

Curtains of water sprayed high as Stevie Brooks pushed the jetboat to the limit. He cut the wheel to starboard, turning the boat as though doing wheelies in a parking lot. Water sprayed eight feet high behind him. More than once, Stevie swept near a few smaller boats and soaked the occupants, much to the amusement, and dismay, of his girlfriend Lara.

Dressed in an American flag style bikini, Lara leaned back in her seat, drinking an orange juice/vodka mix. Ten in the morning? Who cares?! She was on vacation, and she was going to enjoy every second of it. Stevie certainly didn't mind. The tipsier she got, the more open to suggestion she was. And despite the hangovers, she never had any incidents that required cleaning.

Lara watched the ocean through her pink sunglasses, embracing the power of the wind through her hair. She had four more days of bliss before they had to return to Indiana. Then, she'd be back to managing Starbucks and explaining the difference between a latte and a cappuccino to customers who really ought to be drinking smoothies. At least that job helped her to meet Stevie...before he was fired for telling a customer that very thing. It worked out in a way, since company policy prohibited co-workers from engaging in relationships.

Now, Stevie was a manager in his own right, in charge of a McDonald's, which he also came close to getting fired from. He wasn't an angry person, just a natural wiseass, with no care for his finances, as proven with his twenty-thousand in credit card debt doing things like buying vacations he couldn't afford or renting jetboats on the fly. As long as he made that minimum payment, he was usually eligible for another card.

Her brown hair flapped in the wind as her boyfriend completed another turn.

There were a few other speedboats and yachts out a half mile to the east, most of them performing the same routines. Further out were a few love yachts and fishing boats. Stevie zigzagged between a couple of them, the jets of water spraying the decks before he aimed the boat north and fled. Laughing hysterically, he held his middle finger up to the disgruntled boat owners now behind him, who wouldn't see it due to the big jet of water that splashed over their windshields.

"Ah-ha-ha! What's the matter? Get a little wet?" he shouted. He could barely even hear himself though the roar of the engine and constant splashing all around him.

"Come on, babe! Don't get us in too much trouble," Lara said. She was laughing as she said it, but she might have had a point. He glanced back, making sure none of the speedboaters decided to make chase after his little stunt. One of them followed for a few dozen yards, but quickly gave it up.

Stevie watched the group in his mirror. Maybe Lara was right...maybe. Pissing other people off, especially strangers, was just too much fun for him. It was one of the reasons he hated the retail and fast food industry.

It looked like the boaters behind him had cooled off, at least enough so to not do anything about it. Still, better to keep making some distance. He raced another mile northeast, then spotted a yacht with a couple of jet-skiers buzzing all around it like flies. There was two other people sitting on the aft deck, all college age by the looks of it. The deck was about three feet off the water...low enough for his jets to clear the gunwale. He smiled mischievously.

Stevie had been told that he was born an obnoxious prick, and the thoughts going through his head justified that statement. No way would that yacht catch up with him, and anyone would be stupid to pursue a jetboat on a jet ski. What would they do? Leap onto his boat like some 80's action hero?

He started aiming the bow to starboard, then felt Lara slap his arm.

"Don't even think about it," she said.

"What? I don't know what you're talking about!" Stevie lied.

"Uh-huh. You're thinking of spraying them."

"A little water never hurt anybody."

"Yeah, but it might piss them off," she said. "We don't know any of these people. One of these days, you're gonna piss off the wrong person."

"Oh, they won't do anything. I've already thought it through!"

"Stevie! There are jet skiers all around. You could crash. *Please,* turn away."

Oh, she had to ask like that. Stevie stuck his tongue out at her, then aimed the boat away. After passing the boat, he continued northeast.

"Looks like you need a refill there," he said, pointing at her glass.

"Hey. Don't judge."

"I'm not. I'm actually jealous. I could use one myself," he said. He performed another tight circle, splashing nothing but air and ocean. *I must be a prick, because this isn't as exciting if someone's not getting pissed off.* He looked longingly at the yacht to the southwest and the jet skis moving around it.

Lara leaned over and smiled, already halfway to being drunk.

"Oh! Well, all you have to do is ask," she said. Stevie whooped and completed the spin, then finally slowed down to a stop.

"Hey baby! Would you be so kind to lean down," he winked, "and make me an early bird cocktail?"

"I can do that," she said, "if you let me drive the boat." She leaned in for a kiss, which Stevie quickly pulled away from.

"Hell no!"

"What?! What do you mean 'hell no!?' You think I can't drive a boat?"

"Not in your current condition," he argued. "You know the rules. *I'm* the one who put the money down on this thing—nobody drives this bad boy but me."

It only took eight seconds for the mood to go from exhilarated, to sensuous, to plain hostile.

"You remember the agreement when we moved in together," she said. "What's yours is mine. What's mine is yours."

"I remember saying we aren't married, so that isn't so," he retorted.

"You're an ass," she said, then whipped herself back into her seat. She crossed her arms and looked away.

Stevie smiled, feeling victorious as he pushed the throttle. "Face it. You love my ass."

After several seconds, she looked back at him.

In another eight seconds, that hostile look transformed back into a sensuous smile.

"Maybe a little." She pinched two fingers in front of her eye. "You're still a prick."

"Yeah? What are you going to do about it?"

"Not make your drink," she said.

"I can live with that," he said. He sped the boat again. The bow raised a couple of feet, the jets intensifying behind him. He slowly turned to starboard and glanced back at Lara. She was watching him the whole time, tilting her shades down, hypnotizing him with her stare and grin. It was clear to him what card she was playing. And that smile was genuine, because she knew it would eventually work. The happier she was, the better the next 'activity' would be. Already, his mind was playing a dozen different pornographic scenarios featuring the two of them, and one that included her last roommate. *Damn, I wish she'd be that open minded again.*

"Alright, fine!" He slowed the boat to a stop, then stood up. "But I want that drink first."

"Oh, you want a drink?" Lara laughed obnoxiously—never a good sign. "Here's your drink!" She stood up and pushed him over the edge. Stevie summersaulted backwards under the water, his curses lost in a series of air bubbles. He emerged along the surface then scowled at his live-in girlfriend, who had moved over to his seat, her laughter echoing to the blue sky.

"And I thought *I* was the dick!" he said.

"Oh, you are. And I can see why. It is kind of fun!" she said. She started fixing a drink. At first, Stevie thought it was for him until she started sipping from it.

"Hey!"

"How does the water feel, babe?"

Stevie smirked, stroking his arms to the side. "Be better with you in it."

"No way," she said.

"Why not?!" He backpaddled a bit.

"Stevie, you know me! I watch too many shark attack documentaries."

"Then you should know you have a better chance of being struck by lightning," Stevie said. "Come on. Get in the water with me. It'll tone that sexy body of yours up."

Lara shook her head. "Hmm-mm, no way."

"If you're so worried about sharks, then why'd you push me in?" he joked.

"Because it's funny! And I'm tipsy."

Stevie started to paddle to the boat.

"Maybe I'll find it funny if I pull you in with me!"

She backed to the other side.

"Nuh-uh!"

"Oh, for crying out loud. There aren't any sharks!" He jerked suddenly, his eyes wide, mouth gaping, as though about to let loose a horrible scream. "Oh no! There is! Lara, you were right! AHHHH!" He splashed back and forth, mimicking struggle. "It's got me!"

Lara crossed her arms and shook her head. "You're a dork."

Stevie laughed. "See? My splashing would've alerted any sharks that would be nearby. As you can see, there are no sharks." He mimicked being attacked again. "Wahhh. Wahhh. WHHAAAAHHHHH!"

Lara cupped her hands over her mouth and screamed. The huge shape seemed to materialize out of nowhere. It rose up out of the water, with Stevie impaled in its jaws. Blood spurted from his abdomen, coating the side of the boat. Stevie reached out to her, only to vanish beneath a huge splash as the shark crashed back down. A swell hit the boat, knocking Lara back into her seat.

Her heart pounded and her mind raced. With trembling hands, she pulled herself to an upright position and looked for the swells. The shark was now on the starboard side, with a red cloud trailing behind it. She looked over and screamed again. With one mighty swing of its head, the shark tore Stevie in half. His upper body was thrown several feet ahead of the beast. To Lara's horror, it looked like he was still trying to swim. His arms stroked, his teeth clenched. Before he slowed into a deathly pose, the shark snatched the rest of him up, chomped a few times, then swallowed.

Lara's screams intensified when she saw the arm float away to the side before sinking. The ocean was now completely red. Buzzing and surging with adrenaline, she sat in front of the helm and felt the controls.

How does this work? She found a lever that she remembered Stevie pushing, then shoved it forward. The boat gunned, the bow lifting slightly. Caught off guard by the sudden motion, Lara leaned back in her seat. She grabbed the helm and spun it to the side. The boat turned sharply. *Too* sharply. She pulled back, barely preventing herself from flipping over.

Now, she was at risk of tipping over on the left side. She throttled back, then adjusted her steering. Already, there was no sense of direction. All she saw were boats way off in the distance, none of them close enough to know what was happening.

To the left was the red cloud, comprised of her boyfriend's blood. She must've circled all the way around. She remembered the way they came. If she went directly ahead, she should eventually return to the beach.

Before she could gun the throttle again, she felt the shudder of impact beneath her. All of a sudden, she and the boat were airborne. The bow flipped upward, flinging her into the water. She skidded along the surface and sank.

The water itself was like a wind, spinning her around. She threw her arms out to fight against the current. Her eyes opened. The jetboat was nearly broken in two, the sections held together by a small piece of hull. She felt another jerk of the current.

Something had moved past her, and was circling back behind her. She spun around, then let out a muffled scream.

The fish came directly at her and bit her across the middle. Blood bubbles erupted from her mouth as she was shaken side to side. Her legs came off first. Then her midsection, leaving only her shoulders and head, which were quickly snatched up and eaten.

Scar swam around the blood cloud for a few moments in search of any remains. He was still hungry, and the water was full of prey. It was just a matter of catching, killing, and devouring.

CHAPTER 15

David Hummer watched the water ripple behind the police vessel. He and the Sheriff were almost a mile out by now. They could see the atoll about a quarter mile ahead, roughly seven degrees off the port bow.

By nine a.m., the waters around the island were teeming with boaters. All around, they could see parasails in the sky, fishing lines trailing fifty yards behind yachts, a few vessels simply drifting, while their occupants conversed. So far, no sign of Pete Drier or Rosco Kusmer.

"Unit Three? You see anything yet?"

"Would've radioed you if I had, Sheriff," Roper replied. He was patrolling somewhere on the southeast end. *"Found a small yacht adrift. Thought it was Pete's for a second. Then you should've seen the young feller who came bursting out after I flashed my lights. Barely managed to pull his shorts on. Mad as a bull!"*

"Fabulous," Nick said. He put the mic down and watched the water.

"Sheriff, you think we'll even find them out here in all this?"

"That's our job," Nick said.

"It's a big ocean," David said. "Even if these people were actually missing, what are our odds of finding them?"

"It doesn't matter," Nick said. David hesitated before asking the next question. Usually, when the Sheriff sounded irritated, it was when he was setting somebody up for a joke. This time, though, it was especially hard to tell if it was genuine.

"Pardon me for asking, but I think it matters in the sense of how we stretch our manpower," David said.

"Kid..." Nick looked back, "I know our spot is laid back and all, but you need to understand that this job is not all sunshine and rainbows."

"Sir, don't get me wrong. I'm not trying to be a prick. I just think it might be wise to wait another day to see if these guys come back."

Nick turned around. His expression, while not angry, was a bit stern.

"Here's a quick story for you, kid. We had an APB in Ann Arbor alerting us that somebody was missing in Southfield. The person was the kind of person who went off on their own, so most people didn't think of it to be a big deal. Except the dude's mother. The guy was supposed to stop by at a certain time to help her with the sink or something. Never showed up. Didn't answer the phone. Turns out he was jumped outside of his office and left to die in an alley a few blocks down. Coroner said if he was found three hours sooner, he might've lived. The cops in that district waited four before they started looking."

David nodded. *Point taken.*

They continued past the atoll, passing the time by chit-chatting about fishing, police work, and sports. Around here, the water wasn't nearly as busy, which would make spotting boats a little easier.

Figuring this would be a longer trip, Nick was smart enough to pack a cooler.

"Want a water?" He held one out to David.

"Sure." David held his hands out to catch it, his fumbling hands nearly knocking the bottle over the side. Nick cackled and turned to face the helm.

"You ought to play for the Tigers with those catching skills," he said. David leaned against the transom and twisted the cap.

"Hey, I may not catch for shit, but I can curve a ball right past your bat. You'll think it's a straight shot, until your swing hits nothing but air."

Nick glanced back again.

"You play baseball?"

"Back in High School and College," David said. "My last game, I had three innings in a row where nobody even nicked the ball! And two three-pitch innings!"

"Yeah? I had a game where I had four of each," Nick said, unimpressed. David's smile faltered. Nick grinned. "Just kidding. Not bad kid. Provided that's not a fish tale you're spewing."

"Hell no. Here, I'll show you." David pulled his smartphone from his belt clip and scrolled through his video archives. "Here we go. Check this out." Nick took the phone and watched. It was a far-off view from the bleachers, which obscured David's face. The pitcher leaned forward slightly, ball clenched between both hands. He reared back, then launched it at the batter, who swung and missed. The audience clapped their hands as he repeated the process.

After watching a few more pitches, Nick handed the phone back.

"Could've been anyone," he joked.

"Ha-ha," David said.

"You should've kept at it. Maybe you would've gone pro," Nick said.

"Eh," David looked away while putting the phone back on the belt clip. "Probably would have if I stuck with it a little longer. I was just doing a two-year program, and frankly, I hated school, so…"

"I think I'm hearing some sort of excuse," Nick interrupted.

"Maybe," David said. "Eh…" Nick had seen that look many times.

"You tried out, didn't you?"

David sighed then sat down. "It was June of last year. I went in thinking I was gonna kick ass. Then, all of a sudden, this anxiety takes hold of me when I show up at the camp. My first pitch went wide. Second went high. Tried batting, and I could barely graze the ball." He took a swig of his water. "Worst freaking day of my life. After those games I showed you, I should've had it in the bag. But for some reason, I let the shakes get hold of me."

"Pick a different word. Makes you sound like an alcoholic," Nick joked. They shared a laugh. "I'm gonna ask you a question, and I want you to be honest. Is that why you're here?"

David hesitated to answer. It felt like a trick question.

"It played a part in it. I had a dream. I thought I had it in the bag. Then I watched that dream slip through my fingers. I was majoring in criminal justice and I was close to my degree. I just wanted to get away, because every interaction for months included somebody mentioning the tryouts. 'Oh, I can't believe you didn't get in.' It was like rubbing salt on a wound. Of course, I lied to them and made it sound like I lasted longer than the hour I did."

"Ah! So, you quit?"

"I didn't quit. I failed."

"Another word for quitting, in my book," Nick said.

"Sheriff, you can't tryout more than once."

"That's not what I'm getting at—though to respond to that point, I think you could've tried out with another team. But let me ask you this: why did you want to get involved with baseball?"

David shrugged his shoulders. "Well, uh…"

"There's no wrong answers, Dave. Were you wanting to get rich? No harm in saying yes."

"That's always nice, I won't lie. But, really, I just like baseball. I really like the sport, and wish I could make some kind of living at it."

"Well, shit, David. Why are you here? With a little practice and time investment, you could probably coach on a junior league, then work your way up to college level. If you like being in the sport, you should've kept with it. Instead, you picked the easy way out."

"Isn't that what you did?" David asked. He gulped, thinking he may be overstepping his bounds.

"Not particularly," Nick said. "I like it here. No stress. The job pays well and allows me to practice my hobbies—guns. I love shooting. It's my thing. Hence, I'm always offering practice sessions to you and the guys because I really enjoy it. I love shooting guns so much, I might have to start a *YouTube* channel. Eh, on second thought, I'd probably get blacklisted and demonetized after the first upload. The point is, I get to do what I like, while maintaining a proud family tradition. I can't get enough of shooting at the range. It's my Zen, so to speak. You need to find the same thing for yourself. Believe me, buddy, do not SETTLE for something. It's a long, LONG life if you simply *settle* for something."

David smiled and nodded, feeling a warm feeling of sentimentality. It was always helpful to hear encouragement from others, especially an employer who saw him as more than just a name on an employee list.

His gaze swept past the Sheriff at a shape in the horizon.

"Sheriff?"

Nick turned to look. He squinted.

"Am I seeing what I think I'm seeing?"

There was a yacht about a quarter mile to starboard—what was left of a yacht.

"The wheelhouse...the cabin...it's...DEMOLISHED!" David confirmed. Nick accelerated the patrol boat. Still, he thought he was seeing things. With every few meters gained came more details. Nick could see glimpses of the yacht's interior beneath the wreckage. There was some furniture intact. Maybe a bed as well—it was hard to see exactly. What wasn't hard to see were the indentations in the hull. Something big had repeatedly collided with the yacht. There were no paint markings, nothing to suggest collision with another ship. The fragments all matched the design of the vessel in Nick's memory.

Even stranger, there was a fishing pole on the aft deck with no owner. The portside guardrail was folded down right along the middeck, as though a giant support beam had been dropped on it.

He circled around to the front, catching the letters under an equally ravaged bow. *Morning Anthem.*

"Dave, start taking photos of that right now," Nick instructed, while grabbing his speaker mic. "Boat One to Dispatch."

"Go ahead, Sheriff."

"I've located Pete Drier's vessel, about a half mile northeast of the atoll. It's heavily damaged. Some sort of impact, but nothing that makes sense. I'm gonna climb aboard and have a look inside."

"Ten-four, Sheriff. Do you wish for me to alert Fire-Rescue?"

Nick stared at the front of the pilothouse, and the dried blood that stained the white paint.

"Go ahead. More importantly, we'll need a tugboat out here. And forensics."

"Boat Two copies. Sheriff, you want me to head that way?" Roper said.

"Please."

Nick circled the boat around to the starboard side. Nick lined the vessel up with the boarding ladder and brought the patrol boat to a stop. Dave reached out and grabbed the ladder, keeping the boats from drifting apart. Nick grabbed a rope secured to the railing, then started climbing the ladder. During the short climb, he kept his right hand as close to his Colt Trooper as possible.

He reached the deck and tied the line around the railing, securing the boats together. David climbed to the deck, then followed the Sheriff to the aft side. There, he dug through the wreckage, before ultimately finding a woman's purse near the seat, along with some sandals. Nick walked past the seat and stopped.

"Cigar," he said. He knelt down. The tip had been lit, but it hadn't been smoked for more than an inch. David checked the bag and found an ID.

"Jane Warner."

Nick gave the deck another glance. No other belongings—no sign that anyone else was here. *Perhaps Amanda's suspicions were well founded.*

He turned around to gaze at the massive hump of wreckage. Fragments of the walls were sticking up out of the boat like teeth. The only thing that made sense was some kind of explosive...except there were no noticeable burn marks. Plus, an explosive would've damaged the outer decks...and it also wouldn't account for the cavities in the hull. In addition, the portside railing along the side-deck were crunched downward directly below the breach.

Much of the debris had fallen into the ocean, making a complete analysis impossible. All he could do now was sort through the wreckage in case anyone was buried underneath.

Nick pushed into the interior of the vessel until he was standing in what was previously the owner's cabin. With David's help, he pushed aside large chunks of steel and wooden planks until he had the bed unburied. Among the wreckage was various belongings, all of which seemed normal...except the huge bloodstains all over the carpet.

"Jesus!"

David hurried next to him, then cupped a hand over his mouth. The floor was a red-brown color, dried and cracked from exposure. They looked at some of the other fragments, which were also caked with blood.

"Holy shit. Sheriff?"

"I don't know," Nick said, answering the unspoken question of 'what could've done this?'

There was something on the floor…something white and shiny, but not metal. Whatever it was, it was triangular and edged. It didn't resemble jewelry of any kind. In fact, its surface was coarse and the edges serrated.

"What is it?" David asked. Nick stood up and stared at the object.

"A shark tooth."

CHAPTER 16

"I don't understand. Why are you so far away?" Lisa said. She kept peeking at her computer as she drove the boat. The pod of orcas had moved further out, while the two stragglers remained behind. Even more confusing, they had barely changed position since the last time she checked the computer. Something was wrong.

She pinpointed Charlie's location. He was somewhere to the east of the atoll, not too far from where she usually met with the pod. Freddy was somewhere south, though it would be more difficult to maneuver through the intense tourist activities. Best to visit Charlie and see what was going on there.

As usual, Lisa had packed fish to bring to the pod, which would likely have to be placed in a freezer if the orcas didn't return.

She steered her boat through a mile-long stretch of water rife with tourist activity. Up in this area, she could see fishing vessels going by, as well as a few parasailers in the distance. She saw the atoll further to the north. Just a half-mile to go.

Charlie was somewhere in this area. The signal indicated that he was slightly north. She turned the wheel to port and watched the infinite stretch of blue. She glanced again at the monitor. She was close. A thousand feet or less.

Lisa watched the waves, looking for that majestic dorsal fin. Nothing straight ahead. Nothing to the right, nor left. No spraying from a blowhole. No head popping out in search of the day's snack. She was looking at a derelict ocean surface.

Perhaps the tag broke off.

She nodded. It wouldn't have been the first time a specimen lost its tag. Once, she was tracking a whale shark's movements all the way from the coast of Florida to Bermuda, only for the tag to eventually be found detached. It was a disappointing day, as she feared the fish had been caught by fishermen for its fins, which weren't even a delicacy in most of the world, but used as displays.

She turned further to port.

Just a few hundred feet out, the water was splashing against something. Like a log in the water, the object rolled with the swells, its two ends wheeling along the side.

Lisa's heart felt like it was sinking into her stomach.

"No. Charlie?" It couldn't be!

But it was. Lisa slowed the boat alongside the dead mammal, then hurried to the main deck to examine it. It was Charlie alright—no mistaking that dorsal fin. His bloated body was filled with gas, which would inevitably deflate and cause him to sink to the bottom.

Lisa leaned over. Her face was wrinkled with shock. There were bite marks all over its body, exposing the pink internal organs. Some of the ribs had been exposed, washed perfectly white by the saltwater. Both flippers were torn away, as were the eyes.

"Jesus!"

There was no mistaking the type of bite wounds she was looking at. There was a distinct pattern. These were shark bites.

The scientist in her started debating internally. No shark was remotely large enough to inflict this kind of damage. Especially not to the leader of a pod. Even if he was somehow outmatched, the others should have rushed to his defense.

Charlie's corpse bumped into her hull. Lisa sighed mournfully. It was a safe bet that Freddy was dead too. The pod was undoubtedly in mourning, especially Daisy.

Lisa went into the cargo hold for a rope. If Charlie's body were to be left here, it would possibly drift close to the island, which wouldn't be appreciated by the tourists. It was best for him to be laid to rest by her.

She stepped back on deck, yellow rope in hand, and grabbed a pole to steer the orca's fluke close to the stern. The pole struck the water, missing the lobes entirely. She reached further, smacking the blubbery flesh. She rotated the orca a few inches before it slipped.

One last try. She reached down and smacked the water. The tip of the pole angled around the fluke, the side lodging against its edge. Lisa pulled down and back at once, maintaining the downward angle while steering the tail closer. It was a strenuous effort to steer a six-thousand pound creature. The orca spun clockwise until its tail slapped the diving platform.

Lisa knelt down with the rope. She reached forward, looped it around the tail, began to knot it...

Then screamed.

The shape appeared out of nowhere. For a split second, it looked like a dark blue cloud. By the time she saw the red eyes, the cone-shaped head exploded through the surface.

She fell backwards over the transom and landed face-first on the deck. Water trickled down on top of her as she sprang to her feet. In the swirling water was the beast that killed the orca. Charlie, though he would never know it, had saved her life, as the shark had bumped into his underside in its attempt to snatch her off the boat.

It traveled along the surface, as though showing off its immense body to its new victim. The eyes were blood red, as was the scar that traveled over the right one. The teeth were at least two-inches in length. The tail, while shaped like a typical great white's, looked as razor-sharp as a sickle blade. The fish was larger than Charlie.

It turned and went straight for Charlie. Lisa gasped, witnessing the immense jaws extending, pink gums glistening in the sunlight. The beast sank its teeth into the dead orca's midsection and shook him side-to-side, as though punishing him for interfering in its attempt to seize its human victim. She could hear bones popping and flesh peeling. Scar yanked his head to the side, pulling out a mouthful of stomach contents and intestines.

The caudal fin slapped the vessel, creating a rippling effect that nearly knocked Lisa to her feet. Two sides of her brain were screaming at her. First, was the scientist side, which demanded she get footage of this beast. The other side, however, yelled at her to get the hell out of here.

The shark made the decision an easy one.

Another surge of water splattered the deck. Following it was the shark's massive bulk, which had been launched from the water like a missile. It crashed down on the stern, smashing the transom as though it were comprised of toothpicks. The bow catapulted upward. Had Lisa not already been grasping the frames of the pilothouse door, she would have been flung right into the creature's mouth.

The boat teetered backward like a ramp. Lisa hyperventilated. She was looking right into the shark's mouth. Bits of flesh dangled from its teeth. Her feet scraped against the deck. Water was climbing. The boat was sinking, both from the water intake, and the shark's weight.

As she kicked, she noticed another detail in the shark's teeth. There was something frayed and stringy, but it wasn't organic. It was fabric. It had killed before and had developed a taste for human flesh.

The shark bit at the air, writhing to inch closer to her. Something snapped underneath it, causing it to lose its traction. The beast rolled into the water, sending a huge swell crashing into the pilothouse. The ship rocked forward, though was still teetering back. Lisa was sinking.

She grabbed the boat radio and found the police frequency.

"Sheriff! Nick! This is Lisa! I need your help!"

"Lisa, what's going on?"

Oh, thank God he answered quickly. "My boat is taking on water! There's a huge shark! I'm close to where we met yesterday, a quarter mile east of the atoll."

"Fire a flare if you have one. I'm coming now! Just hang on!"

"I'll try," she said, out of breath. She fumbled around the console until she found the cabinet with the flare. She opened the chamber and loaded a flare. She looked to the back entrance, then hesitated. The back of the ship was sinking further. Regardless of whether she shot the flare, she needed to be outside. The ship was going down no matter what, and being trapped in the pilothouse was not conducive to escaping.

She turned to the forward section and looked at the window frames, which were now starting to face skyward. She climbed over the instrument panel and reeled the window open wide enough to push herself through. Pushing her foot against the helm, she lifted herself through and fired the flare high into the air.

****

Nick slid down the yacht ladder and rushed toward the helm. David was only halfway down when he started the engine, and the rookie was barely in the boat when he throttled.

He steered the police boat around the yacht and aimed south. Arching down in the air like a burning star was Lisa's flare.

"I see it," he said. "Boat Two, we have mayday. Research boat half a click east of the atoll reported to be taking in water. We have a report of a vicious shark. Be aware."

"Copy that, Sheriff. I'm coming in," Roper replied.

David shook his head. "What kind of shark would sink a boat like Dr. Robinson's?"

"I have no idea," Nick said. He grabbed the shotgun, then pushed the boat to its full speed. After twenty seconds of travel, he could see her vessel off in the distance. With the bow pointed up, it resembled an iceberg drifting in the current, gradually sinking lower.

Just another minute. Hang on, Lisa.

****

Lisa stood up on top of the vessel, with one foot on the forward deck, and another on the other windshield panel. She held the flare gun in one hand and two spares in the other. She opened the breach and loaded one of the cartridges, then gripped the weapon as she did Nick's pistols during gun practice.

She saw the flashing lights to the north.

"Hurry up," she muttered. She swept the water with the muzzle of her gun. The boat shook under her feet. The water level was climbing, the surface embracing the rear of the pilothouse.

She saw another set of red-and-blue flashers coming from the southwest. Her heart thumped hard in her chest as though trying to escape. Her hands quivered, shaking the weapon. Sirens struck the air.

Nick's boat was a thousand feet away now.

A wall of water obscured her view of the boat, but not the gaping mouth that angled her way. Lisa screamed and fell backward into the water. The shark's chin smashed the windshield, the jaws slamming shut inches from her body as she fell out of reach. She twirled underwater, briefly lost to panic, then snapped back to her senses. She swam to the surface and inhaled.

The beast was thrashing on the boat, cracking bits of the bow with its weight. The pilothouse submerged, allowing the shark to barrel roll to the side. A resulting swell lifted Lisa, sparking a terrified gasp. A second one escaped her lungs as she watched the dorsal fin emerge and turn toward her. The shark closed in, the eyes glowing under the surface.

Despite the terror gripping her, Lisa extended the flare gun and squeezed the trigger. A fiery red ball pierced the ocean and skidded over the creature's face. Blinding red light flashed over its right eye, sparking an instinctive reaction to turn away. Splashing water with its caudal fin, the shark raced to Lisa's right.

Kicking her feet to remain afloat, she struggled with the flare gun to load the last cartridge. She opened the breach, only for her fingers to slip and lose her last flare.

"Shit!" She reached into the water and grabbed for it. Tauntingly, it brushed the tips of her fingers, barely out of reach before descending to the depths. Lisa looked back to the east. The fin was circling back. The boat was completely submerged. There was nothing between her and the fish except three hundred feet of open water.

Rifle shots cracked the air. Lisa jerked, unaccustomed to hearing the cracks without ear protection. Bullets struck along the beast's right side, forcing it to turn away and dive.

Strobing lights glimmered across the water as the police boat pulled up alongside her. She saw David Hummer reach over for her, while Nick scanned the water with his rifle.

"Get her in," he barked.

Lisa swam a little further and reached up. To her relief, their hands clasped tightly on the first try. David clapped his other hand over her wrist and hoisted her up. His eyes widened after looking over her shoulder, at the two glowing eyes on each side of an angular head. With one final tug, he pulled her into the boat.

The shark breached and slammed itself into the side. The boat teetered to the verge of flipping over entirely. Nick grabbed the helm, keeping himself from tumbling back. As the boat rocked back to starboard, he thrust the rifle out and let out a volley of shots. He saw the shark twitch from each impact, but there was no blood. The bullets were nothing more than mosquito stings to it. They stung just enough to drive it away.

The shark dove out of sight, slapping the vessel with its razor-sharp caudal fin. The boat spun like a top until Nick pushed the throttle.

"You alright, Lisa?"

"In one piece, so far," she replied.

"What the hell kind of shark is that?" David asked. He grabbed the shotgun Nick had given him and aimed it into the water.

"I seriously have no idea. I've never seen it before. It's not like anything ever recorded."

"Judging by its eyes, I say it came from hell," Nick said.

"Then I suggest you push this boat like the devil's after you...because it fucking is," David said. Nick looked over his shoulder. Twenty feet behind them was the shark.

"Son of a bitch." Even at twenty knots, he couldn't outpace it. "What kind of fish is this thing?" He snatched the radio off the console. "Dispatch! This is the Sheriff. Order everyone out of the water now! This is an island-wide emergency. I want everyone out of the water, including boats."

David fired a shotgun blast into the shark's face, angling it away. The report reverberated into the radio transmission, alarming the dispatchers and all other deputies listening in.

He whipped his head back after hearing David discharge another shell. The beast flinched, no more so than he did after getting a mild zap from touching something electrically charged. With the shark gradually closing in, he cut the wheel to starboard, taking them south toward the atoll. The creature followed, then turned away.

"Where the hell is it going?" David said. He started loading fresh shells into the shotgun, while watching the dorsal fin move to the south...right toward Roper's approaching police boat.

Nick clutched the transmitter. "Roper! Cut to starboard! It's coming right at you!"

The fish dove, then vaulted upward in an upside-down U-shape. It ascended with amazing speed, rolled its eyes into its head, and made impact with the keep.

Roper never knew what hit him. The boat cracked in half, each side vaulting in opposite directions. Flying among the debris was Roper, flailing madly.

"NO!" Nick shouted. He cut the wheel back to port, but before the bow was pointed toward the wreckage, he saw the shark breach the water. In his mouth was Roper. Blood sprayed from the edge of the jaws in thick streams. Roper's screams traveled far and wide, expressing the pain and agony of a man whose flesh was being sliced and his bones crushed.

The evil fish splashed down with its prey in its mouth, then shook its head side-to-side. Lisa cupped her hands over her mouth as arms and legs detached from the body.

The shark swallowed the bulk of its prey, then raced southwest.

Nick, Lisa, and David stood frozen with shock.

"Where—" David felt like he would vomit any moment. "Where's it going?"

Lisa took a deep breath. "It's going for easier prey."

Nick followed the shark fin with his eyes, then gazed out ahead of it. The ocean was alive with vessels. Some of them would hear the radio call and head in, others would ignore it, and the rest would probably not even be aware of it.

All of them had no idea that they were the special of the day.

CHAPTER 17

Scar's world was rife with the vibrations from the human operated machines. He was an alpha predator, determined to strike down at the land-dwelling species that invaded his ocean. He had no motive other that it was his biological imperative to kill. There was no notion of pity or empathy, nor did he feel a consideration for consequence. He was a born killer, and he was ready to unleash his fury on the world above.

Buzzing like flies directly ahead were three humans on jet skis, moving a few yards away from a yacht nearly three times his size. He felt no fear: he had destroyed a vessel of similar size and design. They had no weapons, and their rigid shells could not withstand the blunt force of his attack.

Scar closed in, keeping a few meters below the surface. Like a missile, he increased speed, zeroing in on the one furthest out.

The vehicle flipped, its operator snatched from the seat as the great fish breached the water. The two companions screamed, as did two others who stood aboard the yacht. Scar swam along the surface, carrying his prize, as though demonstrating the fates of those who were next. The person kicked and flailed, then spasmed in intense agony as Scar chomped repeatedly. Warm blood rinsed his gills. With a quick shake of the head, the body split apart, then rolled into his gullet.

With a burst of speed, Scar went for the next jet skier. The terrified human tried angling to the left, but nearly crashed into her companion, who, in an attempt to avoid collision, shot inadvertently toward the shark's jaws.

Scar rolled his eyes back and let his snout absorb the blow. The jet ski skidded over his face, rolling like a ball in midair. He opened his red eyes and spotted the human angling for the water. Before going for the easy prey, he turned left to close in on the remaining jet ski. Its operator screamed at the sight of his hideous snout, then tried to speed away. With a swing of his tail, Scar accelerated into the trajectory, then bashed his head against the underside like a bull raising its horns.

The jet ski and its owner flipped over. Scar raised his body out of the water and snatched the flailing human out of the air, then splashed down. Gurgling screams had no impact other than to inform his brain that his teeth were properly doing the work they were designed for.

Before he was finished tearing his victim apart, he was already focusing on his next target. With the struggling human clenched in his teeth, Scar raced for the yacht at forty miles-per-hour, then plowed through the hull.

The humans on board screamed, both from the sudden turbulence, and the sight of their companion literally exploding into red mist after being bashed against the hull, which was now gaping open. Scar swallowed the mashed victim, then shook his body until he was free of the crater. The struggling movements of nearby prey drew his attention to the right. The remaining jet skier splashed the water, yelling for dear life. Those screams intensified as Scar edged closer. The prey turned away and paddled in a fruitless attempt to put distance between himself and the fish.

Scar bit down and pulled. He felt the pop of a cracking bone, which was immediately followed by a sudden loss of resistance. Scar spun back, the severed leg of his victim clenched in his teeth. The human sank several feet, his screams masked by air bubbles while he clutched the stub of his thigh. He saw the shark through the cloud of his blood and tried paddling for the surface. The effort was as fruitless as his other attempt to escape.

The fish plucked him as a bat would an insect. He chomped once, savored the taste of blood and meat, then swallowed.

The yacht dipped to port, its terrified occupants rushing to the opposite side. Scar circled and waited, only for the arrival of another boat to catch his attention. It was a fishing charter, with one man on the helm and two on deck. With their eyes on the sinking vessel, they never noticed the fish accelerating.

Scar struck the bow, flipping it backwards. The Captain flipped head over heels before crashing down fifty feet back. The boat smashed down, crushing one of the fishermen in the blink of an eye, the other carried toward the yacht by the tremendous swell. Drawn by the smell of blood, Scar went for the dead victim. He passed the other, turned sharply to the right to find his prey. In doing so, his tail smacked the live one, sending him hurtling face-first into the yacht. The man hit with the force of a meteor, splattering over the white hull, coating it red. Arms and guts riddled the deck, leaving the occupants silent. They had fallen into a state of shock by this point, their brains forever numb to the world around them.

Scar felt the vibrations of the struggling Captain. With just three strokes of his caudal fin, he crossed the fifty feet of distance and snatched the human in his teeth. With a few violent jerks of his head, he split the man in half.

There was more. So much more. The water was filled with victims just waiting to be slaughtered by the evil shark. But first, there were those aboard the yacht.

The waterline climbed up to the deck. The stern was almost completely submerged. As far as Scar was concerned, it was low enough for him to snatch the humans off. They stood together, frozen like statues, their faces void of emotion. Like a bass catching a dragonfly in a pond, the shark leapt over the deck, snatching both humans in a single bite. Their corpses merged into a single cloud of blood and guts as he ripped them apart.

He was full now, but not ready to finish his rampage. The need to kill was still prevalent. It was no longer about sustenance, but about dominating the sea.

Scar continued further southwest. The waters were becoming shallower. There was land in sight. Along the shores were hundreds of humans, many of which were in the water. Separating him and them were numerous vessels moving like a school of fish that had been alerted to the presence of a threat. There were red and blue lights coming from the land, and soon, his lateral line picked up the fluttering movements of humans racing ashore.

He dipped under the water and watched the vessels from underneath. The surface was full of them, with fifty yards of distance between each one. He settled on a twenty-foot sailing boat and ascended like an astro-rocket. The boat split in half at the center and toppled, drawing screams from the nearby vessels. Scar found the human piloting the vehicle and snapped his jaws shut over his neck. A quick jerk led to a *snap*, and the head detached.

Leaving the decapitated body to sink, Scar raced for the next vessel and charged. There were two people on this one, one in the cabin, another on the fly deck, looking at the water in search of the beast. He spotted him, right as Scar leapt from the ocean and snatched the target from the deck. His tail struck the boat as he crashed down, tossing it into a spin. The helmsman struggled for control, while looking over his shoulder in search of his companion. What he saw was an empty deck, with bloody water clouding around the ship, then a dorsal fin turning toward him. The last thing he saw before feeling the vessel crack beneath his feet were the red eyes rolling back.

Scar swam through the wreckage, nudging the splintered cabin with his snout in search of the human. Feeling the water displacement to his right, he turned, spotted the target, and closed his jaws over it. The man screamed, tongue fully extended from his mouth, his breath lost in a burst of air bubbles and blood. Scar tore him in half at the waist, spat out the twitching legs, then sped for another boat.

This boat was faster than the others, and jetted forward unexpectedly. The person controlling it was as clumsy as he was terrified, as he quickly lost control and found himself rocketing into a yacht. The two boats burst into a volcanic cloud of debris, gasoline fire, and smoke. Tossed among the debris were human bodies, some intact and alive, others in pieces.

Scar moved in with laser precision and ripped open the body of a three-hundred pound vacationer, ripping his right shoulder clean off. He snatched his prize at the midsection and turned violently, slashing down the chest and belly of another boater. His head, left shoulder, and left ribcage separated from everything else, and the diagonally split body twirled into the depths.

CHAPTER 18

A thousand screams pierced the air at once, making Officer Doug Maggard unable to hear the Sheriff's instructions over the radio. Never in his fifteen years of law enforcement had the forty-year old officer seen such mass panic and confusion. But there was no denying the cause.

The explosion could've been seen for another mile had it been that far away. But it wasn't. It was a quarter-mile at most. There were boats speeding for the harbor in unison, fighting for space, smashing into each other. Some of them simply raced for shore, not caring whether their boats would get lodged in the sandbanks.

"Everybody, please get out of the water," a lifeguard repeated over a speakerphone. An exodus of people raced to shore, spurred by the chaos and the terror surrounding them. There were shrieks from all over the beach as people fled to avoid the incoming boats.

To the north, Doug watched a jetboat come racing in, bumping over a dozen people without care.

"Stop! Stop! Stop!" he shouted, racing to the shoreline. The boat was running aground, but was still coming. The officer dove out of the way, narrowly avoiding fatal injury as the boat skidded onto the sand. Now out of harm's way, the man aboard was only now grasping the sense of consequence of what he had done, which led to a new panic. He leapt from the cockpit and started running, only to be tackled and cuffed by another Deputy.

Bodies were dragged ashore, with several of them covered in blood. Cries and screams flooded the air, making communication nearly impossible. Doug joined the lifeguards in wading into the water and assisting the injured. Within a few seconds, another boat came racing ashore.

Doug pulled an elderly man out of the way, grabbing his wife in the process, then sprinted with an arm around each, taking them from the boat's path. They could hear the thuds of bodies bashing against the hull.

Then, a new wave of screams echoed, followed by a booming crash. Doug turned, then joined the screams as he watched the boat flip repeatedly. Behind it, a large torpedo-shaped body crashed into the water. The crescent-shaped tail swung high over the water before following its owner beneath the waves.

The dorsal fin sliced the air. It was a shark. A giant, bloodthirsty, devil-eyed shark from hell.

He watched it emerge again and snatch a swimmer out of the water, then smack another with its caudal fin. A fountain of blood soared high, followed by a broken body, tossed by the fish in favor of another victim.

Doug and a few other officers watched in silent horror as another person was disemboweled and tossed aside. The sense of duty returned, and the men drew their pistols and waded into the shallows.

"We need boats in the water. Draw off the shark!" It was the Sheriff's voice. Doug glanced to the northeast and saw the flashing lights. *"I need all available units on the water, fully armed, with at least two gunmen. Draw it away. Leave clearing the beaches to Fire Rescue. Use armor-piercing rounds. Dispatch, any officers off duty are now ON duty."*

Doug turned to his men. "You heard the man. Get in the boats right now!" The officers raced to their interceptors, passing a line of firetrucks and ambulances on their way to the harbor.

Red strobes lined the roadway along the beach as the emergency vehicles stopped along the road. The personnel hesitated a moment after disembarking, seeing the mass of bodies invading the sand, and the enormous fish wreaking havoc behind them. Among the bunch were several bleeders, as well as people with cracked ribs and limbs from being trampled. Some people writhed on the sand in agony, their bodies swollen into human balloons after being struck by boats.

Their work was cut out for them today. The Fire Captain barked orders like a Drill Sergeant, hastening the crew to treat the wounded. But even he jolted at the crack of shotgun blasts in the distance.

Beyond the incoming crowd of swimmers, a Cross Point Island Police Department vessel sped to the south, slowed enough for the two officers on deck to blast the shark and get its attention, then led it out to the open water.

****

Lisa Robinson pushed the police boat to twenty knots, shuddering from each thundering crack from the firearms behind her. There was nothing but open ocean ahead of her. Most of the vessels had circled around to the south harbor. The ones further out had received the message to return to the island, and would circle wide in order to avoid interception by the fish.

Nick popped off several rounds into the shark's snout.

"Jesus, why won't this fucker die?!"

"This is a nightmare! It's gotta be a nightmare," David said.

"Don't lose it, kid!"

David fired another blast, pumped the shotgun, then fired again. *Click.* He swallowed. The weapon may as well have been a tennis racket at this point.

"I'm *trying!*" he replied, dropping the empty weapon to the deck. He drew his sidearm and fired off a few shots.

The shark showed no sign of injury, but the repeated shots were visibly inducing pain. It jolted repeatedly, the nerves lighting up from the blows to its many pores, which prevented it with jetting to a ramming speed. A few more stings landed, and finally, the fish turned away.

Nick watched its silhouette turn around and head to shore.

"Shit, it's going back. Lisa, bring us around."

She made no argument, despite the crushing fear in her stomach. Lisa cut the wheel to starboard, facing the bow west, and throttled after the fish. Nick hurried around the cockpit to the forward deck, rested the rifle barrel over the gunwale, then fired a few shots. He saw the twitch in its caudal fin. After another few hits, the fish turned around. They had its attention once more.

The downside to this was it was coming right at them. Nick fired the last few rounds in his mag, but it wasn't enough to deter the creature from making impact.

The boat lurched backward, knocking all three to the deck. The shark turned and smacked the hull with its tail, spinning it to the right.

Lisa was on her knees, with one hand gripping the wheel. Another impact rocked the vessel, rolling David over his shoulder. Nick fumbled for his magazine, slapped it in place, then stood up. He let out a dozen rounds, stinging the beast like a wasp. If only his bullets were as poisonous... Unfortunately, all he could inflict was a bit of pain against bulletproof skin.

Lisa stood up and gasped after seeing the crumpled bow. The engine had flooded and quit, forcing her to turn the key. It turned over once then quit again.

"Come on," she said. She tried again. Same result. The third time was the charm. It roared, sounding clunky, but it worked. She turned to port and accelerated north.

The fish was right behind them, and closing in fast. This time, it wasn't allowing itself to be deterred by bullets. Nick cringed. He landed every shot he had against its nose and back, yet the demon was not slowing. He watched his last round ricochet off its back, leaving him with an empty rifle. He dropped the weapon and drew his revolver.

David emptied his mag. He looked at the open breach, then back at the shark, which had closed within twenty-feet. Nineteen.

"Sheriff..."

Nick blasted all six rounds. "I know!" He looked over his shoulder. They would not make it to land at this rate. He thought fast for some kind of solution. Only one came to mind.

He fell to his knees and yanked the cargo hatch open.

"Keep shooting," he told David. The Deputy loaded a fresh mag with his shaky hands, then resumed hitting the shark with nine-millimeter rounds. Nick dug around in the cargo hold until he found the red-and-yellow nylon zip-case. A yellow ripcord dangled from the side. He reemerged, kicked the hatch closed with his boot, then stepped beside David. The young Deputy was gritting his teeth, tense with horror. The shark closed within five feet. Four. Three.

It reared its head and opened its mouth.

Nick pointed the zip-case. "Nibble on *this!*" He yanked the ripcord, rapidly inflating the emergency raft, which extended right into the shark's jaws. It bit down on its 'prey' and turned to the side, allowing Lisa to put a little more distance between it and them.

The raft popped. The shark continued tearing. Chunks of red rubber flew in the air. The fish regurgitated to free the fragments caught in its throat, spewing out pieces of recently consumed meals.

It flexed its jaws, allowing its stomach a moment to unfold into its normal position, then resumed its chase.

"I can't believe it. It's still coming after us," David said.

"This isn't normal behavior," Lisa said.

"Doesn't take a doctorate to realize that," Nick said. He ejected the empty cartridges from his revolver and loaded six fresh rounds. "We've hit it with enough rounds to put down a whale. I don't suppose any species you know has skin like that?"

"No," Lisa said.

"Maybe we just need more bullets," David said. He pointed to the northwest at five police vessels speeding in from the north side of the island.

Nick watched the shark for a moment to make sure it was still following them, then stepped beside Lisa.

"Lead it to them. If we pump it with enough lead, we ought to land at least one lucky shot."

Lisa veered to port and sped toward the incoming boats.

"We're on our way, Sheriff."

"We're leading it right to you," Nick replied. "It's fast and mean! Hit it with everything you've got. Don't let it ram you. It split Roper's boat right down the middle."

"It killed Roper?!" another Deputy asked.

Nick hesitated, realizing this was the first everyone was hearing of it.

"Yes. Now focus! Kill the thing."

The police boats spaced into two-by-two formations, each group lined up directly with the other, while the fifth vessel hooked to the south. Lisa could see the officers positioning their rifles to blast the fish as she led it between them.

Except it broke off to the left…instead choosing to go after the vessel that veered around them. Nick spun on his heel and watched the dorsal fin cruising through the water.

"Boat Six. It's coming right toward you! Move to port."

Lisa covered her eyes, but still yelped as she heard the devastating *thud*. Boat Six flipped over, launching its officers into the waves. The fish swam around the sinking boat and seized one of the deputies. His two companions screamed, forced to watch as their helmsman had his midsection completely torn free. He floated along the surface, just long enough for everyone to see he had no stomach, then sank.

The fish went for the next Deputy, clamped its jaws over his shoulders, then thrashed its head left and right, swinging his legs. After the fifth time, his lower half broke off and skidded for a few feet before sinking.

The boats closed around the fish, the riflemen blasting away at its flesh. Bullets bombarded the shark's back and side, alarming it to potential injury that would occur if the assault continued. A few of the rounds started chipping flesh, then finally drew blood.

It dove, then passed underneath them. Bullets plunged into the water, some hitting their mark, others going wide. The fish reared its head, swung its tail, then struck one of the boats at the stern.

Boat Four catapulted, sending one of the riflemen barreling right through the windshield of another boat. The shark struck again, puncturing the hull with its snout.

It didn't bother waiting for it to sink. It raced toward another boat, taking a few rounds to the face, one of which split its skin below the eye. It dipped, arched upward, then breached. Its body flapped once in midair before crashing down on the center of Boat Five, crunching it into a V-shape.

Deputies flailed in the water. A smack of the shark's tail sent one twirling into another vessel.

Nick's men were dying before his very eyes.

"Get everyone out of the water! Everyone, back to shore!" He reached over and pulled one of his deputies on board. A scream made him look up. The shark had another one of his deputies in his mouth. The man was flailing, fingers coiling, his tongue extending as the teeth sank deep into his stomach and lungs. It dove out of sight with its victim in tow, leaving a trail of blood in its wake.

The boats gathered the survivors and raced back to the island.

Nick knelt by the injured Deputy he had pulled from the water. The young man wasn't much older than David. His leg was swollen and his breathing was labored. Possibly a broken rib. He would live, unlike several other deputies and civilians.

The Sheriff stood up and watched the water. Broken boats drifted along the surface along the entire east coast of Cross Point. He didn't even want to speculate how many had sunk. The body count would be impossible to determine at this point.

How could one animal do all of this? What kind of shark is this thing?

CHAPTER 19

Two Hundred Miles Southeast of Savannah Bay, Georgia
Cruise Liner *Adventurer*. Return trip from Grand Turk.

The excitement aboard the nine-hundred foot cruise liner was starting to dwindle. The seven-day trip around the Caribbean was now drawing to a close. By the end of the day, the ship would dock and unload its eight-hundred-and-fifty passengers.

From the depths looking up, the ship looked like an asteroid gliding across the surface of a young star. The world beneath it was quiet, dark, and hundreds of feet deep. A few fish and sharks glided between the seabed and the ship, all of which evaded its presence in fear that it was a giant predator that would swallow them at any moment.

The only creature that did take an interest did not have gills. In fact, it was bound by the land, only able to venture into the ocean through craftmanship. Blue flippers waved up and down like the natural ocean dwelling mammals, though the creature's speed was mostly provided through the use of a propulsion vehicle.

The diver had departed from a mile out. In twenty minutes, he would return to the location where he had dived, and vanish, not from a ship, but a plane. First, he had to reach his prey. Unlike the other creatures around him, there was no fear of the leviathan above. This predator knew how and where to strike. He was not looking to kill, though he had the means to do it. It was not through teeth or crushing limbs, though he had both, and had used both in his forty-one years of life.

Instead, his method was through the inventions of his species. It was an evolution from the spears his ancestors constructed to take down sabretooth tigers and woolly mammoths. That evolution led to bigger spears, then to arrows, and into swords, and eventually to muskets and cannonballs, then eventually bullets, artillery, and ultimately, population-destroying weapons. The one this predator chose was only a tiny fragment of such power. His intent was not to destroy, but to harm—to do *just* enough.

Terrify.

The shape grew larger as it ascended. Eventually, it got so close that it blotted out the bright sun. The diver traveled along its belly, then settled near the port quarter, where he implemented his instrument of death. To the untrained eye, it looked like a small nylon block, harmless as a child's toy. But in its belly was hellfire, waiting to be unleashed.

He secured the package to the ship, then accelerated with his propulsion vehicle to the extraction zone. It was fifteen minutes of continuous travel before he reached his destination.

The aquatic plane swooped down like an eagle. Its rear ramp opened wide, and two men dressed in black gear reached out to help him in. They could see the cruise liner nearly a mile out.

"Has Farcas hit the cruise line to Bermuda?" the diver asked.

"Detonation was two minutes ago," one of his comrades replied. The diver pulled his mask and gear off, while a couple of other men secured the diver propulsion vehicle and air cannister. They lifted the ramp, then harnessed themselves into seats while the plane took to the sky.

The diver watched the cruise liner from high above. Less than half an hour ago, it was a titan cutting through the ocean like a razorblade. Now, to his eye, it was no bigger than a pebble.

"Roark has secured payment?"

"He ensures us it'll be substantial. We'll receive transfer once his mission is complete."

"Better be substantial, considering we'll have the whole Air Force and Navy gunning for us. We en route to Columbia?"

"Yep. Hope you're in the mood for a year-long vacation."

"As long as the money comes in."

The diver pulled the detonator from his belt, activated it, then pressed the button. From this altitude, he could not hear the deafening roar of the C-4 explosion. He watched the vessel dip to port, with smoke billowing from the stern. The propellors had been destroyed, the hull breached, the engine critical. By now, the SOS signal was being sent out.

The plane turned south and raced out of U.S. jurisdiction.

"Call Roark. Tell him the deed is done. If we don't receive payment in forty-eight hours, we're coming for him."

****

"Uh-huh. New York too? Good, well done. You'll receive payment to your offshore account in three days." Roark rolled his eyes as he listened to his associate, Jeff Calmes, make his usual threat of what would happen if the money wasn't received. He tilted the speaker away to not be heard, "Blah, blah-blah, blahhh...yeah-yeah, you'll put your knife in my ass. I've heard it all before..." Finally, the tirade stopped.

"I better hear from you in seventy-two hours, Roark," Calmes concluded.

"You will. Now, enjoy your vacation." Roark hung up. "Jackass." He turned around and saw Olivia standing on the fly deck beside him.

"It's done?"

"Yes, it's done," he answered. "This fish better be worth it to you. The whole country's on alert right now because of what Calmes did."

Olivia smiled. "Excellent. That's what I wanted."

Roark chuckled then watched the ocean splash the bow as they continued northeast to Cross Point.

They had received news on the radio of the incident at Cross Point. Several boats were reported to have sunk. Numerous people were dead or injured. The mentions of a killer shark were vague so far, but the incident was severe enough to draw attention of the authorities…unless they were diverted. Luckily, Roark had contacts along the East Coast. Planning had to be quick and large promises had to be made. The hardest part was convincing him to make the calls.

There was no way around it; this was pure terrorism. Of course, Olivia tried to justify it that minimal lives would be lost in the process if the bombs were placed correctly. Minimal lives—as long as they didn't get in the way of her catching that shark!

What could Roark say? After all, he went along with it. Money spoke louder than morals, and his associates shared the same philosophy. Each team would receive two million dollars, to which Olivia was confident she could convince Skomal to pay.

Roark's expression soured. There was no turning back now. He was committed to this assignment. If not, he'd have two teams of highly trained mercenaries hunting him down. As usual, Olivia got her way. It didn't matter the cost, or who paid it.

"It must be one hell of a shark if it did all of that," he said. Olivia's smile turned into a sneer. She didn't like his tone; it sounded like that of a man who was second-guessing his decision.

"Is that a problem?"

"Doesn't matter now," he said.

"I told you…I'll double your money."

"I know. You told me thirty minutes ago," Roark replied.

"Only if it's captured *alive*," she said. There it was again, another reminder. It was probably the hundredth time she said it. Roark thought of a few smartass replies, but instead looked at his watch.

"We'll be there in a little over an hour. We'll hang to the east, out of their jurisdiction until dusk. All boats are grounded, so if we search during daylight, we're bound to attract attention."

"Fine. As long as it's done." Olivia returned to the pilothouse, made an 'ugh' sound after seeing Heitmeyer, who was at the helm.

After rolling his eyes, Roark looked off into the distance. *I should've negotiated another romp in the sack, just to piss her off.* He smiled. *She would've done it. She would've done anything.*

CHAPTER 20

"No, no, you're not listening to me. We need a ship sent here today! You...no, Commander. Nets won't hold it. Yes, I heard what's going on, but it doesn't change anything. We need a damn cutter...Yes, I understand it sounds crazy, but this is no ordinary shark!"

This was Nick's third conversation with the U.S. Coast Guard, and for the third time, his blood pressure was rising. Nobody was believing the details he shared regarding the fish, despite the footage that was leaking onto the internet by some of the tourists.

Nick listened to some more babbling from the so-called officer on the other end of the line, then slammed the phone down.

"Jesus, Nick, what the hell's going on?"

Nick ran his fingers through his short hair, then shook his head.

"Two cruise liner bombings, one off the coast of New York, the other coming in from Georgia...all at the same time we get hit by a shark on steroids."

"Do they think it's terrorists?"

"Definitely no coincidence," Nick replied. "The military's been placed on full alert. They've got Navy ships patrolling twelve miles out. Nothing that'll help us."

"So, we're on our own, I suppose."

"Nothing more than the air-rescue support we received. With everything that's going on, they can't divert a cutter to take out a shark," he explained. He looked out of his office window, hoping to let the scenery calm him down. Instead, the view of the ocean only seemed to heighten his anxiety.

The hours following the attack were almost as brutal as the incident itself. It was a rush of tending to the casualties, most of whom had been shipped to the mainland. Even so, the local hospital was overloaded.

The majority of the injuries were actually due to the mass panic that ensued, leading the authorities to believe it was mass hysteria that led to the event. When the dust settled, Nick found himself facing another school of sharks, armed with microphones and cameras. The reports of a killer shark were already facing scrutiny, with many believing it to be an exaggeration. During the press conference, Nick had to fend off against a wave of questions, some of which were baiting him to sound like a lunatic.

"How can one shark cause so much damage?"

"Sharks don't have red eyes."

"The largest great white on record was twenty-six feet. You claim this one is over thirty. Care to comment?"

"Sheriff, I understand you lost some men in the hysteria?"

Hysteria. This is what passes for news these days. Unfortunately, many people were foolish enough to buy into it. Among those skeptics was the Coast Guard.

"So, what do we do? We can't let that thing swim around free out there," Lisa said.

"No, we can't," Nick said. "We need to kill it ourselves. You don't have any poison that can kill it, do ya?"

"I'd have to get up close to it," Lisa said. "Considering how fast and strong it is, forgive me for not wanting to get that close."

"No arguments here," Nick replied.

"What about explosives? We know its skin can be broken with enough force. A good blast should do the trick."

"Yeah, I did try to get Town Hall to equip my patrol boats with five-inch Navy deck guns, but they wouldn't do it. Cheap bastards," Nick quipped.

"Nick…" Lisa said.

His fake smile faded. "You're probably right. I would like to see that bastard blown to hell, but I don't have access to any explosives."

"Yeah, but I think we can find someone who does," Lisa said. Nick gazed up at her. He realized who she was referring to. He gripped a pen on his desk and pressed his thumb against it until it snapped in two.

"Oh no. HELL NO. I wouldn't trust that guy if-" Nick said.

"He's the only source of dynamite we know of around here," Lisa said. Nick leaned back in his seat and stared at the ceiling. A headache gripped his brow and squeezed his temples together.

"I'd rather stick my head in that shark's mouth than ask Barney Grey for help."

****

"Before I even consider helping *you* with anything, I have some shit that I need taken care of," Barney Grey demanded. In his mind, Nick was putting the scrawny fisherman in a headlock. He tilted his head to the right, just long enough for Lisa to see the 'I hate you' look.

It also provided an excuse to turn his eyes away from the pigsty that was Barney's old shack. It smelled of rust and mold. The floorboards were showing signs of decay, as was the front patio. The dock wasn't much better. Several boards were missing, as well as one of the legs. It amazed him that the thing was even sturdy enough to keep his boat from drifting away.

Nick cleared his throat. "And that would be…?"

"First, I want my net replaced," Barney said.

"Not a problem," Nick answered. He was relieved to hear a surprisingly reasonable request.

"I want funds to repair, maybe even replace my boat," Barney continued. Nick nodded. Again, reasonable—ish. But the guy was risking his neck to solve the problem, so Nick didn't mind too much.

"I think I can convince the island Mayor," he replied.

"I want a sixty-five inch flatscreen television! Two-years subscription to *Netflix* and *Hulu*."

Nick smirked. *Can't get those yourself?*

"Don't forget the six-burner propane grill."

"Okay, Barney, I think we're going a little bit overboard," Nick said.

"Oh!" Barney said. "Well, it was good to see you. NOT! Get the hell out of here, then!" Barney shooed them away like a couple of pests.

"Oh, good lord, Barney. Just give me the dynamite you use for your depth charges."

"What is this? Eminent domain?" Barney said. "Not happening here! Assuming I actually own dynamite…"

"Don't think I'm an idiot, you wiry bastard. I've had numerous reports that you've used it in the past."

"Then don't think I'm an idiot to think I'm just gonna hand it over to you," Barney said. "Do you even know how to use it?"

"Yes," Nick replied.

"It's more than lighting a wick and letting it blow up," Barney replied. Nick squinted.

"What else is there to it?"

"There's, uh… timing! You have to know how to time the blast right, or you'll never get it near the fish."

Nick had already grown tired of this conversation. "Fine! I'll get you all those stupid things you want. I just need the dynamite to go out and kill the shark."

"Kill the shark, huh?" Barney chuckled. "That bad boy did a number on a lot of people today. And the Coast Guard actually thinks it's mass hysteria…which is hysterical!"

"Only in your sick head," Lisa said. Barney chuckled, then led them around to his shed. He opened the splintering doors, lined with loose nails and screws, revealing a lawn mower, a few drums of fuel, and several cases of dynamite.

"Holy shit, Barney. You own a mine, somewhere?" Nick asked.

"My granddaddy did," Barney said, handing one of the cases to the Sheriff. "So. You have a plan in mind? Or are you just gonna go out there and try your luck?"

"I'll figure something out," Nick replied.

"I hope you do, for your sake. The way you describe that ol' shark, ramming boats, taking down your deputies, outpacing every boat he comes across, I think it'll be more complicated than tossing a few sizzling sticks into the water."

"You just let me handle that," Nick said.

"I ought to," Barney said. "It'll be hilarious to watch you blow your ass up!"

"Keep it up, Barney. I'll just shoot you and take the dynamite."

"Nobody here will miss ya," Lisa added.

Barney stepped back. "Well, golly! Didn't think you had it in you, Sheriff." He passed along a couple of cases of dynamite. "You know you're gonna need a plan. Or else, you'll be tossing them sticks all day long."

"I'll figure something out," Nick said.

"It'll have to start with a boat," Lisa said.

"The island's full of fishermen," Nick replied. "I think I can get a couple of them to volunteer their trawlers."

CHAPTER 21

Tyler Monclova was the polar opposite of Barney Grey. He had an excellent figure, well-groomed face, was well-spoken, and respected by the island. From the age of twenty-two to thirty-one, he was a Deputy in Madison County, Virginia, where he learned to engage with people in a variety of scenarios. He liked people, so much so in fact that he hated seeing them at their worst twenty-four-seven. His passion for law-enforcement faded around the age of twenty-nine, though it took a couple more years for him to finally work up the courage to leave it and make his own destiny. When his peers learned that he was moving to Cross Point and making a life as a fisherman, they laughed at him. Hardly any of them had ever seen the ocean, despite only being a few hundred miles from it. He had no wife or kids, and no debts to tie him to Madison County. He was free to do what he pleased. So, he did.

Tyler was forty-three now, but by his features, he had hardly aged a day since he first bought his home on Crooked Peak, located on the southeast corner of the island. Those fellow officers of his probably had the opposite luck, especially in the present climate. In his day, he had met a few superiors whom he swore were in their fifties, only to learn they had barely broke forty. He believed it was a noble profession, but that didn't mean he was sorry for leaving it.

Today was the first day in twelve years Tyler Monclova was grounded. He had spent the late morning assisting EMS with bringing in the critically injured after the incident. Now, as late afternoon faded into the twilight hours, he found himself seated on the middeck of his seventy-foot trawler, the *Star Blaze*. He stared out into the ocean, thinking about the horrific events. Only once did he get a glimpse of the fish that caused it. It was larger than any shark he had ever seen, aside from a forty-foot whale shark swimming fifty-miles off the coast of Florida. But this was no whale shark. At first, he thought it was a great white, but it was too big. He chalked it up as his eyes playing tricks on him. It seemed reasonable; he had just witnessed numerous boat collisions that resulted in devastating injuries. Blood was in the water. People were screaming. Boats were zipping in every direction like fighter jets in the Pacific Theater. He didn't try to overthink the bizarre details he noticed, like the scarred face, the pigmentation of the skin on a shark that resembled a great white—and who would forget those eyes?

It was easy for him to chalk it up to a figment of his imagination, until Sheriff Nick Piatt arrived at his dock with three deputies, a marine biologist, and…Barney Grey?!

Now things were REALLY weird. And yet, it was only the tip of the iceberg.

"So, it really was a shark that did all of that?" Tyler asked, after listening to Nick explain the events leading to the disaster.

"Some kind of shark," Nick said. "We shot it over a hundred times before we inflicted even the tiniest bit of damage. It *can* be hurt, but we need something stronger than shotguns and rifles. Going toe-to-toe with that thing would just result in more lives lost."

"It can split a boat down the middle like a .308 through a soda can," David Hummer said.

"Really? So naturally, you want to use my boat?" Tyler said.

Nick cleared his throat. "Yes." Tyler bit his lip.

"How do you plan on killing it?"

Nick pointed a thumb at Barney. "He's got dynamite."

"Hell, everyone knows that," Tyler said.

"Eat dick, Tyler," Barney burped.

"Barney, behave," Nick said.

"That's asking a lot, Sheriff," Tyler added.

"I'm asking for more than I care to, today," Nick replied. "Fact is, the Coast Guard's hands are tied. For how long, God only knows. What I do know is that your boat is the only one on the island that might stand a chance against that thing. At least, long enough for me to kill it."

"If you don't blow *it* up first," Tyler said. "It's not like the movies. You won't see the fish half the time. When you do, it'll be when it's about to attack. You need a real plan. Can't just toss dynamite in the water nonstop."

"That what I said," Barney said.

"Oh God. You and I actually agree on something? The world really is a mess," Tyler said.

"He is right," Lisa said.

"Yes! Yes! I get it. I was gonna worry about that *after* I got the tools I needed in order. Tyler, what do you suggest?" Nick asked.

"A net," Tyler replied.

"Hey, I had a net. The thing ripped right through it."

"No shit. Cheap ass nets like the ones you use, a trout could punch through it. No, I'm talking a heavy trawl net, like the one I use," Tyler replied. "My winches are designed to lift twenty-thousand pounds of fish.

I'm positive my nets can hold it long enough for us to place a charge on it, unless it has a chainsaw on its snout."

"Only in its mouth." Lisa mimicked a tooth with her fingers.

"Listen, man," Nick said. "I'm not asking you to come along. The Island Counsel will compensate you for any damage. But I need to go out and…"

"Oh no. This boat doesn't leave this dock unless I'm on it," Tyler said, prodding himself in the chest with his thumb. "You want my help, those are the conditions."

"You don't want money?" David Hummer asked. Tyler chuckled at the rookie.

"I just want to get back and fish. It's what I love, and that damn shark is keeping me from doing it. There's nothing like doing what you love and getting paid for it. The only word I can think to describe it is 'freeing'. No, better—'Living.'"

"So, we have a plan? Net the shark and blow it up?" Barney said.

"Don't tell me he's coming," Tyler said, pointing at the scrawny, tobacco smelling fisherman.

"Part of the deal," Nick stated. Tyler rolled his eyes.

Great. That prick will be aboard my boat. Now I'm DEFINITELY coming.

"If we're gonna lure the shark to the net, rather than the boat itself, we're gonna need bait," Lisa said.

"We're fishermen," Tyler said. "We've got plenty of it."

"I have a sneaking suspicion that tuna and squid aren't going to do the trick," Lisa replied. "I saw how that thing attacked. When it came after me, I was inspecting the body of a dead killer whale."

"Oh, he got them too, eh?" Barney chuckled. Lisa resisted the urge to sock him in the mouth.

"When it attacked, it came right for me. There was enough meat to feed that shark for a week. Yet, it wanted live prey," she explained.

"So, if we put conventional prey in the water, the fish will probably ignore it," Tyler clarified.

"Correct."

"Then what do you suggest? And don't say 'shark cage!'" Nick said.

"I'm not sure yet," Lisa said. "I'm sure I'll come up with something by the time we leave."

"When will that be?" David asked.

"Tomorrow afternoon. I'll be busy with press in the morning, as well as the Island Counsel. Plus, I'll want to visit a couple of the deputies who are in the hospital."

"I'll be set to go by thirteen-hundred hours," Tyler said. "I've got to make up some chum in the morning anyway."

"We'll need a lot of it. It may be a violent fish, but it's still a big ocean to hide in," Nick said.

"Sounds good. Gives me time to make a beer run," Barney said.

CHAPTER 22

They were close. Olivia Zoller's tracking monitor showed that the fish was lurking somewhere nearby. The ocean was an empty sheet of glass, the island appearing as a thin line in the southwest, encompassed by the orange glow of the setting sun.

Roark leaned on the edge of the fly deck, his sunglasses shielding his eyes from the glare of the setting sun. Streams of gold stretched across the Atlantic, creating a taut ghostly figure with the vessel's shadow. Olivia was somewhere below deck, while the men were on the main deck with nets and cables in hand. Heitmeyer was at the center, scooping chum into the water. A few feet to his right was Jacques, who watched the water with his statue-like glare. Mason and Lowery stood on the left, both of them chuckling from one of Heitmeyer's jokes. The ramp door was half-open, the pumps primed and set to go. Dorn was at the helm, carefully steering the boat in a wide circle.

Trailing behind the vessel was a rope tied to the tailfin of a two-hundred pound tuna. The bait was loaded with tranquilizer, which, according to Olivia, would take effect as soon as fifteen minutes after being ingested.

Laughter filled the deck as Heitmeyer entertained the group while chumming.

"So, did you guys hear about the constipated accountant? He couldn't budget, so he had to work it out with a paper and pencil."

"Ah, I've heard that one before," Lowery replied, waving his hand.

"Yeah, but you don't know about the guy in the exam room," Heitmeyer said. "Doctor comes in the office, sees the patient, says to him 'uh, sir, I have some bad news.' He pauses. 'You're gonna have to stop masturbating.' The patient says, 'Oh no! Why, doc?' To which he replies, 'because I'm trying to examine you.'"

That one sparked more laughter from everyone except Jacques, who stood at the transom with a rifle.

"Good God."

Roark turned around and saw Olivia step out onto the fly deck.

"Not much space for you to hide," he said to her.

"I tried waiting in the holding chamber. But with that ramp open, those idiots may as well have been sitting next to me."

"I have a feeling that's not the only thing that's bothering you," Roark said. Olivia sneered.

"It was a one-time thing," she said. "Don't expect more."

Roark raised his eyebrows and smirked.

"I wasn't thinking about *that*...though I might start." He chuckled. "No, I'm talking about the waves your fish made today."

"We lucked out," Olivia said. "Most of the footage was of boats ramming into each other, injuring swimmers. And right now, any news of the incident is being drowned out by the reports of the cruise liner bombings."

"Is that why Skomal wanted that fish?" Roark said. "To sell it as a weapon."

"You saw the wreckage, didn't you?" Olivia said.

Roark nodded. As they approached the island, they passed numerous sunken vessels in shallow water.

"Makes me a little nervous to keep going after this thing, if it's responsible for all of that."

"I didn't know you got nervous," Olivia said.

"Anything you're up to in that lab makes me nervous, especially if I'm sharing the water with it." Roark lit a new cigar, took a couple of long draws, then gazed down at the side of the vessel. "You sure this vessel can sustain a hit by that thing?"

"Yes," Olivia said. Roark turned toward her.

"You don't sound convinced."

"All we need is for Scar to take the bait. Once he does, the rest of the mission will be quick and painless. In his chamber, he won't be able to budge, let alone snap his jaws at anyone."

Roark leaned on the guardrail and watched Heitmeyer toss another scoopful of chum in the water. The sun sank lower, then disappeared, creating an orange tint in the sky that would soon turn to black.

The mercenaries put spotlights in the water, aiming two at the bait and chum trail, and a couple of others streaming over the sides. McGuinness and Mason gradually panned the white lights back and forth, hoping to spot that jagged dorsal fin.

Olivia watched Jacques, who was as motionless as a statue.

"Your man there isn't intending to blow my shark out of the water, is he?"

"Not unless he has to," Roark said.

"I've warned you of what'll happen if any harm comes to Scar," she said.

Roark snorted. "Yeah. You won't become a VP. And you'll have to find some other company to try and worm your way to the top of."

"Would she start by serving coffee?" Mason shouted. The resulting groan came out as though she was punched in the gut. The laughter following her annoyed reaction made her veins protrude from her skull. She wanted to go on a tirade, but had just enough self-control to not take the bait.

"This how you run your operation?" she whispered to Roark.

"I don't choose my mercenaries based on their personalities," he replied. "You want your shark? But if we have to kill it, then so be it, because I'm not dying for your pet project. I don't care how much money you dangle in front of me...or whatever else you use to entice me." His eyes traced over her body, taking notice of the subtle twitches of anger. She had nothing to hold over him, making her completely at his mercy. The only thing Roark enjoyed more than that very fact was how pissed off it made her.

"I don't know what you're so uptight about, since you're so confident the fish will go after your bait. I suggest you pull the stick from your ass and be patient. Then again, that's asking a lot, isn't it."

Olivia started walking back into the pilothouse. "Just find my shark."

Roark scoffed and watched the door slam shut behind her.

"Aye-aye, your royal bitch-ness."

****

As the next hour came to a close, the mercenaries were shrouded in night. The shark was circling, roughly a hundred meters out. Heitmeyer's jokes had come to a close, though not by choice, but by instruction from his superior.

Roark lit another cigar and supervised the operation from above, while keeping an eye on the tracking monitor.

"What the hell is this fish doing?" he muttered.

"I say it's scared of us," Heitmeyer said.

"Or it's got brain damage from all the boats," Mason said.

"Maybe it's full. After all, it ate a lot of people," Dorn added. A couple of mercenaries chuckled.

"Knock it off," Roark said. He watched the shark's movements. It was circling them. It was aware of their presence, and was sizing them up. But the bait was far enough away. The shark wasn't smart enough to know it was being set up...was it? Perhaps Dorn had a point: it had fed significantly today, so perhaps it wasn't hungry.

Roark looked around for Olivia, who was still waiting in the holding area. He grabbed a two-way radio.

"Doc? This thing's not going for the bait. Perhaps it's full?"

"Impossible. It hasn't fed in hours." Her voice echoed across the deck.

"Damn, if it eats that much, I hate to see its shit," Mason said. He panned one of the spotlights over the bait. "Here, fishy-fishy-fishy."

Mason watched the monitor again. The target stopped circling. It was now headed toward them, albeit slowly. *It's interested.*

"Mason, keep doing what you're doing," he said.

"Fishy-fishy, in the lake, won't you please bite my bait," Mason continued.

"Don't know if you realize, but we're in an ocean, not a lake," Heitmeyer said.

"It's how my dad used to say it," Mason replied.

"Pay attention to what you're doing," Roark said, then switched to his radio. "Doc, get that drone of yours ready. Your pet is approaching."

"Copy that."

Roark glanced between the monitor and the light. The shark was over a hundred feet beyond the tuna and closing.

Mason wiggled the light again. "Here, fishy-fishy-fishy. Got a snack for you."

Like a bullet from a gun, the shark accelerated—right past the bait, toward the transom. In the instant before it breached, its glowing red eyes shined in the dark water. Then it leapt.

Its head smacked down on the transom, splintering it. The ship rocked, throwing the mercs about. The fish lurched to the right and snapped its jaws shut, around Mason's waist. The mercenary let out a scream and beat his fists against the creature's snout. It thrashed him left and right, feeling his legs kicking the back of its throat.

He yanked his knife from his vest and slammed the tip down against its snout. The blade snapped.

"Fucking shit!" Heitmeyer shouted. He and Jacques aimed rifles at the creature and fired. Bullets crunched against its flesh, triggering the protective eyelid to sweep over the red balls.

Mason screamed again as the shark thrashed him to the left, bashing his head against Heitmeyer. The fish rolled over its side and fell into the water, carrying its victim into the depths. The ship rocked forward. Water bubbled several meters out. Lowery hurried to the port spotlight and aimed it at something floating around the bubbles. It was Mason's arm.

"Holy shit," he said.

The water erupted again. Lowery fell backward, barely out of reach before the creature struck the vessel. Its teeth snapped shut inches from his face before it rolled over the side. Jacques and Heitmeyer blasted several rounds at it.

Running feet echoed from inside of the ship. A fiery Olivia Zoller burst onto the aft deck, her face red with fury.

"No shooting!" she demanded.

"No shooting?" Heitmeyer said. Suddenly, the wannabe comedian wasn't so comedic. "I don't know if you noticed, but that thing just ATE MASON!"

"There's risk to the job, hence the payrate," Olivia said. "Now, get back to it!" Heitmeyer looked to Roark, not for instruction to proceed with the hunt, but for permission to '*shoot this bitch?*'. To his disappointment, Roark shook his head.

"Fact is, we're fucked now, gentlemen," Roark said. "We're committed to this, whether we like it or not. Only shoot the fish if absolutely necessary. If not, we'll be trading one problem for another."

He glanced to the screen. The shark was circling around the bow of the ship.

"It's coming around again. It's probably gonna make another go for you guys on deck."

"It's not going for the bait," Lowery said.

"No, it's not," Roark said. He gave Olivia a stern glare. "It's going for live prey."

The geneticist caught her breath, then looked at the bait, then at Mason's blood on the deck. Roark was right. It was ignoring the bait.

"This is a new development," she said. "Has to be due to his exposure to the wild. Scar's attracted to movement. And lights."

"Didn't take a PhD to figure that out," Dorn shouted from the helm.

"Where is it?" Lowery asked.

"Moving away," Roark said. "Two hundred feet off the port bow. Doc, you have something we can stick its mouth with?"

"I have a hypodermic needle connected to a rod. We'll have to wait for him to make another go," Olivia said. "I'll run down below and get it."

"Well hurry up because—" Roark glanced back at the monitor, then stared at it. The blip was coming straight at them. He looked to the northeast and saw the dorsal fin. It was racing at the ship like a rocket. "Brace for impact!"

The shark struck the vessel, knocking the bow to starboard. Roark clung to the railing, feeling a brief sense of weightlessness as the boat leaned far to the side. The side deck came within inches of the ocean before rocking back. Before it steadied, Scar struck again.

Olivia was on her hands and knees, only to be knocked completely on her stomach by a falling Lowery.

"Get off me!" she shouted.

"Boss!" Dorn shouted from the pilothouse. "We're in trouble! We're taking on water!"

Roark steadied his balance, then climbed down to the forward deck. It had to be along the portside bow where the creature struck. He hurried to the side, checked for the shark, then leaned over. He could see the upper edge of a large crack.

"That's not good."

"What do we do, boss?"

"We don't have many options," Roark said. "Dorn, there's a tiny island just a mile northeast of Cross Point. Full throttle to that."

"What? You're gonna beach us there?" Olivia said.

"Would you prefer we swim with your fish?" Roark replied. "You go first. Be my guest. Just make sure you have that hypodermic needle on you so you can jab it before it tears you in half."

Dorn pointed the boat west and pushed the engine as hard as it would go. Roark pointed the forward spotlight ahead of the vessel and scanned for the little atoll. It was around here somewhere. He had seen the damn thing.

He panned his light to port.

"Over there. Twelve degrees port."

Dorn turned the wheel. Almost there.

"I see it!" Lowery shouted. Gunshots rang out. Despite Olivia's objections, they unloaded into the fish, which was less than twenty feet behind the stern. The shark hooked to its right, arching around the vessel, and with a flutter of its huge tail, it closed in until its head connected with the hull. The ship pitched to port, knocking the helmsman away from the controls.

Seizing the opportunity, the shark dove, only to angle back up and accelerate.

Lowery had just reloaded his rifle and aimed it over the side, exposing his head and shoulders. In the split-second he saw its glowing red eyes, he realized he had made a mistake.

The water exploded and separated like curtains. The shark was airborne, having snatched the mercenary in its jaws. His legs kicked from its mouth, then with a mighty jerk of its head, everything below the waist separated. Still kicking, the legs and groin hit the transom and skidded into the water, only to be grinded by the propellers.

"Goddamnit," Roark snarled. "Dorn, get us to that damn island now."

The helmsman throttled to the south until he had the island on his right shoulder. He then steered to starboard, hooking it around.

The dorsal fin emerged behind them, the eyes glowing in the dark like two dying stars in the night sky. The fish was faster than the boat. Again, it was closing in.

"Hurry up," Roark said, though Dorn couldn't hear him through the roar of the engine. The fin closed in at forty feet. Thirty. Roark turned to look at the island. There was a dock on its south side. Almost there.

An explosion drew his attention to the rear. He ran to the aft deck and found a screaming Olivia slapping Heitmeyer across the face. At his feet was the pin and lever to a hand grenade. The shark had turned back, drawn off by the explosion.

"You bastard, son of a bitch. You're not receiving a dime," Olivia said.

"You really have a hard-on for that fish," Heitmeyer said. "You know, I read a story once about some chick who fucked a dolphin. Wait till they hear the story *I've* got in store for them."

"Alright, that's enough," Roark said. The boat slowed and pulled up along the dock. Roark climbed out. The water was shallow here, shallow enough to keep the shark at bay, as well as grant him a better view of the damage.

"Looks like we've found our hotel for the night," he said.

"Can it be fixed?" Dorn asked.

"Yeah, we'll weld patches over it," Roark replied. "But we'll also have to check the engine." He walked up onto the shore. "Well done, Heitmeyer, by the way."

"Well done?" Olivia said. "He might've injured my shark with that grenade."

"One more hit, and we would've gone under," Roark said. He found a rock and sat down. "Don't know if you can see far enough past your ambition to realize it, Doc, but a sunken ship is not conducive to your quest of becoming VP."

Olivia took a deep breath.

"Fine! How long until you have the boat up and running again?"

"Morning maybe. Possibly later in the day," Roark said. "In the meantime, we'll have to develop a new strategy. Something that'll involve live bait."

"I have a candidate," Heitmeyer said.

"Fuck yourself," Olivia replied.

Heitmeyer leaned close. "By the way, you don't decide if I get paid."

"Just do your job." She watched the ocean, catching only a glimpse of Scar's dorsal fin in the moonlight. As she got ready to head to her cabin, she noticed Dorn leaning over the side of the fly deck, then heard the sound of unzipping, followed by a stream hitting the water.

"Sorry Doc," he said. "Just relieving tension."

"Ugh!"

The mercs shared a laugh as she disappeared into the boat. They gathered by Roark, bringing along some welding supplies, and a bottle of whiskey.

They each took a slug, performing a funeral of sorts for their fallen comrades. It was as close to mourning as they would ever come, as dying was not unusual in their profession.

Now for the important aspect in life: finish the job and get paid.

CHAPTER 23

"Oh, my day keeps getting better and better," Nick said as he observed the weather forecast on his computer monitor. The storm front that had been forming around Bermuda had hooked west and was making a B-line right for Cross Point. Had yesterday not been so chaotic, he would've learned this information at a more convenient time. The storm would not be extremely severe, but it would put a damper on things should the hunt proceed later into the afternoon.

Nick had stopped at home after his morning obligations with the department. He made his press release at nine a.m. Luckily, it was only local press, as the major news organizations were still sidetracked with the cruise liner incidents. The rest of the morning was spent visiting the families of the deputies who had died. Some were welcoming, understanding that their loved one had died performing a heroic act. Others weren't so kind.

His face was still sore from the slap he received from the widow of Deputy Roper, who blamed him for her husband's death. Nick didn't take it personally. She was a kind woman going through the worst of times right now. However, it certainly made the sting of Roper's death throb more in his mind.

It was a half hour till noon. Nick had received the text from Tyler Monclova that the net and bait was ready. Barney Grey was probably there right now with his stash of dynamite.

Nick still wasn't keen on taking these civilians with him. He had lost enough people in the past day, and the thought of losing more was almost too much to bear. Except, maybe Barney, only because he was annoying as hell.

He chuckled at the thought. *No, I don't actually want him dead.* He then laughed at the fact that he had that follow-up thought. He was always so on guard in today's environment, that even in the privacy of his own house he felt the need to correct himself from being too controversial.

He turned off the computer and stood up. No more time for distractions. Now, he was off to go kill a shark and avenge his deputies, who were also his friends. He changed out of his uniform and got into something a little more comfortable for the mission. Jeans, black t-shirt, and a sweater to wear over it. That ocean wind, even at this time of year, could get a little chilly.

He clipped his duty belt around his waist, holstered his Colt Trooper on his right, while arming himself with a Glock 17 in his left thigh holster. He delved into his collection, grabbing a couple of knives, lighters, boxes of ammo, put them all in a bag, then went to his truck. He'd already packed a few M4 Carbines from the station, and made sure to have plenty of loaded magazines on standby.

With a little luck, this mission would be quick. Maybe the shark would seek them out and go right after them, and fall right into their trap. Judging by its heightened aggression, it might do just that. Hopefully, it would go for the trap, and not the boat.

Speaking of the trap...

Nick checked his phone. He hadn't heard from Lisa. Hopefully she figured out the riddle of the bait, because if not, it was not going to be a pleasant encounter with the fish.

****

When Nick arrived at Tyler's residence, he garnered laughs from the group about being late, even though it was only a few minutes to noon. Tyler and Lisa were up on the main deck, with Barney spitting tobacco from the fly deck.

"Dude, what did I tell you about the chew?" Tyler said.

"It's over the side," Barney said.

"If I see even a pin-sized stain on my deck, *you'll* be the live bait!"

"Aye-aye, Captain," Barney replied, making a two-fingered salute. Tyler's expression improved when he saw the Sheriff approach the dock.

"Hey, Piatt," he said.

"You guys all ready to go?" Nick asked.

"We are," Tyler said, pointing his thumb at himself, Lisa, and, with hesitation, Barney. He then pointed a finger to the right past Nick.

The Sheriff turned around and saw David Hummer standing by the back porch. His arms were crossed, his eyes firing a burning stare up at the boat's owner.

"What are you doing here?" Nick asked.

"Come on, you guys are gonna need help. Look! You brought THREE rifles! You clearly need more people on standby to watch for the thing, and fend it off in case it attacks."

"You're not going, kid. Captain Monclova won't allow it anyway," Nick replied.

"Not exactly true, Sheriff," Tyler said. "I know how you feel about taking more Deputies out...and he's a kid who's been on this island for…what? Six months? If that? Not really enough time to make him an able seaman."

"Hey, man, you know I can help. If things go wrong, I'll be right there putting bullets in the thing. I know its skin is tough, but maybe I'll land a good shot. I just don't want to sit on the sidelines."

Nick shook his head, not to deny what David was saying, but to himself. He had lost enough deputies. He wasn't about to lose any more. Hell, if it was possible, he'd go out there on his own. Unfortunately, that was impossible.

"I wasn't finished," Tyler said. "What I was gonna say, was that I wasn't sure if the Sheriff wanted you along, for the reasons I mentioned. That said, I can't complain about having an extra rifleman on deck, and Lisa did say you were able to shoot straight when that thing was on your ass yesterday. So, as far as I'm concerned, if the Sheriff's fine with you going, then it's good enough for me."

Nick closed his eyes. *Thanks, Tyler. Had to turn it around on me, didn't you?*

"Come on man, I was right there with you when the shit hit the fan," David said.

"Dave, if things go wrong, we're as good as dead out there. There won't be any backup coming. And I'm not sure about our odds."

"Odds don't matter. It's the job," David said. "You said it yourself, this job isn't all sunshine and rainbows."

Nick looked away. *Damn it, I hate it when that happens.*

"Hey! We going or not?!" Barney shouted from the fly deck, spitting tobacco onto the dock.

Tyler pointed a finger up at him. "Hey! What I said about that chew applies to all my property, you damn scarecrow."

"We do need to get going, Nick. I don't know if you saw the weather…" Lisa said.

"Yes, yes, we're going," Nick replied. He gave David one last glance. Finally, he relented, and waved him over to follow him. "Don't make me regret this. Come on."

The two cops climbed aboard.

Nick glanced at the line of clouds in the horizon. "About the weather; you guys sure you don't want to put the trip off for another day?"

"You pussying out, Sheriff?" Barney said. "Can't stand a little rain?"

"I can, but I don't speak for everyone," Nick retorted.

"No, we have to kill it today if we can. If that thing moves off to find new hunting grounds, there's no telling how many people it'll kill before it's stopped. Hell, the storm might actually cause it to migrate north or south."

"I agree," Tyler said.

The Sheriff nodded. "That's all I needed to know." He inspected the large net hanging from the pylons. The cords almost looked like extension cables, and felt just as strong. Then again, they were dealing with a shark that could sink boats ten times its mass.

"You guys confident this'll hold it?" Nick asked, directing the question more at Lisa than Tyler, as he hadn't experienced the shark's wrath.

"Long enough for us to complete the mission," she replied.

"Good enough for me," Nick said. "Speaking of which, have we decided how we're gonna pull this off?"

Lisa smiled. "I had to pull some strings, but I managed to get just the thing. You're gonna owe me ten more dinners for this, because I had to go to the mainland, kiss some major Navy ass, and get it back here in time to cast off."

"I'd be more impressed if I knew what you were talking about?" Nick said.

Lisa led him to a large, metal case by the transom. At first, he thought it was a large, oddly expensive container for the chum—until he saw the plastic tubs to his left. The metal case was about five feet long and a yard wide. She opened it and watched his expression.

"It's a shark," he replied, shrugging. "It's a dead shark—oh, wait..." He was fooled, thinking she was showing him a shark carcass for bait. Then he noticed the metal texture and glassy eyes. It was a machine. He looked it over, saw the receivers on the dorsal fin. He looked back at Lisa, who sported a control pad in her hands, and a smile on her face. Nick finally laughed. "Holy shit. It's a drone that looks like a shark! I never knew they made such a thing!"

"It's called a GhostSwimmer," Lisa said. "It was developed by the Navy back in '14. They actually put it to work off Virginia Beach. It's easy to use; just move the joysticks, and the thing will actually move like a shark."

"How deep will it go?" Nick asked.

"Down to three-hundred feet, max," Lisa answered.

"Good enough," Nick said. "How did you convince them to let you use this?"

"I know the guy running the Navy base in Virginia Beach..." Lisa said. Barney chuckled up on the fly deck. Her expression became a disgusted one. "No! You freaking pig! God!"

"Barney, I've only been here a few minutes, and I'm already *this* close to tossing you off the boat." Nick pinched his finger and thumb together, with a tiny space in-between. "And I'll keep your dynamite, by the way."

"Good luck," Barney said, before strutting around to the foredeck.

"Wouldn't be hard," Nick muttered. He shook his head, then looked over at Lisa again.

"I helped them with a few search and reconnaissance missions in '18, before coming here," she explained. "I told the Base Commander about the shark."

"Something tells me there's an aspect to this plan you didn't tell him about," Nick said. Lisa looked a tad guilty.

"Rather than net the shark and toss dynamite down at it, Tyler and I decided with a simpler, and much more reasonable solution. We'll strap the dynamite to the bait! Let the shark go after it, and secure it in the net to make sure it doesn't let go right away. We'll have to be quick, because the shark will realize the drone's not real as soon as it bites. Once the net is secure, we let it drop to a safe depth, then blow the charge, which'll ignite the dynamite. Then *boom*, no more red-eyed shark." Lisa cleared her throat. "So, yeah, I might've left out the dynamite portion, though not entirely out of dishonesty…but with the bombings, I figured it probably wasn't a smart idea to bring that up."

"Good call. They'll be pissed, though," Nick said.

"Maybe, but I have the money for the fine. And once we recover the shark's body, we'll prove the case that it was needed. Besides, nowadays, they can make a new one for ten-grand. You know the government; they spend that kind of money on ink pens."

"Don't get me going on that," Nick replied. He looked to the eastern horizon. "Alright, we have a solid plan. And, honestly, I think it'll work."

"Damn sure hope so," Tyler said. "Let's get this party started and find out!" He climbed into the pilothouse and started the engine, while Lisa and Nick pulled in the tie-off lines. "Off we go!"

Tyler steered the *Star Blaze* east. Up ahead was the thin grey line— the first sign of the storm to come. With a little luck, they would find the fish and kill it before the bad weather rolled in.

CHAPTER 24

Sparks zipped across Roark's face as he pressed the torch to the patch. Inch-by-inch, the metal fused together as one. By noon, the patch was complete.

Dorn and Jacques tinkered inside the engine room. Water had seeped into the vessel through the night, forcing them to pump it out before performing an oil change along with other emergency maintenance needs. Metal clanged together as they replaced damaged components.

"Same saltwater corroded the fuel filter," Dorn called out.

"We have a replacement," Olivia replied. She was standing on the fly deck, staring out at the storm to the east.

"Only so many, Doc," Heitmeyer said. He stepped onto the main deck, his outfit drenched from hours of pumping out water. He glanced down at his boss. The patch was near completion, but he couldn't help but take note of the thin metal that made up the sheet. "It won't take much for your fish to bust that back open. We can only do so many patches before we're dead in the water."

"Can't stay here," Roark said. "Even if we sat and waited, the Coast Guard would be on our ass." *Not to mention we'd exceed the timeframe I promised Jeff Calmes.*

"Fine. I'm up for catching the damn thing," Heitmeyer said. "But in the twelve-plus hours we've been here, we've never discussed any plan of catching the shark. The doctor claimed it would go after the bait. We know how that worked out. It went straight past it in favor of the fresh meat aboard our ship."

"I'm working out a plan," Olivia said.

"Yeah?" Roark applied the last few touches of the patch job, then lifted his goggles. "What would that be?"

"We learned last night that Scar prefers live bait. So, that's what we'll give him."

"That's fine and dandy, Doc," Roark said. "But to capture that thing, the bait needs to be loaded with whatever tranquilizer you're planning on dosing it with. The amount you're probably requiring is far more than the necessary amount to overdose a fish of any size with. When something overdoses, it dies. And last time I checked, a dead fish doesn't make for good live bait."

"I'm aware of this," Olivia said.

"Let me guess," Heitmeyer said. "You're gonna lower an anti-shark cage and try to stick it in the mouth?!"

Olivia peered down at him and smiled.

"No. I'm not. *You* are."

Heitmeyer's smile disappeared. "Yeah, you can forget it."

"What's the matter? Afraid that cage won't protect you?" Roark teased.

"YES!"

"Don't worry, I'm of the same opinion." Roark climbed aboard then looked up at Olivia. "Yeah, lady, you can forget it. You saw what it nearly did to the boat. You saw the wreckages. A dinky little cage won't last ten seconds."

"Fine!" Olivia replied. "Then I'd like to hear *your* plan. Use one of these stupid jet skis?" She pointed at the other side of the dock, where two abandoned jet skis were chained.

"Put that damn drone of yours to use," Roark said. "If it can attach a clamp or a hook, it can carry a syringe needle. Get the thing in the water, stick the shark in the mouth when it draws close, then while it's down there, attach the cable and reel it into the holding chamber."

"And if the drone is too damaged to do that?" Olivia said.

"I'll dive down there myself if I have to, as long as the damn thing's asleep," Roark said. "But no way are any of us going into that water while it's at full strength."

"We'll want to stay in shallow water," Dorn said, brushing his hands against his pants legs as he emerged from the engine room. "Any time it takes to dive increases the likelihood it'll wake up. And if you're in the water when it wakes up, then I'll be the new boss."

"You'd like that, wouldn't you?" Roark replied. Dorn shrugged, then smirked.

"Maybe a tad."

Olivia scoffed, which sparked a laugh from the mercenary leader. Even now, with not only her career, but her LIFE at stake, she hated not being the smartest one in the group. Roark could read her mind like a diary. *I'm the one with the Ph.D! I'm the one with understanding of genetics and biology, and whatever the hell else I studied. These guys are just apes, doing brainless work that anyone could do...except me apparently, even though I preach 'fight the good fight', girl-power, and whatever other bullshit I believe in.'*

Unfortunately for her ego, she couldn't deny Roark's plan made the most sense.

"When are we going to be up and running?" she said impatiently. Roark was tempted to reply with the smartass answer 'got a date?' but realized he didn't want to listen to her tirade about getting back to the floating lab on time. He glanced at Dorn.

"How's it looking?"

"Gotta add new oil to it," Dorn replied. "Maybe another thirty, forty minutes."

"Sounds like a typical auto shop," Roark commented. "Alright, fine. Finish it up. I'm starting to feel like *Gilligan*."

"You can be him. I'll be the millionaire," Heitmeyer joked.

"If he's *Gilligan,* would that make her *Mary Ann*?" Dorn asked, pointing up at Olivia.

"I don't know," Heitmeyer said. "If she's *Mary Ann*, then Roark would probably be the professor…"

"Alright, fun's over," Roark said. "Keep this up and I'll feed you to the fish myself." He glanced up at Olivia. "Hey, *Mary Ann*?! Is your pet still swimming around out there?"

Olivia scowled.

"Yes."

"Good," Roark said. He grinned as he looked away. "Let's finish this up, boys. Our scientist has a career that's at stake."

Dorn cackled as he returned to the engine room. Olivia waited alone on the fly deck and watched the water. Only Roark remained on the aft deck. The others were busy with repairs. She took the advantage of their distraction to make her way to the holding chamber. There, she collected her drone and syringes, and began rigging up a harness to utilize Roark's plan.

She arrived on the aft deck with the expectation that he would badger her some more. To her surprise, he was looking out to the south. He wasn't simply watching the water; he was looking at something specific.

"We're not alone out here," he said. Olivia walked to the transom. He pointed to the south at a large trawler. At almost two miles out, the boat almost looked like a brown speck moving across the water. Olivia had to squint hard before she could see it.

"So what?" she said.

"*So what?!* Weren't you the one making a big deal about being inconspicuous?" Roark said. "Whoever that is, they might see us out here when we resume our hunt."

"As long as we capture the shark quietly…with *no* gunfire, they won't even suspect what we're doing," she said.

"Yeah, I understand that," Roark said. "But *what if* they see us?"

"That's where you come in. No witnesses. Can't afford the issue. Do what you have to do," Olivia said. There was no emotion in her voice. She spoke with the casualness of a grocery store manager addressing staff about stocking the shelves. "Any problems?"

Roark looked over at her, amazed at her coldness. He was in no position to judge. He'd done it before. He preferred strikes against armed subjects, not civilians, but with the right amount of money thrown at him...

"No problems. If they come over here, I'll take care of it," he said. He leaned on the transom and watched the distant vessel travel further to the east until it was out of sight.

He couldn't help but grin. *Damn. She never fails to impress.*

CHAPTER 25

"I think we should start here," Tyler said. He glanced up at the clouds. They were gradually starting to darken. The first wave of storm winds were already sweeping over them. The ocean was calm when they left. Now, there were mild swells rolling against the trawler.

"Here is fine," Nick said. "Fish finder set up?"

"Always," Tyler said.

"Alright. Barney, you're up. Time to chum!" Nick said.

"Wait...what?!"

"You heard me."

"And make sure you do it from the side," Tyler added. "We need the fish to come in from the front."

Barney sneered then groaned, then sneered again after hearing Tyler Monclova chuckling in the pilothouse. Nick was almost afraid to watch the idiot drag the chum to the starboard middeck. He was so wiry, his arm looked like it would snap off with the slightest tug.

Nick climbed up into the crow's nest with his rifle and a set of binoculars. Lisa explained that sharks can smell a molecule of blood in a million molecules of water. Assuming that was true, it would have no trouble picking up on this chum trail.

Tyler lowered the net into the water and let it descend for fifty feet. All Lisa had to do now was get the drone into the water. With a few screwdrivers, they were able to get some dynamite sticks inside, which would be triggered by a remote charge that Barney was able to rig. While useful for this current operation, it still nearly infuriated her. How many depth charges has he been using? How much damage had he done to the ecosystem around here? More importantly, was he planning on using these explosives on her killer whales? She knew the answer, and it took every ounce of her willpower not to confront him about it.

"Need help lowering that into the water?" David asked.

"Please," Lisa said. They each took an end then lifted it onto the dive ramp. Lisa knelt down and gradually slipped the drone into the ocean, but not before double checking its receiver and joints.

Looking at it from up above, had David not already known it was a drone, he would've mistaken it for a small shark. Then, when he saw the thing move by, swaying its caudal fin back and forth, he was definitely certain he would've been fooled by it.

"God! Think of all the practical jokes we could play on people!"

"Hope your whales don't decide to come in and steal it like they tend to do with my catch," Barney said.

Lisa groaned. It didn't take long for the remarks about her pod to come flying out of his mouth.

"Why do you hate them so much?" she asked. Barney snickered.

"I thought I just explained it," he said.

"You really asking him that question?" Tyler said. He chuckled. "I have the answer for you. It's *Barney*! He hates everything."

"And everybody," Nick added, his eyes not wavering from the ocean.

"No, I'm genuinely curious," Lisa said. "You *really* think they tear up your nets?"

"I've seen them do it. Alright, the last time may have been that shark for all I know. But there have been other times…" Again, he came close to mentioning his drift nets, which he didn't want to do. Lisa was fed up by the evasive language.

"Yeah, I know you use drift nets. You know why the orcas tear them up?" Barney didn't answer, again, out of interest of not incriminating himself. "Because they nearly lost a baby in one of your nets. Yeah, the runt you saw in that pack, he almost drowned if not for his family…and me."

"What's it matter? They're just animals. They're a dime a dozen. You'd find others to gush over," Barney said. He tossed another scoopful of chum into the water.

"I guess I see other living things as more than objects to gush over," Lisa said. Barney chuckled as he tossed out another scoopful.

"Oh, boy! Let me guess. You're one of those tree-hugger types. Probably get your panties in a bunch if a hunter kills a jackrabbit. Or a fisherman hauls in some tuna."

"Not at all," Lisa said. "I'm a meat-eater, in fact. I don't blame humans for eating fish any more than I blame a killer whale for eating a seal."

"Or Barney for eating worms," Tyler joked. David covered his mouth to hide his laugh. Unsuccessfully.

Barney was surprisingly quiet. Everyone figured he'd have some sort of quip. A sly comeback. A witty remark about the orcas. Instead, he just continued launching chum into the water.

Finally, a remark broke through his breath, or rather, a question: "You ever use seals?"

Lisa squinted, unsure if he was somehow setting her up for a joke.

"You mean, to train? Or use in research?"

"Research," Barney said. "Haven't you ever used one to get video?"

Lisa shrugged. The fact that she was even getting a semi-intelligent conversation out of Barney Grey was a scientific breakthrough in itself.

"I was in Alaska once and we used trained seals to get video of the ocean terrain," she said. "I didn't take part in the training. That was done by my associates up there."

Barney continued to chum. His eyes were fixed on the water.

"Any killer whales come eat your seals?"

Now Nick was looking down. He had one eyebrow raised. Barney was never one to be trusted, though there didn't seem to be any 'gotcha' moment. No punchline. It was as if Barney was expressing some degree of...grief.

The fisherman glanced around. "The hell are you all looking at me for?"

Nick lifted the binoculars back to his eyes and scanned the water. Tyler was back at the helm, though he kept the windows open to eavesdrop on the conversation.

Lisa knelt by her tablet to monitor the drone's movements.

"To answer your question; no. We did see killer whales up there, but we never lost any seals to them." She glanced over at Barney. "You seem to have an interest in seals, of all things."

"That a problem? I thought it was good to love animals." A drop of spit flew with each word.

"Not a problem at all," Lisa replied. "You're the one who brought up seals. I thought you were making a point."

"Eh, never-mind," he said. He continued scooping until his chum trail stretched for a half-mile out. Lisa thought of pressing the subject, but worried about triggering his hot temper.

What did seals have to do with his hate for killer whales. She highly doubted he had one as a pet. Still, there was something there, and she found it fascinating.

"I saw a movie where a killer whale was avenging the death of its mate," Tyler said. "Came out during the '*Jaws* rip-off era' as I call it."

"Bastard had it coming," Barney muttered. Tyler burst into a fit of laughter.

"Dude's getting bitter about a *fictional* killer whale! He REALLY hates them."

"Ever been to Iceland or Norway, Barney?" David asked. The fisherman snickered.

"I know what you're gonna ask me: Have I ever eaten whale?" David ginned, then nodded. "The answer is yes." Barney immediately looked over at Lisa to see her reaction. Aside from shaking her head unapprovingly, she didn't express too much condemnation. "Have you guys ever eaten elk?" Nick raised his hand. "It's somewhat similar to that. More exact to moose. Not bad, though. Not bad at all." He glanced again at Lisa and grinned like a comic book villain.

Instead she decided to turn the tide.

"What about veal?" She directed the question at her peers, while watching Barney in her peripheral vision. He didn't appear to care. Regardless, she kept pushing.

"I have," Tyler said. Nick and David shook their heads.

"It's a bit more tender than beef," Lisa explained. "I bring it up because that's how cooked seal meat tastes."

"Damn, Lisa. Never thought you were the type to go for cooked seal," Nick said.

"Hey, I knew a farmer once. He loved cows. Loved them like family. Didn't stop him from eating beef. I've spent most of my life on the coast. You tend to get a lot of seafood in your diet. I've tried a bunch of different things. That includes seal."

Still, Barney didn't provide much of a reaction. Lisa began to think she was using the wrong method to dig out the answers she wanted. Barney wouldn't care what she ate. Even if he had a fascination with seals, he probably didn't care about them as a whole.

Yet, he asked about their use in research. Whatever the issue was, it had something to do with *trained* seals.

"How much do you know about seal training, Barney?"

"What do you care? You're the scientist, you should know far more about it than me," he said.

"I'm curious."

"That why you became a biologist? Curiosity?"

"You're deflecting," she said.

"Lisa, let it go," Nick said. She ignored him.

"You asking me if I can balance a ball on my nose?" Barney said.

"Now *that's* something I would pay to see," Tyler remarked. Barney flipped him the bird.

"No, no," Lisa said. "I'm thinking of getting trained seals to help me film the local populations. Of course, handling them takes money and manpower. I can't just hire anyone off the street. It has to be someone who knows how to interact with them."

Barney looked her in the eye, trying to judge whether she was serious or pulling his leg. He suspected the latter, but took the bait anyway.

"What holding facility would you have for them? They need space. Can't be cooped up for too long in little cages."

Tyler cupped his mouth to suppress his laugh. *Ol' Barney Grey, jackass of the sea, who uses drift nets and depth charges, suddenly cares about cute little seals?! Am I in a cartoon?*

"What's so funny?" Barney said.

"Nothing. Nothing at all," Tyler replied. Barney glanced back at Lisa.

"Why do I get the feeling you're putting me on?"

Now, even Nick was snickering. *Because she is.*

"So, you do know something about them," Lisa said.

"A little…"

"I could use your help, then," Lisa continued. "I plan on getting a few to film the reefs, help me map out a few underground caves, maybe document dolphin and orca behavior…"

"No!" Barney exclaimed.

"Huh?"

"Not feeding your seals to the freaking whales," Barney said. Lisa was silent.

It all made sense now. His knowledge of seal handling; his hate for killer whales; his specific phrase of 'feeding your seals to the freaking whales'.

"I see why you hate them," she said. "It happened when you were a kid, didn't it? You knew a trainer, or a researcher, or both. Helped with the caring of the seals. Learned a few tricks in the process. More importantly, you got attached to one. It went out for an assignment, then had a run-in with a killer whale."

Barney wrinkled his nose. "What? You trying to go all *Dr. Phil* on me? Wanna know how I feel? Fine. I was right there with Dr. Moore. Milo started his dive. As usual, he had an underwater camera on his back. Dr. Moore always let me watch. He was passing over some reef. All I remember was that he moved to the surface, then suddenly turned around. I saw the jaws on the monitor. Heard Milo's squeal before the screen went to black."

"Milo? Was that the name of your pet seal?" Tyler chuckled.

"Go stick a pinecone up your ass," Barney snapped.

"Alright, that's enough. Tyler, mind not egging him on, please?" Nick said.

"Whatever you wish, Sheriff," Tyler said. He stepped back into the pilothouse, amused by Barney's story.

Lightning flashes in the far distance eliminated his humor. By the looks of it, that storm was coming in faster than they thought. He checked the fax for any updated weather reports.

"Hey, guys, we better find this fish in the next couple of hours."

"Don't tell me it's increased to hurricane levels," Nick said.

"No, but according to the updated report, it's right on the cusp of being a tropical storm," Tyler said. "Not conditions I want to be hunting a killer shark in."

"Great. Just great," Nick said. He took a breath and said, "Let's proceed. Hopefully we'll find it and kill it before the weather gets too bad. If it gets to be too much, we'll call it quits."

"Pussies," Barney muttered.

CHAPTER 26

"Come on. Hurry it up," Olivia demanded.

"Calm it down, Doc," Roark said. He finished the last few touches on the welding patch, then climbed aboard. He made his way to the foredeck, then signaled for Dorn to start the engine. The vessel came to life with a metallic clatter. A puff of black smoke escaped the exhaust, then gradually lightened up after several moments. Roark blew a sigh of relief, which was lost in a gust of wind. He watched several flashes of lightning in the distance. "Even if we caught your fish, are you sure you want to push this boat through that storm?"

"What's the matter? Afraid of a little rain?" Olivia said.

"With *this* engine, maybe a little," he replied.

"I'm sick of reminding you that we don't have the luxury of time," Olivia said. "Let's catch Scar and finish the job. The tracker shows him to the east. Let's get going. Sooner we find him, the better."

"You sure about that?" Heitmeyer said. He picked up Lowery's rifle.

Roark climbed to the fly deck. "Dorn. Back us out."

Dorn put the vessel in reverse and gradually backed the boat away from the dock, then pointed it out to open sea. Olivia was kneeled on the aft deck with her drone in front of her. She equipped the arm with a large syringe and loaded it with sedatives. The cables and winch were already prepped to haul in the prize, and a scuba tank was prepared for Roark for him to make the dive.

All I need to do is get Scar to come after this sucker.

They proceeded east for several minutes, the helmsman being careful not to be too hard on the engine. Olivia was the tracking monitor. Scar was going everywhere: north, south, west, east, shallow, deep. He completely dominated the water like it was his own fortress. In a way, Olivia felt proud, like a parent did when their baby first walked, rode their first bike, presented their first report card, and ultimately took on the world. That's what Scar was doing: taking on the world. He was doing better out here than she ever would have predicted. In a way, she was almost sorry to be snatching him out of his new environment and containing him in the artificial one in the lab. At the end of the day, Scar was just a product; a stepping stone to bigger and better things. And Olivia Zoller would supervise the creations of those better things. Her products would bring in buyers from across the globe. Skomal Corp's stocks would ascend to the heavens, and all because of her.

Then, she could spit in the face to all of those who tried to hold her back. Her ex-husband, her in-laws, her parents, professors.

"You really sure you want to crossbreed different species?"

"Is there really a market for this?"

"Why is this so important?"

"You're letting that shark attack dominate your life."

"I never see you."

All of their voices rang in her mind, especially that bastard ex-husband. He never saw the bigger picture. She tried to let him come on board, but he was too narrow-minded. Then came the issue of her abortion. She remembered how he freaked when he found out. Like she could focus on having a kid right now? A kid she didn't even want in the first place, no less. The good thing that came from that incident was that it made them go their separate ways. Better yet, it got her half his income for five years thanks to a good lawyer and judge who saw the world as she did. So nice that his business took off during their marriage; made it easy to allege she was crucial in its development.

Olivia smirked. Who cares what he put into it, or that she didn't know anything about it? He was a thorn in the side of her ambitions, and in her mind, that was the price he deserved to pay. Another victory for her.

There were a lot of victories, lately. None of which would compare to that of delivering Scar back to the lab. Then Skomal could suck up to his sponsors, get more money, then she would earn that title of Vice President.

They were getting close now. Scar was lurking another mile off, maintaining a standard pace. He was ascending now. Olivia wondered if he was hunting for squid that lived a thousand feet down. He was experiencing so much in such a small period of time.

He was going south now. In a few minutes, he would probably turn west towards them.

She stood up and switched on her drone.

"We're getting close," she announced. "Let's get ready. I need a man by the winch. Roark, you all set to dive?"

"Let's worry about giving your fish his nighttime medicine first," Roark replied.

Heitmeyer moved to the winch controls, while Jacques stood ready with his rifle. Olivia grimaced, barely holding back the argument about not killing the shark which had been done a few times already. It didn't matter; the plan would work. They just needed to get a little closer. Once the drone was in the water, Scar would go after it, receive his injection, then be hauled on board.

"How far now?" Roark asked.

"Three quarters of a mile due ea—" her voice trailed off when her eyes went to the monitor. Not only was Scar continuing south, he had accelerated. Already, he had added a half-mile's worth of distance. "No, no, no…" she muttered.

"What?" Heitmeyer said.

"He's running off," Olivia said.

"He's running?" Roark said. "You mind elaborating?"

Olivia groaned. "He's going south."

"So what? We'll start chumming and draw him to us," Roark replied.

"No, he's moving fast," Olivia said.

"Ha!" Heitmeyer exclaimed. "He probably sensed we were coming and thought, 'nope. Don't want to deal with them again!'"

"He fears nothing," Olivia said.

"Yeah? Then why is he running?" Heitmeyer shot back.

"I don't think he is," Olivia said. "He only moves this fast when he's hunting. There must be something drawing his attention. Maybe a whale or a…" A realization hit her. "Roark, that boat you saw—where is it?"

"How the hell should I know?" Roark replied. "It was two miles south of us, heading due east from what I could tell. I can't see it now."

"What kind of boat was it?"

"Do I look like I have enhanced vision or something? Is that something you're working on in the lab?"

"Roark!"

"I have no way of knowing. Probably a fishing trawler," Roark said.

"Scar's going right toward them," Olivia said. "The fact that he's going that fast means they might be chumming the water. I think they're hunting for him."

"How many boats did he sink during the rampage? You're worried he won't be able to handle just the one?" Roark said with a laugh. Olivia's expression intensified. Roark's laugh turned into a groan. *Great. Now I get to shoot civilians. I'm sure that'll look great on my resume.* He went into the pilothouse. "Dorn. Turn to starboard. Full speed."

CHAPTER 27

Barney Grey tossed another scoopful of chum into the water. It splashed down and immediately was carried away by the waves, which were now pushing west. He tossed another one out, only to watch the same result. The chum trail was hardly a trail anymore. Rather, it was just a wide seascape of oil and fish guts with no obvious point of origin.

"This isn't going to work," he muttered.

"Barney, we haven't been at it for very long," Nick reminded him.

"I know, Sheriff. Of course, we could've taken our time a little more had you gotten out of your precious press conferences this morning."

"Hey, if you want to help run the island, be my guest," Nick replied. "Now, back to chumming the water."

Barney mumbled a few curse words, then dipped the scoop back into the bucket. As he leaned to toss it into the water, the wind kicked up, pushing some of the chum right back into his face.

"Son of a dick!" Barney muttered. Tyler was the first to break out in laughter, followed by everyone else. Barney wiped his face with his sleeve, then glared at his companions. "Something funny?"

"Only your face," Nick said.

"Got some up here," Lisa added, pointing to her left eyebrow.

"You know, all you need to do is go to shore like that, and you'll make a ton of new seal friends!" Tyler said.

Lisa covered her mouth, but couldn't help herself. She laughed intensely at Barney's misfortune. Her laughter put David over the edge as well. His face was red as he cackled.

"I—I'm sorry, Barney. I know you love seals, but that's just too funny," he said.

"Kid, you're about to look like me. Only the guts won't be from FISH!"

"Hey, come on now," David said. "Shouldn't you be mad at Tyler?"

"You all suck," Barney said.

"Ah, nothing new there," Tyler said. "Barney always hates everybody. And everything. Except seals, apparently."

"Come on now," Lisa said. "It was a cute story."

"Hey, some good came out of it. Someone got fed!" Tyler continued.

"Alright, don't badger him too much," Nick said. "Barney, go clean yourself up. David, you take a turn with chumming."

"Oh…" David muttered, his eyes going toward the disgusting mixture.

"Hey, you wanted to come along…" Nick reminded him.

"Yes, Sheriff," David said. He approached the bucket. Pieces of fish floated about in the mixture. He saw intestines, skin, pieces of grounded meat, and in the corner, one fully intact eye. He felt as though he would turn green.

"Got a problem there, Rookie?" Tyler asked.

"None." David sucked in a breath. Silently, he was grateful he took the Dramamine, or else he wouldn't be able to hold it together. He clenched his jaw hard to avoid making whines of disgust, then thrust the scoop into the bucket.

"Can definitely tell he's a mainlander," Tyler joked.

"So are we. He'll learn," Nick said. He watched David's awkward technique in tossing the chum out. "Though I will say: he might take a little longer."

Tyler Monclova snorted, then stepped back into the wheelhouse. He put on some music and kept the boat steady. All the while, he watched the weather gradually intensify. The clouds were turning grey, the horizon behind them pure black with the exception of numerous white lightning flashes. The swells were growing larger and more intense. The rain had not started yet, but Tyler could feel the humidity coming off the clouds.

He glanced up to the sky. *Hey, God, did you feel like you needed to make this a little extra challenging? Are all the angels up there placing bets?*

"I've got five on the shark," he mimicked in a deep voice, then switched to a higher voice, "Put me down for twenty on the guys with the boat!"

He smiled at his own joke, then saw the sonar monitor. On the upper left side of the screen, a green speck of light occurred. Very gradually, it was moving toward the center of the screen. He looked up at the ocean. There was nothing on the surface that would cause this blip, and no marine life ever rushed his vessel at such a speed. Even the largest of sperm whales turned around at the sound of his motor.

He glanced up at the sky again.

"I better get a cut of the winnings if I end up visiting you guys," he muttered. He stepped out onto the fly deck and waved a hand to the team. "He's coming from the north."

All eyes turned to him.

"How fast?" Nick asked.

"Fast. Like pissed-off-fast," Tyler replied. "He's less than a mile out."

"Holy shit," David said. He shuddered. The situation felt real now. "I hope this works."

"It'd be weird if you didn't, youngster," Barney replied.

"Keep chumming, David. Keep him coming to us," Nick said. He looked north with his binoculars. So far, he couldn't see anything.

"Are we sure it's the shark?" David asked.

"Nothing else would be coming at us at such speed," Nick answered. "Mr. Monclova, I'd recommend facing our bow at him."

"Already on it," Tyler replied. He spun the helm to port. The vessel rotated, the two-foot swells battering the hull and erupting into salty mist.

"Lisa, how's that drone doing?" Nick said. The marine biologist was at the transom with the control mechanism. She watched the camera feed on her laptop monitor as she maneuvered the drone.

"Looking good, Sheriff," she replied.

"Good." Nick continued to watch the water. So far, there was no sign of the fish. "Tyler. How far off is it now?"

"Three-quarters of a mile and closing, Sheriff. It's coming fast. It's definitely the shark!"

Nick still couldn't see it. "Lisa, we're gonna have to rely on the camera feed for visual. Barney, lower the nets."

"Hang on," Lisa said. "We're going too fast. The drone's lagging behind."

"Oh shit. Tyler, slow it down."

The Captain cut back on the throttle.

"It's almost here, guys."

Barney moved to the winch and placed his hand on the lever. "We can't wait much longer, fellas!"

"Hang on," Lisa said. She could see the vessel on the monitor. She just needed to get the drone another few hundred feet closer. "I'm almost there. I'm almost…" She leveled the drone to face directly north. She could see the evil red glow of the shark's eyes. "I see it. It's coming right at us."

She regretted saying that with such urgency. Barney clutched the lever and pulled down.

"Wait!" Lisa's words fell on deaf ears. The net struck the water…right on top of the drone. Instinctively, she thumbed the joysticks in hopes of steering it in front of the net, only succeeding in tangling up their bait. "Damn it, Barney!"

"What happened?" Nick said.

"Raise the nets. The drone's tangled. It won't get the shark's attention," Lisa said.

"Just wiggle it free," Barney said. "As long as the fish goes down to get it, it doesn't matter if it's—"

A thunderous *crack* echoed across the ship. The bow jolted to starboard, the lines bending with slack. Barney saw them folding into the water, right where the propellers were.

"Oh shit!" He climbed to his feet and pushed the winch lever forward, reeling the nets in.

In the pilothouse, Tyler turned the wheel back to port. So far, the vessel seemed to be operational. Nick had climbed down from the crow's nest and hurried to the forward deck. He looked over the gunwale to see if there was any obvious damage.

"I think we're fine," he said.

"At the moment," Tyler replied. "Another hit like that and we're done for. Where the hell is it?"

Nick and David shouldered their rifles and took watch, with the rookie taking the portside.

"Well, this isn't going as planned," he said.

"Knock it off, Hummer," Nick replied. "You get a shot, take it."

The net raised over the transom, with the drone caught along the bottom. Lisa stood up and reached for it. The netting had wrapped around the tail and dorsal fin.

"Damn it, Barney. You could fuck up a wet dream," she muttered.

"Hey, if you didn't screw around and try to wiggle it free, we could've gotten the net off before it tangled," Barney retorted.

"You're seriously gonna blame me?" Lisa said.

"What's going on?" Nick asked. Lisa threw her hands up in the air.

"It's tangled in the fishing net," she replied. "I've got to get it out."

"Fabulous," Nick muttered. He suppressed his inner desire to chastise Barney, instead focusing his energies on looking out for the fish. "Just get it untangled and back into the water."

The rolling waves clashed around their vessel. The wind picked up to over thirty-miles per hour. The lightning flashes grew nearer and more intense. Thick white bolts streaked across the black clouds. Cracks of thunder sounded off like artillery fire.

Beyond the wind was the sound of rain battering the ocean. It hadn't reached them yet, but they had minutes at best.

The next loud *crack* rocked the ship, for it was not thunder that struck, but a ravenous shark. Its snout struck the starboard quarter, spinning the stern to port. Nick pointed his rifle at the red eyes and fired off several rounds. The fish lashed its body to the left and dove, but not before slashing the vessel with its caudal fin. Nick staggered with the impact. After regaining his balance, he aimed again at the water. There was nothing but rolling waves.

"Tyler! Where is it?" he yelled at the pilothouse.

"He's circling wide. Coming up on the portside," Tyler replied, his eyes fixed on the fish finder. Nick and David took firing positions.

"You should've stayed on shore, kid," Nick said. David shook his head.

Kiss my ass, Sheriff.

The ocean broke and those red eyes came up at them.

"Jesus!" David shouted, blasting away at the open jaws. Nick grabbed him by the collar and yanked him back.

The shark raised its head from the water and slammed it down on the side of the vessel like a hammer, crunching the gunwale right down to the deck. The boat teetered.

Lisa gasped, finding herself sliding toward the portside. She felt a hand grab her by the shoulder. A moment later, she was lifted up the slope. She winced, as those fingers pinched her skin in the process, but didn't care…as long as they lifted her away from those two-inch triangular teeth.

She glanced back to see her rescuer, thinking it was Nick…only to realize it was Barney of all people. He had one hand on her shoulder and another on the cleat, and was straining to keep his grip on both.

"You gonna grab onto something? Or am I expected to dangle you over his choppers like a hors d'oeuvre?"

Lisa threw her arms out and curled her fingers around the edge of the gunwale.

The ship teetered further. The waterline was almost up to the coaming. The shark twisted violently. It struck its huge caudal fin against the waves in an attempt to propel itself up the deck to get the meat on the other side.

The vessel shook. Water slowly began to dribble over the port gunwale.

David's feet scraped the deck. He was almost dangling at this point. He tried to point his rifle at the beast like a pistol, but another hammer-like pounding by the beast shook the boat again, as well as the weapon from his grip. It hit the deck and slid to the other side.

His grip on the weapon was not the only thing to falter. He could feel his wet hand peeling away from the ledge.

"Sheriff? SHERIFF! NICK!" He threw his other hand for the bar but was too late. His grip slipped, and he found himself sliding toward the mouth of the scar-faced fish.

Nick lunged, barely managing to grab the rookie's fingertips. David panted, dangling like bait on a fishing pole. A single meter below his boots were the hyperextended jaws of the fish. Pieces of meat and clothing dangled from their serrated edges, a taunting reminder of the fate that awaited him.

Nick strained to hold on to him. He could feel his grip starting to weaken. "David, you're gonna have to grab something! Anything! Just reach out."

With seconds left, David glanced around for anything he could hold on to. The only thing within reach was the cargo hatch coaming, a small ledge protruding a few inches off the deck. He swung himself as though on a tree vine, then lunged for the ledge. With a triumphant yell, he grasped it with both hands.

With the rookie out of the way, Nick grabbed his sidearm and pointed it at the beast. Two shots entered its open mouth, spurting red mist. Another shot skidded over its shout. A fourth punched through its tooth. None of these shots deterred the beast. It cocked its head to the left to snap at David.

Nick aimed for its eye and fired, only for the fish to move at the last second. The bullet struck a few inches low and split into shards, which rained uselessly onto the deck. With one shot remaining, he aimed again.

"The gills!" Lisa shouted. "Aim for the gill slits!"

Nick didn't waste time with questions. He panned the muzzle to the left and fired. The bullet punched through one of the gill slits, resulting in a small explosion of flesh and blood. The shark jolted, its nerves flaring. It teetered further to its left, then rolled off the boat, disappearing into the ocean with a tremendous splash.

The ship rolled back to starboard, the momentous force throwing the crew about.

Barney grunted as his body thudded on the deck. He was the first one to be back on his feet. He approached the portside to gauge the shark's position. Rolling waves scattered the newly created blood trail, but there was enough for him to see that it was moving further out.

"Monclova! Can you see it?!"

Tyler had been thrown against the bulkhead, and required several seconds for his senses to return. He glanced at the fish finder, then peered out onto the deck.

"It's coming back. Portside again."

"We can't take another hit like that again," Lisa said.

"Damn straight. We're turning back," Tyler said.

"There's no point. We'll never outrun it," Nick said.

"The plan's not working, Sheriff," Tyler replied.

"It can work. Let me get the drone untangled," Lisa said. She dropped to her knees and started working the net out from around the artificial caudal fin.

The boat shook from underneath, knocking her backward. Water sprayed high into the sky.

Nick knelt, barely keeping his balance. When he straightened his stance, he saw the shark's dorsal fin emerging on the starboard side. It circled back and rammed the boat again, rolling it hard to the left. All hands stumbled to port, then back as the vessel rocked.

"Son of a bitch!" he shouted.

"The hull's breached," Tyler said. "We're taking on water. I can patch it, but not with that thing down there. I'm telling you, we need to make a run for it."

"You do that, you might as well serve yourself up to that thing," Nick said.

"Sheriff, this plan's dead! It won't work!"

"Oh, for the love of God! You two are like toddlers who won't shut up," Barney said. He opened a case of dynamite, grabbed a stick, then dug in his pocket for a cigarette lighter. "Time to go back to the old plan."

He watched for the shark, then saw the red glow under the rolling waves. He broke off a piece of the fuse, leaving only a few second's worth, then sparked a flame with his lighter.

"Nibble on *this*." He tossed the flickering stick of dynamite into the water. A tremendous explosion rocked the ocean. The shark arched back and dove.

"Tyler?! Where is it?" Nick asked.

"Diving low. It's running. Five hundred feet..." Tyler said.

Barney smiled victoriously. "Ha! Leave it to me to fix things!"

"Yeah, don't forget, you're the one who mucked it up to begin with," Nick said, cocking his head at the net and drone.

Barney glanced at it, then shrugged.

"It's coming back," Tyler announced. "It's ascending fast. Coming in for another run."

Barney smirked. "He has no fear." He lit another fuse and moved to the edge. He couldn't wait to see the shark... by then, it would be too late. He tossed the dynamite into the sea, then ducked as the resulting explosion launched a wall of water at the boat. As the mist and smoke cleared, they waited for Tyler's update.

"That did it. It turned away," he said.

The Captain took a breath and changed course to take them to the atoll. As the bow faced north, he noticed something roughly a thousand yards out. It was another vessel, and it was speeding right toward them.

****

Olivia watched the event through long-range binoculars, baring teeth in anger as the explosive echo swept past them.

"They're using dynamite," Roark said. He spoke nonchalantly, as though it was just another day at the office.

"Fishing vessels don't typically carry dynamite. They're hunting for it. They're trying to kill my shark!" Olivia said. "Hurry up! Get us over there."

"We're already at top speed. This boat can only go so fast," Roark replied. Olivia dropped the binoculars and grabbed him by the collar with both hands.

"What the hell am I paying you for?"

Roark smirked. "Damn. I thought you were gonna kiss me."

"Ugh!" Olivia pushed him away. Roark grinned and started for the pilothouse, where he kept a special rifle case.

"Yeah, as if the thought of that actually disgusts you," he muttered. He entered the pilothouse, opened the case, and attached a scope to his M4 Carbine.

****

Lisa pried the net lines apart, then pulled the drone's caudal fin free. She undid some of the tangling around the head and the dorsal fin, until finally, the machine was free.

"Nick. I'm set to go," she said. They lowered the net back into the water. The current got hold of it, expanding the trawl net to its full width.

"Tyler, keep it slow. Turn us to face the shark," Nick said.

The Captain glanced back, and saw that the team was ready to continue the original plan. He measured the shark's position, said a brief prayer, then swung the boat to starboard.

Nick rushed to help Lisa lower the drone into the water. She steered it under the boat and lined it up with the net.

Her laptop had fallen near the portside corner of the stern when the shark leapt onto the boat. David opened it up for her and switched it on. The monitor was cracked, but still managed to display the drone's camera feed.

Nick and David reloaded their rifles. Up on the fly deck, Tyler was standing ready with his. He looked like an Army soldier, ready to make a last stand against an overwhelming invasion.

It was a sentiment that Nick felt in the back of his mind.

"This better work," he said.

"It'll work," Lisa replied. She moved the drone around in tight circles. She flipped the joysticks, creating sharp, erratic movements to mimic the movements of an injured fish.

Tyler peeked through the window. "It's moving in."

Barney held on tight to his case of dynamite. He latched it shut, while holding a few sticks in his hand, ready to light the fuses in case the plan failed. He stuffed a pinch of tobacco in his mouth and chewed nervously, while also smoking a cigarette.

"Five hundred feet..." Tyler counted. "Four hundred. Three. Two...it's going low. One hundred. It's passing under the bow."

Lisa faced the drone forward. Behind the crack in the screen were a pair of enormous jaws. They engulfed the entire image, which then shook violently, before becoming a grainy, grey image.

The net lines went taut, then shifted back and forth like a fishing line with a three-pound largemouth at the end of it.

"We got him!" Nick said. "Close the nets."

Laughing wildly, Barney pulled the lever, winching the lines back just enough to close the net around the shark. Tyler came rushing down from the fly deck.

"That's enough. Let's drop it down." He arrived at the controls and lowered the winch slowly, dropping the shark low to keep them out of the blast range.

Barney glanced around the deck. "Where's the detonator?"

The group looked, realizing it had fallen from place after the shark nearly capsized the boat. They shuffled around in search of the small, black device.

"Here it is!" David shouted. He tossed a case of dynamite aside from the base of the cabin, then grabbed the detonator. He flipped a switch, activating the device. A red light came on. All that needed to be done now was to hit the trigger. He looked to Tyler. "We all set?"

"It's deep enough. Blow that sucker out of the water," Tyler said.

"You got it. Goodnight, you red-eyed piece of sh—"

An explosion of blood ripped from his shoulder, followed immediately by a deafening gun report.

Time seemed to slow down as the group saw a bloodied David Hummer fall to the deck. Several meters behind him was another vessel, slightly smaller than theirs. It looked like a simple yacht. However, the people on board, judging by their tactical gear and weaponry, were clearly not casual boaters.

"Get down!" Nick shouted. He grabbed Lisa and threw her to the deck. Bullets struck the hull and pilothouse, splintering metal and shattering glass.

"Christ!" Barney shouted, diving into the cargo hatch. Bullets grazed his thighs and back as he disappeared into the ship.

The boat shook, then was dragged backwards. The gurdies broke apart and the tag lines whipped freely, scraping the transom. The outriggers bent back to stern.

The fish was thrashing its tail left and right, slicing the strange confining object encompassing its body. After a minute of biting and thrashing, it ripped through the net and swam free.

Like a bull that had been cruelly prodded by its handler, the predator shot for the surface, then struck the enemy vessel as though it was a surface-to-air missile.

The hull split, separating the stern from the rest of the ship. Nick and Lisa were flung toward the bow, while Tyler was launched several meters over the starboard side.

The bow drifted for several feet, then sloped back into the ocean. Nick pushed Lisa toward the ladder to get her to climb for the fly deck. Bullets struck inches from her hand, sparking a scream.

There were three men on the mysterious vessel, each armed with automatic rifles. On the fly deck was a woman. She had an average height, black hair, and a tattoo of a shark poking through her black tank top. Standing right next to her was a scar-faced man, whom Nick believed to be the commander. Though, this was no standard military op. These were clearly private contractors. Mercenaries.

"Hold up," the woman said. "Take these two with us. I know a way we can use them."

The scar-faced man glanced at her. "You sure?"

"Yes."

Their helmsman steered the boat closer, while the squad kept their guns on the couple.

"Who the hell are you?" Nick said. The scar-faced mercenary answered with a gunshot. The bullet whizzed right past his head, making him flinch.

"Save your questions," the merc said. He kept his guns fixed on the Sheriff while the mercs reached for Lisa. At first, she refused to approach. The mercenary leader scowled, then fired another round, this time landing a bullet inches from her skull. "You have three seconds before I decide you're not worth my time. Three. Two..."

"Alright!" Lisa put her hands up and approached the edge of the boat. The mercs grabbed her by the shoulder, hauled her over, then waited for Nick.

Nick turned to the back of the deck, where David was lying face-down. He started to reach down for him, only for another gunshot to warn him away.

"This man needs medical attention," he shouted.

"What a shame!" the mercenary leader said. "He's dead weight. Get aboard, or you'll suffer the same fate." He pointed his rifle at Lisa's stomach.

The boat continued dipping into the water. Nick looked down at David one last time. A scream from Lisa drew his attention back to the yacht. With no other choice, he raised his hands and crossed over.

A rifle butt immediately struck his midsection, knocking him to his knees. Two of the mercs bent his arms behind his back and tied his wrists together, then did the same to Lisa. Nick grunted as he was forcefully lifted back to his feet.

The woman stepped in front of them.

"I see you met Scar," she said, smiling sinisterly.

"Scar?" Lisa said. "That's your shark?"

"What? Is it your pet?" Nick said.

"Not exactly," Olivia said. They looked back to the water after hearing the sounds of struggle.

Lisa gasped. "It's Tyler!"

"You need to get him aboard," Nick said to the woman.

She scoffed. "No. I don't need a third body." She stood and watched as Tyler stroked through the wreckage. Rolling waves lifted him up. The rain was coming down hard now.

One of the mercenaries aimed a spotlight on Tyler. The sight of the man struggling sparked a chuckle from the leader.

"Wait for it…wait for it…there!"

The dorsal fin emerged and the eyes glowed bright, like the red beacons of an airliner. Tyler reared back and screamed as the jaws clamped down on his waist. Suddenly, he was airborne, along with the shark whose jaws he was in. The fish twisted in midair, then splashed down. Rolling waves carried Tyler's blood west. The fish breached once more, shook the dying man as though showing off for its creator. Tyler let out one more scream, which ended in a squealing noise. Even through the wind, they could hear the snapping of his spine. Tyler's upper body fell into the water.

The fish gulped everything still in its mouth, then dove to chase after the rest.

"You want to start your plan now?" the mercenary leader asked the woman.

She shook her head. "No. Throw a couple of grenades into the water. Drive it away for the moment so we can better prepare."

"Hold on a second: Heitmeyer did that last night and you threw a fit!"

"He was trying to kill it. I'm just asking you to drive it away so I can prepare a trap," the woman said with an angry sneer.

The mercenary leader shook his head, annoyed, then plucked a couple of grenades off his vest.

"More like you have a stick up your ass."

The mercenary at the spotlight, whose face was marked up even worse than the leader's, aimed it to the right, then pointed a finger.

"There."

The leader pulled the pins then chucked the grenades. They hit the water then exploded, overwhelming Scar's eardrums and forcing him to retreat.

The woman watched the monitor.

"Alright. That did it. Let's move out. He'll be back shortly. Let's head north near the island. He seems to favor that location."

"Who the hell are you people?" Lisa said.

"In an hour, it won't matter," the woman said. She glanced at the leader. "Roark. Take them below."

Lisa struggled as the men grabbed her by the shoulders.

"Don't touch her," Nick warned. The man named Roark smiled, then landed a right hook to his chin, knocking the Sheriff to the deck. A kick to the groin killed any remaining fight he had left in him for the moment, allowing the merc to lift him to his feet and drag him below.

As Nick was lowered to the aft deck, he glanced over at the *Star Blaze*. The bow continued to dip, as though some giant being was slurping it down from under the water. The bow leaned back until it was facing straight up, then tilted to the right, and slowly, it disappeared under the waves.

After securing the prisoners, Roark returned to the pilothouse.

"Alright, take us that way," he said, pointing north.

"We sure we don't want to check for other survivors?" Dorn asked. Roark glanced back at the bits of floating wreckage, then shook his head.

"Nah. If there are any, they're as good as dead anyway."

"As you wish." Dorn turned the boat north and throttled.

CHAPTER 28

David was in and out of consciousness. In the strange void of dreams and storms, he could hear gunshots and screaming. He felt as though he had gone back in time to one of the World Wars. The splashing of water against his face made him think of the documentaries of Normandy Beach he used to watch.

The flash of lightning and the sudden lack of air forced him awake. He opened his eyes and felt the sting of the ocean. A powerful force was throwing him around in the darkness.

David was underwater. The lack of oxygen forced his body to dull the pain in his shoulder in preference of making him swim to safety. Another flash of lightning gave him a sense of direction. He kicked for the surface then drew a deep breath, only to be hit by a huge wave which drove him under again. The rookie rolled backward, found his bearings, then swam up again.

The world around him was a moving mountain range of ocean. Rising and falling with it was debris from the *Star Blaze*. David kicked as hard as he could toward a piece of cargo decking. He threw himself over it, only to continue sinking into the ocean. The fragment was cracked down its center and split, the two halves insufficient to keep him afloat.

Panic was starting to set in. David was losing strength quickly. Being a skinnier person, he didn't float very well. His muscles were burning, and the endorphins that acted as natural painkillers for his shoulder were quickly wearing off.

A flash of lightning illuminated another piece of debris. He swam for it as hard as he could. Water struck his face. Huge waves rolled him backward, while simultaneously pushing the fragment away. It was as if the ocean was actively trying to keep him from staying afloat.

David screamed in terror and frustration, which ended abruptly after the waves dunked him again. There was almost no method to his paddling now. He was throwing his arms and legs in a fit of panic and desperation. He managed to break the surface again, and resumed screaming.

He threw a fist toward the sky as though attempting to punch the storm.

"Fuck you! You wanna drown me? Then do it! Drown me! Piece of shit!" he shouted at the heavens. As though in direct response, another wave struck him, and David was forced under the surface again. Disorientated and exhausted, he paddled again, only to lose steam. He saw a flash of lightning, then closed his eyes and tried to think about something peaceful. He thought about baseball, and the roar of the crowds when striking out a batter.

His mind focused on a particular college game. It was five-to-five up until the ninth inning, when one of his teammates scored a run, taking it six-to-five. It was up to him to eliminate the opposing batters and keep them from tying the score and putting the game into a tenth inning. It was two down, with one to go. The first two strikes went smooth. The second two throws resulted in the batter nicking the ball. It came time for an old-fashioned trick. David drew his throwing arm, thrust it halfway, stopped briefly, then completed the throw. The batter swung before the ball left his hand.

The team went nuts. David remembered his buddies crowding around him and lifting him off the field. The hands grabbing his shoulder felt so real—so real in fact that it triggered the pain in his injured shoulder.

The grip tightened, flaring the nerves. David yelled as he felt himself being lifted. He broke the water and screamed. His hands swung wildly, only to strike Barney Grey in the face.

"Hey!" the fisherman shouted back. "You call me a piece of shit, accuse me of wanting to drown you, and *this* is what I get?!"

"Barney!" David exclaimed. "You're alive!"

"No shit, you dumb kid," Barney replied. "That tends to happen when you remember to wear a life vest." He clung to the injured rookie and paddled toward a large piece of floating debris. It took several minutes, and despite the aid from Barney's lifejacket, it was still an exhausting struggle to reach it. Both men clawed at the piece of decking and rested their heads on it, while allowing the ocean to toss them about.

After several more minutes of catching his breath, David looked at the world around him.

"What are you looking for?" Barney said. David didn't answer right away. He looked over his right shoulder, then his left, then straight ahead.

"There!" He pointed at lights in the distance. The mysterious boat was going north.

"Yeah, you're not gonna convince me to swim after that," Barney said.

"Who the hell are they?" David said.

"I don't know, but they've got the Sheriff and his girlfriend," Barney replied. "Tyler fell overboard and was killed by the shark. I was able to take cover in the cargo hold. Was about to hit them with some return fire—" he tapped on his dynamite case, which he had managed to string over his shoulder with a piece of rope, "but the damn fish struck again."

David caught his breath. "They've got to be after it. No coincidence that these people show up right after this crazy fish appears in our waters. Not to mention the fact that they're willing to kill for it without hesitation."

"Fascinating deduction, kid," Barney muttered. "Doesn't help us get out of our current predicament."

"Paddle!" David said.

"Where?! We don't have any clue where we are," Barney replied. "We've got no sense of direction. Hell, we're probably drifting back into open sea for all we know!"

"The storm came from the east, genius," David said. "It'd be pushing us west."

"Doesn't mean it'll carry us home. We might miss the island altogether," Barney replied.

The fisherman had a point. David rested against the plank, while looking again for the ship. Nick and Lisa were still alive, but David suspected that wouldn't be the case for much longer. After all, they left him and Barney for dead, after shooting him, no less.

"Oh shit," Barney muttered. David whipped toward him.

"What?" He saw that the fisherman looked terrified. He was looking to the left, while gripping his dynamite case with his fingers. David still couldn't see what he was looking at. "What is it?"

"I think our luck's run out," Barney said.

The huge dorsal fin rose several yards out. Barney grumbled several curse words, while David simply watched. The fin moved in a straight line, then arched back. Even in the wind and rain, there seemed to be something different about it.

Barney lifted his case aboard the plank. His thumbs went to the clips.

"Well, if I'm gonna be eaten, I'm gonna make sure I add a little extra kick to my flavoring!"

"Wait," David said, holding his hand up. "I don't think it's the shark."

"The hell are you talking about?" Barney said. They watched the dorsal fin. Suddenly, the creature's head emerged from the water. A mist spurted high into the sky. It was a killer whale taking a breath.

Barney shivered. Another dorsal fin emerged. Then another. They were surrounded by killer whales.

"Oh, we're fucked," he said.

"What?" David said. He shook his head after another wave struck his face. He spat out the water, then watched the whales circling them. Barney fumbled to open his dynamite case. Once again, David stopped him. "The hell are you trying to do?"

"Look at them! They're circling us. They're gonna tear us apart as though we're big, fat, juicy seals!"

"Sharks make that mistake. Not orcas. They don't eat humans," David retorted.

"You've been talking to that scientist lady your Sheriff likes, haven't ya!" Barney clenched his teeth, bracing for the horrible fate of being drawn and quartered by these creatures. "You might be alright, but I'm a goner!"

"Relax," David said. "We'll be fine."

"They hate me! I've netted them! I've tried shooting at them. Now they're here for revenge!" Barney threw a fist toward one of them. "Well, what are you waiting for? You wanna eat me?! Then get to it! What's taking so long? You guys waiting to say grace?!"

They continued swimming around for another minute, while making clicks and pulsed calls to one another. Finally, one of them swam around the human. Barney grabbed his lighter from his pocket, but it was too wet to spark a flame. He shrugged and awaited his fate.

"Fine then." He felt the creature drawing close. Large swells struck their backs, pushed along by its mass. Even David cringed, despite everything he stated in their defense. He took a deep breath and anticipated the horrible pain of being torn in half.

The orca's snout emerged between them. Gently, it pushed against the plank. It paddled its tail against the current, thrusting them northwest.

"What the hell?" Barney said.

"Shh!" David raised a finger to his lips. "Just hold on."

Silently, they rode along the plank while the creature propelled them into the distance. Where it was taking them, they had no idea, but it beat being eaten.

David angled his upper body to look at the majestic creature. Its eye was as big as his fist, and seemed to be staring back at him.

"Do you remember me? From talking with Lisa. You know Lisa, right?"

Barney scoffed. "You're not actually talking to that fish, are you?!"

"Don't you realize what it's doing?!" David shot back. "It's saving our lives. So what if it doesn't understand if we're thanking it. I like to think it does. You ought to give it a try."

"That'll be a cold day in hell," Barney retorted. A wave struck both of them. David shivered.

"Already there," he said.

Barney glanced around him and saw the rest of the pod following along. Finally...begrudgingly, he turned to the right. He looked right into the orca's eye. There, his eyes remained. He didn't say a word for the rest of the journey.

The pod pushed them along through what seemed like the entire ocean, until finally, David pointed a finger dead ahead.

"The atoll! They're pushing us toward the atoll!"

Barney continued watching the orca for several seconds, then looked for himself. A flash of lightning illuminated the tiny island. The orca pushed them for another hundred meters, then backed off, allowing the humans to carry themselves the rest of the way. The waves threatened to carry them off, but they managed to overpower them and arrive at the shore.

David didn't care about the wind or the rain. Never in all of his life did he appreciate dry land as much as this moment.

"I feel like I ought to be on some television show," Barney muttered. He fumbled in his pockets for his cigarettes, which were all soaking wet. "Figures." He crumpled them up and tossed them aside.

David sat up on the deck. Through the next flash of lightning, he could see the orcas swimming about. There was a magical feeling in watching them. Never in his life had he ever felt so much gratitude and amazement.

"My God," he said. It was all hitting him at once. "They saved our lives." Barney spun on his heel, his finger raised, his throat carrying a hundred phrases intended to dispute that point. But all of them would fall flat. Barney didn't say a single word. He lowered his finger and simply watched the creatures swim about. A few moments later, one of the orcas whistled to the others, then all at once, they dove beneath the waves.

Barney's knees buckled and he fell on his rear, exhausted and overwhelmed, though refusing to show it in his face.

"We're alive," David said.

"I noticed," Barney said, his eyes locked on the water.

"Sorry," David said. "I guess I'm just grateful and—agh!" He clutched his shoulder. Barney stood up and rushed over to him.

"Hold still." He examined the wound, tearing away at David's shirt. "Bullet punched straight through. You're lucky it didn't blow your whole shoulder off." He took off his flannel jacket and tore a couple of sheets. "Wouldn't be surprised if it hit bone, though." He tied a sling with the sheets, then wrapped it around David's arm and other shoulder.

David wiggled his fingers. He still had control of his arm, though the range of motion was not great.

"Don't mess it up more," Barney said. He tore another sheet. "Hold still." David yelled as Barney stuffed the wound. "Sorry, kid. Gotta stop the bleeding or else your grand rescue won't amount to much."

"I'm good," David said. He grimaced as Barney completed his makeshift bandaging, then stood up. He walked to the center of the tiny atoll, then looked out to the east. The wind swayed his hair and the rain assaulted his face.

Barney leaned against one of the trees. "Looks like we're stuck here unless someone comes by." He watched David, who continued to stare out into the ocean. "Oh God. You're not gonna find them."

"Nick and Lisa are out there," David said.

"And you're not gonna be able to save them," Barney retorted. "Christ, kid! You've got a hole in your shoulder. Yeah, you still have that sidearm there, but considering it's on your right hip, I assume you're right-handed...and there's no way you'll aim well with that shoulder." He found a pebble on the ground and tossed it into the water. "Besides. That shark will probably find them first."

"We have to do something."

"Like what? Swim? We barely made it here. We don't have anything to get us off this island for chrissake!"

David closed his eyes and let the pain do its worst. In that moment, he remembered the incident he and Nick responded to a couple of days prior.

He turned and found the dock at the southeast side. Tied to the support beams were the two jet skis.

"Yes, we do," he said.

CHAPTER 29

It was like looking at a berth designed for a submarine.

The bindings dug into Nick's wrists as he sat on the side platform within the holding chamber, looking at the mooring in its center. Three large restraints were teetering over it, ready to close down and lock on the other side. On the inner side, opposite the ramp, were two pumps; one for water, the other, Nick wasn't sure.

Since their capture, Nick was able to catch the names of the other mercenaries, as well as that of the woman leading the group. The fact that they made no effort to conceal their identities was a major red flag in his mind.

The mercenary named Jacques was guarding them. He stood at the doorway, his gun pointed at the deck, finger pointed over the trigger guard. He stared at the two hostages. In the time since their capture, they never saw him blink. The man had such a menacing presence, Nick felt he should've had red eyes like the shark. Chemical burns covered his face, sparking questions in Nick's mind as to whether the man was sane.

Nick leaned toward Lisa to assure her they would be okay. Her eyes were fixed on the strange berth.

"This is a holding chamber for marine animals," she said.

Nick nodded. There was no question: these people, whoever they were, were after the shark.

"What's so important about a fish?" he whispered to Lisa. She shrugged.

"I don't think it's a natural born species. Considering the equipment, and the thing's near impervious skin and red eyes, I'm suspecting it's been genetically enhanced."

"Not exactly." The door opened and the woman named Olivia Zoller stepped into the holding chamber, followed by the mercenary leader, Roark. He stood by Jacques, while she inspected one of the pumps.

Nick resisted the urge to spring from the bench and knock her into the berth. His feet weren't bound; he could have. In fact, had they been alone, he would have, but the guns-for-hire were clearly the types who loved to throw a beating. And knowing those devil eyes, Nick suspected it wasn't only *he* who'd get punished. He glanced over at Lisa again. She was calm and collected, though understandably nervous.

Olivia finished her inspection and stepped in front of the prisoners. There was a smirk on her face, like she was proud of what she was doing.

Nick seethed. *God, never in my life have I even considered hitting a woman. But now...*

"So, that thing out there is *your* pet, huh?"

"Only someone with a miniscule education as yours would think of it that way," Olivia replied. "It's more than a pet. It's more than an animal, or an experiment: it's a breakthrough."

"A breakthrough, huh," Nick said. "You aware that breakthrough is responsible for countless deaths? Do you even care? I think I know the answer."

"I don't expect a man like you to understand," Olivia said.

Nick couldn't help it. He lowered his head and laughed.

A MAN like me. He shook his head. "Great. You're one of those."

"There's collateral damage in every scientific venture," Olivia said. "I don't expect you to understand."

"Why? Because I'm just a dumb Sheriff? Or a *man*?"

Olivia chuckled. "Sure. That might play a part in it."

Lisa's fists tightened behind her back. *This bitch. If only I wasn't tied up...*

"I've studied science all my life, Doctor. I'm suspecting you don't understand the point of it. It's about bettering our planet and all living things, human and otherwise, living in it," she said.

Olivia scoffed.

"Go ahead and continue that schoolgirl monologue. I'm sure you're making a major difference counting conks, naming fish, and doing routine tagging on sharks that'll probably get fished out of the water in a year's time."

"Beats creating things that get people killed," Lisa replied. "Oh, sorry. Collateral damage. Apparently, that's the way to progress, right?"

"The dumb man here has a question, since you seem to be chatty," Nick said. "How does creating an overgrown shark pave the road to progress?"

"It's more than a shark," Olivia said. "It is a hybrid. A mix between the prehistoric species Megalodon, whose DNA we were able to extract from fossilized teeth, and the modern day great white."

Lisa leaned back. "You spliced the DNA of an extinct species?"

Olivia smiled. "Impressed?"

Lisa shrugged. *If you weren't such a psychopath, I would be.*

"There's so little we get to recover from extinct species of sharks. Since they don't have skeletons, any fossilized fragments are mainly their teeth. We don't know too much about these ancient species other than their size, habitats, and possibly their diets."

"So...the red eyes? The resilient skin? Can I assume these are traits of the ancient shark?" Nick asked.

"They must be," Lisa said. "With so few remains to study, there's so much we're unable to learn. The red eyes probably help to lure prey when swimming in the deep. The skin? Probably to protect against the jaws of marine reptiles."

"I thought Megalodons were sixty feet or something like that," Nick said.

"They were. She said they mixed it with the genes of a modern day great white, which averages at roughly fifteen feet," Lisa said.

"Still doesn't explain the 'why'," Nick said, looking back at Olivia. "What's the point? Just to see if you could do it? Aren't there less violent species you can screw around with? Like, I don't know, resurrect a prehistoric guppy instead of an insatiable killing machine?" Olivia rolled her eyes. Nick snickered. *Oh, right. A man like me is too far beneath you to question your research.*

"Money," Lisa answered for Olivia. "She's a geneticist, not a researcher. She spliced genes for the biggest creatures she could get her hands on. She picked these sharks because it would gain her the most notoriety within whatever sick-minded company is financing this shitshow. She picked a shark because it'd get people's attentions. I wouldn't be surprised if she added steroids, considering the size and uncontrollable violent rage. Another thing, I'm willing to bet my bottom dollar that somewhere during its development, she fucked with its metabolism. Hence, it's hungry all the time."

"Hungry all the time..." Nick's voice trailed off as he realized what Olivia had in store for him and Lisa. It was obvious. They were bait! "So, is that it? Are we part of that 'collateral damage' that occurs with scientific progress, as you call it?"

"In a sense," Olivia said. "You're going to play a crucial role in helping me recapture the shark."

Well, at least she confirmed it. Sort of. At this point, he wished he'd gone down guns blazing during the initial attack.

"Yeah? How? You gonna put us on a fishhook and cast us out?"

"It'll be a little more elaborate than that. You'll find out," Olivia said. She looked over at Jacques. "If they move, pop their kneecaps. Hurt them so bad, they'll be begging for Scar to put them out of their misery."

"Scar?" Nick chuckled. "You named your fish after a *Disney* villain?"

"Laugh while you can, Sheriff." Olivia walked out of the room with Roark, leaving the prisoners alone with Jacques.

Every fiber in him wanted to rush the mercenary and beat him into the floor with his own gun. Unfortunately, the guy had a hairpin trigger, and would probably not be a breeze in a fight, especially considering Nick's hands were bound behind his back.

His mind went into planning. He could easily slip his hands under his feet. Considering the number of sharp objects on this boat, he could easily cut through the zip tie cuffs.

Might as well try. They're gonna kill us anyway.

However, he couldn't do it. A voice in his mind told him to wait. He was never a religious person, but it almost felt as though some higher power was guiding him. Somehow, they would get out of this. Getting gunned down while bum-rushing the mercenary wouldn't do it.

He took a breath and waited.

CHAPTER 30

"This is dumb, kid. We don't know where they are!" Barney complained. David ignored him while he checked the jet ski battery and cleaned some of the residue off the propellers. Barney stood on the deck, his hands thrown high over his head. "They've got automatic weapons! We've got your peashooter. Nothing else. Not to mention that damn shark is still out there!"

"You can stay if you want. I'm going out after them," David said.

"Kid, you've got balls, but not the brains that go with them," Barney said. "Why not go back to the island and get help? You know firsthand the weaponry those psychos have. Wouldn't it be better to get some reinforcements and come up with an attack plan?"

"Nick and Lisa don't have that kind of time," David said. "People like that don't hang on to prisoners for very long. I have almost no description of the boat. No name. No major details. I couldn't see it in the storm. If that boat leaves, they might as well be gone forever."

"Kid, this is dumb," Barney said. "What are you gonna use? You won't be able to hit shit with that pistol. Besides, I'll address the biggest elephant in the room...or island. Whatever. You need a key to start these jet skis. Looks to me like those key ignitions are empty."

David felt a brief moment of panic, then started to laugh. He dug his wallet out of his pants pocket and opened it. The keys were still there. Being the rookie he was, he had forgotten to place them in storage.

"Responsible and organized," he joked to himself. Barney stared, bemused.

"What the hell? When did you become Houdini?"

David tossed one of the keys to him.

"The Henderson family will probably be pissed." He mounted his jet ski and started the engine, then looked back up at Barney. "Come on. They've got lights on. They'll stick out like a sore thumb. All we need to do is find them."

Barney stood on the dock, shaking his head. David groaned. It was clear that the fisherman had no intention of coming along.

"It's suicide, kid."

"Fine," David said. The temptation arose to tell Barney what a coward he was, but it wasn't worth it. Not like the jerk would even care anyway. It wasn't like protecting and serving was Barney's duty anyway. "Mind if I borrow a couple of sticks of dynamite then?" Barney looked at his case then back at the Deputy. The prick was actually considering keeping it for himself! After several moments of consideration, he tossed a few rolls at the Deputy.

"Hope you can make this work. It's still wet." Barney tossed him his lighter. David flicked the wheel several times to try it out, blew on the igniter to dry it off, then tried again. After a few flicks, a flame came on.

"Thanks, I guess," he said. Barney shrugged. It was no loss; he carried multiple lighters on him anyhow.

"I still think you're a crazy idiot," he replied.

"I guess that's the price I pay for having friends," David said. He sighed. *You'd think getting your life saved would spark a little humility.* He wanted to say it out loud, but he was running out of time, which was something Nick and Lisa did not have. "Stay safe, Barney. The island's that way."

"I know. I've lived here since before you were a sperm cell, kid," Barney replied. He hopped onto his jet ski, started the engine, and without saying another word, throttled southwest. It wasn't long before he disappeared into the storm.

"Whatever," David muttered. He steered his ski to the east and throttled into the storm. Immediately, he was met by a series of crashing waves that threatened to flip him backwards. He bounced in his seat with each hit.

The swells reached at him like demons arising from a hellish pit. He tucked the dynamite into his shirt to keep from losing them, then pressed on. After a few hundred yards, he started to get the hang of it. He thought of it as steering a spaceship through an asteroid field. He veered through the storm, measuring each swell by size and velocity.

All the while, he watched the horizon for any lights. That boat was out here somewhere. He just needed to find it.

CHAPTER 31

Scar swam in defiance of the roaring current. The ocean fought his every move, as though trying to pummel him into submission. He could've taken the easier method of waiting out the storm by swimming deep where the currents were not as manipulated by the winds. However, the instinct to overpower any threat, including the weather, was stronger than any natural force the planet could summon. He was a wraith, a killer of killers, designed to overcome any physical threat.

The price of following his instinct so faithfully was the amount of energy required to do it. Fighting the current was a battle like nothing he had ever experienced. He was a spartan taking a lone stance against the gods. Of course, he didn't think of it so metaphorically, as Scar barely thought at all. He simply knew his purpose. Swim. Hunt. Kill. Persevere. If it moved, he would feel it. If it bled, he would smell it. If it was near, he would kill it.

The storm assaulted his lateral line, compromising Scar's ability to detect the movements of other organisms or vehicles in the water. His eyes struggled to see far past the barrage of crashing waves. However, as usual, his sense of smell never failed him.

Something was bleeding. The scent was strong and near. The furthest reaches of this new trail of blood was carried far by the waves. It had thinned and broken up into tiny particles, but it was enough for Scar to trace to its source. It was a familiar scent; nearly identical to that which led him into combat with the human seacrafts. It wasn't clear to him whether the vessels 'bled' or not—their 'meat' did not contain anything edible—but they did carry humans. And humans, as the shark learned, were very edible.

Scar followed the scent north. As he traveled for a half-mile, his red eyes spotted bright lights. They were steady streams, not the instant flashes offered by the storm. They were barely above the surface, their movements in rhythm with the current. The fish recognized these lights, as they were the same used by the human vessel the previous night.

It had returned, ready to do battle once more. It had stolen its prize from the other vessel, and now it was in the water, 'bleeding'. Twice, it had driven him away with the weapon of intense vibration. But like the most dangerous of predators, Scar learned to adapt. The loud *booms* and their resulting shockwaves were only dangerous within a certain reach. The noise itself didn't hurt him. The humans relied on projectile weapons that generated intense sound. Those weapons, however, were meaningless once their seacraft was eliminated.

The seacrafts were like the flukes to the enemy killer whales and the caudal fins to other sharks. Eliminate the ability to navigate the sea, and the threat was no longer a threat, but a victim—a victim, helpless to the demise Scar would bring.

With a thrust of his tail, he closed in on his prey.

CHAPTER 32

"He's coming," Olivia announced.

Heitmeyer looked up from the transom. The chum mixture swished near his feet, threatening to escape the container. He held the greasy scoop in his hand.

"Should I keep going?" he asked.

"No," Olivia said. As she stood on the fly deck, she watched as Nick and Lisa were dragged out onto the aft deck below her. Nick struggled, only for Roark to drive a fist into his stomach.

"Don't fight," the mercenary said. He nodded back at Jacques, who proceeded to grab a fistful of Lisa's shirt, ripping the collar slightly. "I don't prefer to work this way, but if you make one more move, my pal there will grant your lady a good time before serving her up to the fish. And I'll shoot you in the arms and legs, and keep you alive and conscious just so you can watch."

Every muscle in Nick's body tensed. What dark circle of hell did these guys come from? His inaction was his way of yielding.

Jacques shoved Lisa against him, and the two were forced to stand back-to-back. The one named Dorn approached them with a rope.

"Sorry, *Marshal Dillon*. Shit happens." He slipped the rope under their arms and tightened, squeezing the two of them together. Lisa gasped as her ribs were pressed into her lungs. Dorn proceeded to connect the rope to that on the outrigger, then used the winch to tighten the slack until the human bait were lifted to their tip toes.

"You guys are insane if you think you can control this shark."

"My job's just to transfer it, lady," Roark replied. "Leave it to the doc to try and control it. I just care about getting paid."

"Hear-hear," Dorn said.

"You won't make it that far," Nick snarled. Roark, Dorn, and Heitmeyer all looked at each other, then at the Sheriff, his wrists bound together and fastened tightly to Lisa. All at once, they broke into laughter.

"Look at this guy trying to sound tough before heading out to dinner," Roark chuckled.

"He's right, though," Lisa said. Her voice trembled with each word. She was barely holding it together, but refused to give these killers the satisfaction of an emotional breakdown. "You might kill us, but don't fool yourselves into thinking you won't be next on the menu."

Roark glanced up at Olivia, then held his arms out impatiently.

"You gonna do your thing? Or am I supposed to do it?"

"Do what?" Lisa asked. They waited a minute as Olivia made her way to the aft deck. In her hands were four nylon belts. Tied to each belt were four large plastic bags, each containing a clear white substance. Lisa glanced at the bags for a moment, then back at the crazy geneticist. "What the hell is that?"

"This is what'll keep us from being next on the menu," Olivia replied. She tied the harness around Lisa's legs, then proceeded to tie another around Nick's. Roark leveled his rifle, centering Lisa in his sights to make sure the Sheriff didn't get courageous.

Lisa sneered as she felt the belt tighten around her waist. Judging by Olivia's choice of words and the appearance and texture of the substance inside the bags, it was clear that they were being equipped with a sedative.

"2-Phenoxyethanel?"

Olivia grinned, then fastened the second belt around her knees. She had almost already forgotten that Lisa was a marine biologist. She then proceeded to tighten a belt around Nick's waist. The wind nearly carried it away. She fixed her grip, then reached out to grab the Sheriff, who leaned away.

"Get that away from me."

Roark stepped alongside Lisa, making sure to be in Nick's peripheral vision to reiterate the threat he had made earlier. Nick now REALLY wished he went out shooting back at the *Star Blaze*. He remained still while Olivia tightened the belts around his waist and knees.

"Scar has proven himself to be a formidable hunter," she said. "In fact, so much so, that I believe he'll only be drawn to living prey." Roark and Dorn chuckled, the latter hoisting them up further. Nick and Lisa groaned as the rope dug into their sides. Their feet dangled over the deck. Next, they were swung over the gunwale until they were hovering over water.

Olivia checked her monitor. Scar was still closing in. The drone was ready.

"I really should thank you two," she said. "Thanks to your interference, we are able to continue with our original plan of capture. We just needed to update our bait."

"Nobody's happier than me," Roark said. "I was dumb enough to volunteer to attach the cable to that fish." They watched Nick as he raised his elbows in an attempt to get his hands over the waist belt. The mercenary stepped to the gunwale. "Hey! Sheriff?! What did I tell you?!" He pointed his rifle and fired a series of deafening shots over their heads.

****

David whipped to his left, hearing the *pop-pop-pop* in the distance. That 'thunder' wasn't thunder. *Gunshots!* He steered the jet ski and throttled at full speed. He squinted, ignoring the rain and ocean water that assaulted his face as he pushed through.

There! Lights!

The boat was less than a half-mile out. He placed one of the dynamite sticks between his hand and the bar. In the other, he gripped the lighter. As he closed in, he could see that the lights were mainly on the aft side of the vessel. Something was hanging over the side...

Not something...some*one!*

David checked the fuse. It was longer—maybe thirty seconds' worth. He would close the distance within that timeframe.

For a moment, he felt intense fear. Not for his life, but of failure. If he failed to save Nick and Lisa...or worse, accidentally KILL them...he'd never be able to live it down. He rolled his injured shoulder. That was his throwing arm. The muscles were rigid, but he would still be able to pull off a decent toss. Luckily, he wasn't trying to bring the dynamite near a batter's bat. No, just over the bow rail of a ship; a much broader target. He could pull it off, even in this weather.

"Here goes nothing." David lit the fuse then raced in a semi-circular path, avoiding the reach of the lights as he closed in on the bow.

****

"I'm tired of warning you, Sheriff," Roark said. "Next time, I'll make good on my promise." He glanced over at Dorn. "Go ahead. Lower them."

Lisa quickly looked over at Nick.

"Don't move a muscle. Keep completely still. Don't draw attention to yourself," she said. She spoke louder and more urgently than intended, spurred by the adrenaline she was feeling in the moment.

"Stop," Olivia said. "Bring them back here for a second. I already have a workaround for our friend's scheme." She pulled a knife from her pocket. Dorn swung them back over the guardrail. Olivia extended the blade to Lisa's ankle. "You might trick him with the movement gimmick, but there's no getting around the scent of blood. Once you see his eyes drawing near, any self-control you think you have will go out the window. You'll scream, thrash, and draw him right to you."

"Hey," Nick said, directing Olivia's attention to him. "Did you just assume Scar's gender? That's awfully misogynistic of you. What if he's actually a 'she'?" Roark snorted, much to Olivia's irritation. She glared at the mercenary, then back at Nick.

"You think you're funny. Let's see how hard you laugh when I put this through your calf muscle..." She extended the knife.

"What's that?" Dorn said.

"What's what?" Roark replied. Then he heard it. At first, he assumed it was the wind or the thunder. No...it was something else. An engine...growing increasingly nearer.

The sound of spraying water drew their attention to the front of the boat. A small shape was racing near the bow. Next, they saw a small, sparking light arch through the bow rail and land on the deck. Right then, the object sped away, briefly passing through the reach of the spotlight.

Roark did the math in his head.

"Get down—"

The dynamite explosion shook the boat like a tremendous hammer. Pieces of decking flew overhead like meteor fragments. Dorn and Heitmeyer fell on their stomachs, while Roark and Jacques stumbled toward the transom. Olivia, on the other hand, fell against Nick's legs.

"Here's *equality* for you," Nick said. He kicked both feet into her chin, knocking her backwards. She screamed and fell backwards, the knife shaking from her grip and bouncing on the deck under the hostages. Nick raised his knees and slipped his arms underneath. With his hands now in front of him, he dug his thumbs into the rope and pushed, squeezing his way through the loop. It was a tight squeeze, but sheer will and adrenaline made all the difference. He landed on the deck, immediately saw Heitmeyer propping on his knees prepping to take a shot with his rifle. With a hard kick, Nick knocked the rifle from the mercenary's grasp before swinging his bound fists like a club, striking Heitmeyer across the jaw. As the merc fell, Nick saw Dorn picking himself up. He rushed at the mercenary and threw an elbow into his jaw, effectively knocking him backwards, where he tripped over Olivia.

Nick spun on his heel and found Olivia's knife. He scooped it up, sliced through his bindings, then pulled Lisa down and cut her free.

"Son of a bitch!" Roark said. As he aimed his rifle, he heard the jet ski race by. In that moment, he saw the flare of another stick of dynamite hurtling again toward what remained of the foredeck. The blast shook the vessel, which arched back, then dipped forward as water quickly invaded the hull breaches.

Heitmeyer's rifle slid across the deck and settled near Nick's feet. He snatched the weapon up, pulled back on the cocking lever, then aimed it at its former owner. Heitmeyer drew his Beretta, but never got to aim it, as Nick sent several rifle shots through his chest, which exited out his back in large, bloody displays.

Lisa lunged for the dropped Beretta. All of her gun range training flashed in her mind like a refresher tutorial. She gripped the weapon with both hands, identified her target, then fired.

Jacques saw the weapon pointing his way. Instinct drove him to dive out of the way. It was half-successful—he still caught a round in the right shoulder. The bullet smashed into his joint, causing him to spin and fall over the transom.

He hit the water, sank a few feet, then swam for the surface. Immediately, the current took hold of him.

Jacques kicked his legs and thrust his left arm out, but could not outmatch the waves that carried him away. He heard a few more *pops* from the ship, though the storm prevented him from getting a good view of what was happening. His first priority was getting back aboard.

Another wave lifted him up. He dove forward, riding the back of the swell like a slide, preventing himself from losing too much distance. Another bulge in the water took form. He leaned forward again to perform the same maneuver. That's when he noticed this 'swell' had eyes. RED eyes. And a gaping mouth, which he was diving right into.

For the first time in many years, Jacques screamed.

Scar traced the scent of blood to his victim. He scooped the human into his mouth and closed his jaws. He could feel his prey's appendages clawing his inside. Blood seeped into his throat. Scar dove with his prey, then spun like a crocodile performing a death-roll. The result was the same, except Scar had serrated teeth to help tender the meat. Bones broke. Flesh ripped. The human convulsed violently, then broke into various pieces, all of which were swallowed.

He circled back to the vessel. It was already sinking, sparing him the effort of having to do it himself. The rear was now elevated over the water as it slowly slipped down into the ocean. However, patience was not Scar's virtue. His hunger wasn't satisfied, and the process was taking too long.

He raced for the vessel, closed his eyes, and rammed the underside.

Olivia was back on her feet when the impact happened. This time, it seemed to come from under the ship. Whatever it was, it was powerful enough to knock her clear off the deck. Her back hit the guardrail. She felt herself slipping to the other side. Shrieking, she threw her hands out for anything she could grab. Her left arm found the guardrail right as she fell overboard. She dangled along the side of the vessel, her feet a meter or so above the water.

"Somebody pull me up!" she demanded. Nobody listened. Nobody could hear. The mercenaries were deafened by the wind, thunder, and gunfire exchange.

Roark fired several bursts, driving Nick and Lisa around the starboard side-deck. They moved around the corner, out of sight, but also toward the water. Dorn was on his feet now and assisted in the assault.

Nick tried to aim around the corner, but ducked back to avoid another burst of gunfire. He thrust the rifle out and fired blindly, missing the targets. Bits of the structure exploded as bullets punched through it. They stepped further back. Lisa glanced at the front of the vessel, which was now entirely submerged. The side entrance to the structure was already submerged, preventing them from retreating into the interior. The waterline was only a few feet from where they stood and rapidly climbing.

"Nick," she said. He looked back, saw what she saw, then considered his options.

Can't stay here, can't go in the water, can't go that way...we're really in a pickle.

He fired another burst then ducked back. He checked his magazine.

"Shit." He tossed it down then took Lisa's Beretta. The water was climbing. It was two feet from where they stood now. He peeked around the corner and aimed his weapon, only to find Roark already aiming his. Roark fired a shot, grazing Nick's left arm. Nick jumped back behind cover, checked his injury, then pushed Lisa back further as a few more shots whizzed past the corner.

Lisa's heels hit the waterline. "Shit!" She glanced out to the water in search of Scar.

"I gotta hand it to you, Sheriff," Roark shouted at him, "you're quick on your feet. Had I known better, I'da put you on my payroll! But you've pissed me off. Now, let's finish this quickly. Step on out. Come on."

Lisa put a hand on Nick's shoulder. At first, he thought she was seeking comfort. Then he realized she was pointing ahead. Heitmeyer's corpse was sliding down the deck. On his vest were two fragmentation grenades.

So close, yet going for them would put him right in front of those rifles. Even if he went out blasting his pistol, he'd be torn apart by enemy fire. He looked out to the water.

"Where's David?" He could hear the jet ski in the distance but could not pinpoint its exact location. Another noise he picked up on was that of Roark reloading his rifle. Next were footsteps. The men were closing in.

Olivia was screaming behind them, but the mercs were ignoring her in favor of finishing the fight.

Nick backed up further until his ankles were in the water. He had six, maybe seven shots left. More than enough to take out the two men, but he needed a clear shot and the ability to avoid return fire.

The jet ski engine drew near. David sped near the ship from the stern, dynamite stick in hand. Dorn had anticipated his arrival, and greeted him with a hail of bullets. David veered to the south and sped off, tossing the lit dynamite into the ocean to prevent himself from blowing up.

With the reinforcements driven off momentarily, the mercs took position beyond the corner of the structure. It would be like shooting fish in a barrel. They wouldn't even have to aim.

Lisa took a breath and prepared for the worst. Her eyes went to the knife tucked into Nick's pocket. An idea came to mind. It was a crazy one, but it was all they had. She dug the knife from his pocket, and stepped back. Right then, Roark emerged from around the corner with his rifle shouldered. Nick fired a shot, forcing him back before he could squeeze the trigger.

"What are you doing?" he asked.

"Calling the calvary," Lisa replied. She winced as she ran the knife over her palm, drawing blood. She kneeled and plunged her hand into the water, waving it left and right to create a new trail.

Nick saw what she was doing, closed his eyes, thought *this is insane*, then waited for the inevitable.

The fish was biding its time. The vessel was sinking, the fight won. He just needed to wait and pick off the easy prey taking refuge.

But overwhelming hunger overrode his limited strategic sense. The smell of blood entered Scar's nostrils. Where there was blood in the water, there was prey. His brain demanded a change of plan. Thus, Scar lined his snout with the boat and attacked.

He closed the distance within five seconds and struck the underside of the ship.

The impact knocked the vessel to starboard, throwing Roark and Dorn off balance. The leader staggered and fell against the guardrail, while fighting the momentum to aim his rifle at the human targets. Nick fired, while also fighting against the turbulent motion of the vessel. His first shot zipped high, the second grazed Roark's shoulder, the third struck the frame of his rifle, springing the weapon backward into his face. The barrel clunked Roark's nose, knocking him backward.

"Nick!" Lisa screamed.

The Sheriff looked to his left. The red eyes were rapidly approaching under the dark water. It was coming right for them! He fired his remaining rounds, striking the beast in its face, causing just enough pain to drive it low. The slide locked back. Out of bullets and out of options, he dropped the empty gun and rushed the aft deck like a marathon runner.

As he anticipated, Dorn was there to greet him. The merc popped out from around the corner and pointed his rifle. Nick threw his hands at the barrel, thrusting the muzzle up at the sky right as Dorn squeezed the trigger. They fought over control of the weapon, sending two-dozen rounds into the sky before the mag ran dry.

Nick thrust the rifle into Dorn's nose, then followed it up with a right hook to the chin. Dorn staggered back, his right hand going for his sidearm. Nick rushed again, this time ducking low and grabbing the merc by the waist. He lifted him over his shoulder like a lumberjack, absorbing retaliatory elbow strikes to his head and neck as he charged the transom. Dorn shook as he was body slammed against the guardrail, arching him backward. He jolted again after Nick drove an elbow down into his stomach.

Dorn grabbed the Sheriff by the shirt. If he was going to fall overboard, he would take the Sheriff with him. The tactic worked, and Nick took a step back, unintentionally dragging his opponent off the gunwale.

A left hook caught Nick in the cheek, another in the ribs. The merc went again for his pistol. Nick had less than a second to act. He charged the merc faster than he'd ever ran in his life, tackled Dorn, and threw him back against the transom. The impact tremor shook the mercenary, knocking the pistol from his grip.

Roark rolled to his hands and knees. He checked his rifle. The bullet had struck the frame and damaged the firing mechanism. He saw Nick in combat with Dorn, clearly intending to throw him into the water.

I don't think so.

He drew his Beretta and aimed.

A piercing pain entered his shoulder, accompanied by an intense force. Lisa had charged him from behind, and like a villain in a slasher film, drove the knife into his right shoulder. Roark reared back, clenching his teeth in pain. He tucked his chin down as he felt the biologist attempting to wrap her other arm around his throat. He stood up, shrieking as he felt the knife twist. He threw an elbow back, catching her in the jaw. A second blow knocked her backwards.

Roark turned to face her. He yanked the knife from his shoulder, glanced at the little blade, then back at her.

"You should've gone for the jugular," he said. He pointed his pistol.

A gunshot rang out. Blood sprayed across the deck and water.

Roark stumbled. His hand twitched and wavered, ultimately dropping the pistol. He touched the gaping hole in his neck, then turned around, and saw Nick standing there on the transom, pointing Dorn's Beretta.

"Like that?" Nick said.

Roark scoffed, flabbergasted, yet oddly amused by his demise. His last thought was, *I suppose it's a better way of going out than being torn apart by the shark...*

Frustrated and hungry, and smelling blood, Scar breached the water. He was airborne, angling toward the source of the bloodstream. He struck down like a hammer, his immense weight knocking the boat to port, immediately causing him to lose traction. But before he did, his jaws found the bleeding prey, tasted his blood, and pulled him over the crunched gunwale into the depths, where he proceeded to tear him apart.

The boat fishtailed over the water, then caught a large swell which knocked it the opposite direction. The motion tossed everyone aboard across the deck like rag dolls.

Nick and Lisa climbed for the highest elevation, while Dorn, who lay on the deck in a daze, started sliding for the waterline, which was now climbing past the structure. The touch of water against his face shocked him back to reality. He pushed himself up and looked back, seeing Nick and Lisa holding on to the transom, which had elevated another ten degrees.

Two instincts clashed: one inherent, the other obtained over years of training and discipline. He felt the natural will to survive at all costs, but at the same time, he couldn't stand defeat. All of his comrades were gone. He was the last. No way was he going to allow these nobodies to go home victorious, even if it cost him his life.

He plucked his grenades from his vest, reached for the pins...

...and felt the explosive force of Scar lunging from the surface. He snatched him off the deck like a hors d'oeuvre on a tray.

Dorn screamed, then spat blood as dozens of teeth sank across his torso. With his head resting against the deck, Scar proceeded to chomp, punching new holes in his victim's body each time. Still, Dorn tried to fight. The grenades were knocked from his grip, leaving him only with his knife. He drew the blade and raised it high to plunge it into the shark's eye.

As if anticipating this motion, Scar whipped his head to the right, bashing Dorn's head against the structure. His skull exploded in a meaty spectacle, his arms falling limp as he was dragged under the waves.

"Jesus," Nick muttered. He watched the water continue its climb up the deck. Realizing that there was no way out of fighting the shark, he sprinted down the slope. He dug his hands into the water and found Dorn's rifle, which had been dropped during their brawl. He grabbed the spare magazines off Heitmeyer's corpse, then returned to the transom. He handed Lisa the Beretta and the spare mags that went with it. She tucked the spares into her waistline, then watched the water.

Olivia was still dangling from the side.

"Goddamn you people! Pull me up!"

Nick and Lisa exchanged glances. Was she still speaking to the mercs, or was she actually issuing orders to *them*?

Nick groaned. *God, I hate being a decent human being.*

They rushed to the side and saw the geneticist fighting to keep her grip. Olivia looked up at him, then sneered. Her mercenaries were gone, and now she was at the mercy of the very people she was about to sacrifice.

"Let's pull her up," Nick said begrudgingly. Olivia's natural instinct was to curse them out, but she also wanted to be pulled away from the water, even if the boat was sinking anyway. As the boat slipped, so did her grip. She wasn't simply hanging down, but at an angle, making any sort of grip on the guardrail difficult. She reached for Nick's hand, but faltered as something hit the vessel.

Scar...

Her heart raced. She took the Sheriff's hand and let him begin to pull her over the guardrail. But, like a cruise missile, the shark struck again with devastating force. Nick stumbled, his grip faltering. Olivia shrieked and clawed at him and the marine biologist, but failed to retain her grasp. Her head smacked the hull as she fell beneath the waves.

She emerged on the surface. Right away, she could sense Scar's presence. She moved her arms slowly, doing her best not to generate any struggling motion that would attract his attention. She spotted his fin emerge several yards behind the stern of the vessel. He was going in a straight line, likely lining up for another run at the boat. She just needed to keep calm and find something to float on once the shark had killed the Sheriff and his girlfriend.

All the while, she noticed a peculiar taste in her mouth. Lightning flashed, bringing to view the blood that was spilling from her lip. Her heartbeat intensified, even more so when she noticed the fin turn toward her. A moment later, it disappeared.

Olivia hyperventilated. Memories of her childhood raced through her mind. The triangular snout, the white teeth, the pain in her shoulder...the obsession that followed.

She looked down. The red eyes appeared, growing larger as Scar drew near. All self-control went out the window. Olivia screamed and thrashed her arms in a desperate attempt to get to the boat. Her efforts accomplished nothing, except drawing Scar right to her.

With jaws extended, the shark broke the surface. Olivia rose with him then screamed as the jaws closed down around her back and stomach. Scar carried her along the waves, thrashing his creator back and forth.

He raised his head, and opened his jaws for a better grip, while also allowing his prey to slip further into his mouth. He chomped down again with enough force to break bone. Olivia gurgled, spurting blood from the back of her throat. As the life faded from her, her head cocked to the left. One of the teeth punched through her left shoulder...right through the tattoo. The very same tattoo that covered her first injury.

The jaws tightened. Flesh split and bone crunched, and everything except Olivia's head, neck, and right shoulder slipped into Scar's gullet. The rest descended below, destined to be picked off by the crustaceans and tiny fish below.

CHAPTER 33

With Olivia Zoller and her hired guns dead, there was nothing left for the shark to feast on but Nick and Lisa. They clung to the back of the ship, which proceeded to sink into the ocean. They had maybe ten feet of deck between them and the waterline.

"You said the eyes and the gills were the most sensitive parts, right?" Nick said, while reloading the rifle.

"That and the back of its throat," Lisa replied.

"Yeah, I'm not keen on aiming there."

Lisa found a spotlight attached to the transom and panned it around the water in search of the fish. It was circling the boat, biding its time.

"Hey!" They turned to the north. David was coming in fast. In his hand was a lit stick of dynamite. The fuse was burning away rapidly, with only ten seconds to go and counting. "Where is it?!"

"Follow the light!" Lisa replied. The fish was circling around the rear of the ship, increasing speed after detecting David's movements. He shrieked, not expecting the shark to be so close. He threw the dynamite, which exploded along the surface right above Scar's head. The force of the blast drove the fish downward, shuddering its brain, and forcing an automatic flight response.

Lisa followed it with the spotlight, confirmed it had moved off, then signaled to David the path was clear for the moment. Nick pushed her over to him.

"Get on the jet ski."

She looked at the vehicle. There was enough space for her to cling on to, but not enough for a third person. She whipped back at Nick, who took control of the spotlight. He panned it across the water, while following it with the muzzle of his rifle. It was obvious what his plan was.

"I'm not leaving you here," she said. He looked back and, despite the tension and the rain pummeling his face, gave that charming smile he had.

"You're very sweet. But you've got to go. There's no time. That fish will come back any second now."

"If you stay here, you'll die!"

"If we all stay here, we're all dead," Nick said.

"Sheriff, it'll be a cold day in hell before I leave you here," David said.

"Sorry kid, but this boat's sinking, and you don't have enough fuel to be running back and forth with the shark. At this point, you probably barely have enough to get back." David's eyes went to the fuel gauge. Damn Sheriff was right again, as usual. "I'm giving you an order, Deputy. Get Lisa to safety. I'll keep the fish busy. You got any more of that dynamite?"

David tossed a couple of sticks to him along with Barney's lighter. Nick tucked them in his waist, then started climbing back up to the transom.

"Thanks. Now go."

"But Nick!" Lisa said. Her voice trailed off. There were so many things she wanted to say, but didn't have the time. It didn't matter; Nick knew. He planted a quick kiss on her lips, then guided her over to the jet ski. With reluctance, Lisa climbed aboard. Nick gave David a quick salute. "Thanks, Deputy. You did good work. Now GO!"

David hesitated briefly, nodded his farewell to the Sheriff he admired so greatly, then throttled the jet ski. Right away, he had to veer away, as the fish had suddenly appeared out of the swells.

"Holy—"

Its jaws slammed shut inches from his right leg. As he zipped past it, he felt the reverberation of its tail nicking the back of the jet ski. He glanced back at Lisa to make sure she wasn't injured, then proceeded to race southwest.

Nick didn't need the spotlight to see those red eyes. The beast was turning around to pursue the jet ski.

"Ah-ah, no you don't," he muttered. He shouldered the M4 and rained a dozen bullets over its head. The fish jerked violently, then gave up the chase to go after the easier prey. Nick watched the jet ski. It only took a few minutes for it to speed out of sight. Knowing David and Lisa were out of danger was a weight off his shoulders. Now, it was just him and the damn fish.

"Alright, you son of a bitch. You can eat me if you want, but I'll do my damnedest to make sure you get a bad case of the shits."

Scar raised his head out of the water and smashed through the gunwale on the starboard side. Debris erupted around Nick as though launched from a TNT explosion. The ship teetered, forcing Nick to scoot to the opposite side. He kept one hand on the guard rail. His rifle dangled from his shoulder, threatening to slide off along his arm.

Scar's mouth opened and shut, dripping bits of minced flesh onto the deck. With one hand holding himself up, Nick went for one of the dynamite sticks. The vessel shook underneath him, making it difficult to grab the lighter and get a flame. The one flame he did get was quickly extinguished by the rain.

"Oh, come on!" This couldn't be happening. He was in perfect position, at perfect range…all he needed to do was get that dynamite stick in its mouth. He yelled at the lighter, as though it had a cognitive ability to understand what he was saying. "Riding around on a jet ski, with rain and waves spraying you all the time, you spark a flame no problem. But for a guy simply standing on a deck, NOOOOOO! Gotta be a prick about it!"

Finally, he got a flame. He touched it to the tip of the fuse, which ignited into its small flame.

Before he could toss it at the fish, it slipped back into the water. Nick fell back against the gunwale as it teetered back to port. He still had the dynamite in hand, which was only seconds away from igniting. He looked into the water, spotted the red eyes, then threw the dynamite. He ducked as best as he could, then felt the resulting shockwave.

He looked again, initially seeing nothing but crashing waves. When the lightning flickered, he saw blood in the water. Already, he felt a sense of hopefulness. Was it dead? Did he hit it? Where the hell was it?

Scar answered that question with a bounding leap from the portside. Nick heard the splash and dove down onto the deck. Scar crashed against the fly deck with tremendous force that broke it clean off the ship. Pieces of the deck and pilothouse crumbled down, the weight of the fish driving the yacht into the sea even faster.

Nick pressed his hands against the deck to keep from sliding into the water. He could feel the edge encompassing his left hand. He had only five feet of deck remaining. The fly deck was now in shambles, the structure beneath it crushed like a soda can under a boot. Scar had slipped off and fell into the water again. When Nick got back to his feet, he caught a few quick glimpses of its eyes as it circled for another go. The lightning illuminated his blood trail.

Nick stood up, readied his weapon, and waited for the inevitable assault. Lightning flashed again. Scar was a dozen yards out, traveling along the surface. The dynamite blast had ripped up much of his flesh near his dorsal and right pectoral fin. There was some damage along his head, but not as much.

He aimed the M4, flipped the lever to semi-auto, and carefully aimed for the wounds. He squeezed the trigger repeatedly, punching rounds one at a time into the side of the fish. The first couple struck solid skin. The next one found its mark, vanishing in a small spurt of blood. Scar jerked away and swam under the water again.

"Come on. You're still hungry. I know it. Come on up. I got something for you…"

****

Both David and Lisa shrieked as the storm threw another wave at them. The jet ski rocked back and forth with the water. There was no sign of the island ahead nor the atoll. He had a general sense of direction, but wasn't sure how far he had gone, especially with the storm tossing him every which way.

Each hit they took slowed them down. David, an inexperienced jet skier, made the mistake of trying to drive at full throttle each time he accelerated, which ate up the fuel supply. Only when the engine started sputtering, did he realize his mistake.

The jet ski slowed.

"No," David muttered. He tried to accelerate, only making a few yards, before the vehicle died. "No, no, no! Oh, shit!"

"How far are we?" Lisa asked.

"I have no idea."

Both yelped as they were lifted up by a large swell, which proceeded to drop them like a rollercoaster car down its slope. David tried to think fast, which was difficult considering his predicament. He looked back, hearing gunshots behind the wailing thunder. Nick was still alive and in combat with the beast, which meant it wasn't chasing after them. That was a small relief…though it wouldn't save them from drowning.

He gasped again as another wave crashed from behind. The ocean spun the jet ski like a top, while torturing them with a chaotic mixture of rain, wind, and lightning.

After several tosses, the ocean threw its version of a left hook, which appeared in the form of a rolling wave which struck them from the right. The jet ski flipped over, sparking screams from both occupants before they plunged beneath the waves.

Lisa emerged first. "David!" She looked around but only saw thrashing waves—if she saw anything at all. It was so dark, and all of her efforts were dedicated to trying to stay afloat.

"Here!" His reply was muffled by sounds of struggle. Another lightning flash allowed Lisa to spot his waving hand. He was fifteen feet away. As she swam toward him, she could tell he was on the verge of going under. The pain in his shoulder was too much. In addition, he was losing blood again, and his energy was rapidly fading. She swam over to him and wrapped an arm around his waist, while paddling with the other in an attempt to stay afloat. However, the effort was quickly draining her energy as well. With no sign of land, both of them realized that certain death awaited.

"Well, I'd rather drown than get torn apart by that shark," David muttered.

"Same here," Lisa said. She kicked some more but felt herself starting to slip. She saw David dunk beneath the waves, which generated a few moments' worth of new energy. She grabbed him and yanked him back up. They would fight for every last moment of life they could.

"Come on. Don't give up." Even as she said it, she could feel herself losing strength. "Don't give up." She spoke weakly, like a patient being sedated before a surgery. Like an OR patient, she saw the bright operating lights. Probably the lightning. No…it was steady, not flashing. Probably a figment of her imagination. Maybe it was the first sign of Heaven. The thought was comforting. She listened. She heard something! A faint voice behind that light. God? She always wondered what He sounded like.

She never would've guessed He sounded like Barney Grey.

"I'm getting tired of saving your asses!"

Hope triggered new energy in the duo. Lisa's eyes widened, her vision focusing. She winced briefly as she gazed right into Barney's spotlight. He steered up alongside them with his rattling motor, then tossed them a line.

Lisa forced David to climb aboard first. The scrawny fisherman grabbed him by the shirt and pulled him onto the deck. David sat up and looked at Barney, amazed, thankful, and surprised.

"Barney?"

"Who else would it be?" Barney replied. "I'd say not all that blood is getting to your brain. Makes sense, because your dumbass reopened your wound." He helped Lisa aboard then assisted David into the wheelhouse where they jampacked his wound with fresh gauze. "Where's the Sheriff? Shark eat him?"

"He's back there," Lisa said. She pointed northeast.

"There? What about the fish?"

"He held it off for us to get away," David said.

"And a fine job you did at that," Barney replied. He looked northeast, then groaned loudly. *He's probably dead. Turn back. You did your good deed...* He groaned again. "Hold on." He pushed the throttle to its max. The bow split through the waves, making way for the journey to rescue the Sheriff.

CHAPTER 35

Nick followed the moving shape left to right with the muzzle of his rifle, the deafening reports competing with the intense thunder above. Again, Scar made an attempt to run at him, only to be driven off by well-placed rifle shots through his open wounds.

He had four feet of decking left. The sinking seemed to have slowed momentarily. Possibly an air pocket was keeping the vessel afloat. Whatever the reason, he had more time. More importantly, Nick was still alive and intended to stay that way for as long as possible.

"Where'd you go?" he muttered. He loaded a fresh magazine into his rifle. "Come on, Scar. I have a special treat for you…" He pulled the remaining dynamite stick from his waist, gave himself an inch-and-a-half of fuse, and watched for the fish.

The boat shook underneath him. The stern rose, the slope rapidly increasing. Almost immediately, he was starting to slip down the deck into the water. Nick threw his arms over the transom and hung there, looking down long enough to see that his feet were dangling freely.

He pulled himself over the rail and glanced into the water, catching a brief glance of the shark's bloodied dorsal fin. Its tail whipped back and forth beneath the waves, driving the stern up further.

Son of a bitch! The shark was *intentionally* creating a slope to cause him to fall into the water, like an orca hunting a seal on a floating glacier.

"Did the doc program strategic thought into this damn fish?!" Nick said to himself. He heard a dull *crack* from within the ship, and suddenly, the vessel was starting to sink again. So much for that air pocket.

With one arm over the gunwale, Nick grabbed the lighter and sparked a flame. He lit the dynamite, dropped it into the water, then braced for the inevitable explosion.

He felt the shockwave, then a brief sensation of freefall as the ship rocked back to its original sinking position. There was new blood in the water, along with bits of flesh rising with the swells. The waves were now reaching over the gunwale. Nick had three feet of deck left at most. He put a leg over the transom and mounted it like a horse.

His mind didn't bother with the usual questions of *did the blast kill the shark?* He knew it was alive. Wounded, but alive. And it would not stop for injuries. Injuries would heal. Healing required sustenance. And right now, Nick was the only immediate source of sustenance in Scar's proximity.

Pieces of wreckage floated around him like wasps congregating around a hive. A white bolt streaked across the clouds, lighting the ocean below. Nick watched for movement. His hand twitched near the trigger guard. The anticipation was doing its worst. Did the shark know psychological warfare as well?

Two feet of deck now.

Suddenly, it was obvious…the bastard was simply waiting for the boat to sink! Nick hated himself for using the last of the dynamite, and for not grabbing the grenades off Heitmeyer's corpse.

I could've at least gone out with a bang.

With that thought, the red eyes appeared under the water. The beast was twenty feet to his left and closing in fast. He threw himself over the side and plunged into the water. Scar had made his leap, his jaws finding nothing but decking. Teeth snapped off his gums. The fish battered the empty deck with his face and tail, his weight forcing the vessel under the waves completely.

In that short time, Nick managed to find a piece of the fly deck that was large enough to hold him up. His rifle had slipped off of his shoulder and sank into the abyss. With the exception of that dinky pocketknife he took from Olivia Zoller, he was defenseless.

The spotlights continued to glow underneath the water as the ship plunged to its final resting place. Scar continued to batter the ship, as though angry his meal wasn't aboard.

Nick sucked in a deep breath and held perfectly still, remembering what Lisa had told him before the mercenaries attempted to lower them into the water. He remained frozen like a statue. The only thing that moved were his eyes, which followed those of the shark as it started to search the surrounding water.

He took shallow breaths. His right hand gripped the small knife. If he was going to be swallowed, he'd make sure he'd give Scar a good deal of indigestion before he died.

Scar proceeded to search the water, his dorsal fin appearing, then disappearing, as he checked various depths. So far, it was working. Nick started feeling hopeful that maybe the fish would give up and swim away after a while. He hated that his mind went there, as the rational side of him knew the truth. Scar was not the kind to quit, especially not after the fight they'd just had.

His attention was so fixed on the beast that he never noticed the wave barreling down on him from behind his left shoulder. Nick was suddenly rolled forward, the decking ripped from his grasp.

With the ability to float naturally stripped from him, he was left with no choice but to kick and paddle. His stomach sank as he saw the red eyes turn in his direction.

"Fuck…"

Drawn by his movements, Scar began to close in. His head was above the waterline. His mouth was open, baring razor-sharp teeth that were ready to plunge into Nick's flesh like ice picks.

He winced, accepted his fate, and raised his knife in defiance.

"Bring it!"

Suddenly, Scar stopped, as his lateral line detected a series of approaching movement. Huge swells rolled in from the left. With those swells came earsplitting whistles. Six-foot dorsal fins rose from the water.

The fish didn't even have time to turn and meet the threat, as the pod of killer whales, led by Daisy, swarmed their nemesis. It was a hive mind of vengeance for their lost pod members. For Daisy, it was personal. She was at the front of the group, and was the first to slam into Scar, knocking him away from the human victim he tormented.

Fish and mammal rolled along the crashing waves, sending huge splashes reaching high into the air.

Nick backstroked away from the event, found the piece of wreckage, and grabbed hold of it. Tension gripped his body as he watched the battle ensue.

The orcas learned very quickly that their enemy was wounded this time, and therefore vulnerable. No longer did the fish have the near impenetrable skin that rendered their bites useless. The only obstacle they faced now was each other—as each of them wanted a piece of the action.

But none wanted it as bad as Daisy. With her youngster waiting a quarter mile back with the protection of another pod member, she pressed the attack. Cone-shaped teeth ripped into the open wound along Scar's back. She clenched down, then ripped side-to-side, widening the injury.

Meanwhile, one of her pod members, named Ralf by their human companion, assaulted Scar from the front. He bit on the shark's snout, unable to pierce the flesh, but creating enough of a distraction to allow Daisy to cause more damage to the vulnerable area.

Pain signals raced to Scar's brain. He needed to get out of this predicament or be torn wide open.

With a swing of his caudal fin, he lashed the face of another orca that attempted to bite down on the upper lobe, knocking it away. He swung again to his right, the tip lacerating the flesh under Daisy's left flipper.

She rolled away, driven both by impact and pain. But her need to kill quickly overpowered her sense of self-preservation. The injury was minute; nothing more than a small cut. It would heal within a week. The pain of losing Charlie, however, that was forever. No way would she ever let the creature responsible get away with it.

Scar struck at Ralf with his jaws, missing with the first bite, but succeeding with the second as the orca attempted to dive. His teeth sank along Ralf's upper tail. The orca's upper body swung up and down like a worm, driven by his attempts to wave his tail. Blood swirled from the wounds. Scar began to thrash, using his teeth as saws to widen the injury and sever the fluke.

Daisy struck again and pummeled Scar's gills with her snout, knocking him away from her companion, who retreated to the surface for a much needed breath of air. He sprayed water, filled his lungs, then dove again to rejoin the fight. The other orcas converged on the shark like a swarm of bees.

One of the females, Maureen, clenched Scar's caudal fin, while another, Holly, bit on the left pectoral fin. Scar barrel-rolled, swinging the two orcas with him. The fight led to the surface, where their enormous bodies created waves double the size of those created by the wind.

One of those waves grabbed hold of Nick and pushed him backward. He clutched the wreckage tightly as the force of the swell pushed him under the water. He floated back up, spat out a mouthful of saltwater, then continued to watch the battle take place.

He couldn't believe his eyes. It was the orca pod that Lisa had been feeding.

"God! If only she was here to see this," he said to himself. The words barely left his mouth when his ears picked up on the sound of a rattling engine. At first, he thought it was his imagination. Then he saw the spotlights.

Barney Grey?

The boat was closing in, with one spotlight focused on the marine creatures, while a couple of others panned across the water from the main deck. He saw two figures moving about. He raised his hand and shouted. Judging by the shifting of the lights, they heard him. They waved the white streams around until finally one of them centered on Nick.

"There he is!"

Nick recognized the voice. He thought Lisa should've been back on the island by now. He wasn't complaining, though.

Barney steered the boat up to him. Nick swam up along the portside then reached to grab Lisa's hand.

"Ah-ah!" Barney called out. He leaned over the gunwale at Nick. "You never gave me an answer regarding that six-burner grill!" He grinned, then reached down to help Lisa pull Nick aboard.

"You always were a prick, Barney," Nick said. He never thought he'd be so happy to step aboard Barney Grey's foul-smelling deck.

The intense sound of wailing drew their attention back to the fight.

Scar rolled again, prying himself loose from the grip of the two orcas that tried to pin him. A swing of his tail caught Maureen in the face with an impact intense enough to launch her out of the water.

He spun back, jaws open, aiming for a now-retreating Holly, only to be struck again by Daisy. The two giants raced alongside each other like NASCAR racers, each trying to gain distance over the other in order to position for an attack. Daisy slammed into the fish, knocking him to the left. He returned fire with a similar headbutt, bumping her back to the right. Being the larger animal, his blow was stronger than hers. However, it wasn't only body size that made all the difference in the fight, but brain size as well.

Daisy broke off the chase, but only enough to get Scar to slow down. She waited, saw him starting to circle back, then took off like a rocket. She aimed high, breached the water, then came down, jaws open wide, right on his back. Her teeth found the open wound, which instantly split two feet wider just by the sheer force of impact.

Blood spurted from Scar's back right into Daisy's mouth. Ralf and Holly closed in quickly. Sensing their approach, Scar swung his body with intense force. The timing was perfect. The caudal fin slapped Ralf across the snout, knocking him right into Holly. Both mammals twirled to the ocean depths, momentarily stunned by the blow.

Maureen, also somewhat dazed from the hit she received, raced down to get her companions to the surface for air.

The fight now was between Daisy and Scar.

The fish was stronger, and he knew it. All he needed to do was thrash his body wildly enough and he would be able to pry himself loose. He rolled, twisted, then swam in a wheel-like rotation. He arched forward and back, feeling the pain of flesh ripping from his body. That pain was a reminder that he was still alive...and freeing himself from his opponent's grasp.

Daisy fell away, her jaws clenching a two-foot strip of flesh. Scar swam off, trailing a thick cloud of blood. Despite the bleeding, his speed never diminished. He spun back around, fluttered his tail, and closed the distance. Daisy tried to move but wasn't fast enough.

She squealed in pain as Scar's jaws sank into her flesh, right behind her left dorsal fin. The shark kept moving forward, pushing the bleeding orca along the surface of the water. She wiggled with all of her might, but could not pry herself from his grip. With those serrated teeth embedded in her flesh, each movement achieved nothing but widening the individual wounds. She was helpless, forced to suffer the fate of her mate.

Scar pushed her along, his grip tight, his evil mind knowing he had become the victor in this dispute. Already, he was planning his next kill. He detected the movements of a human vessel, which was less than a hundred feet ahead. He saw the spotlights, which happened to sweep across his face. Near the source of that light, one of the humans stood with a projectile weapon in hand.

Barney Grey put his eye along the iron sights of his shotgun.
"You ripped my trawl net."
He squeezed the trigger and shuddered with the recoil of the weapon. The buck shot struck Scar's left eye, exploding it into a gooey strand of meat.

Pain and blindness struck at once. Scar jerked to the right, his grip on Daisy loosening. Sensing the decrease in pressure, the orca pried herself from his jaws and raced out of his reach.

The fish circled, not understanding why half of his vision had suddenly vanished.

Suddenly, more loud *cracks* filled the air, and all at once, Scar's body was assaulted by the stings of numerous projectiles.

With David's service pistol in hand, Nick fired at the open wound along the shark's back. To his right, Barney blasted at its head, landing some of the pellets inside the exposed eye socket. Lisa stood at the transom with the Beretta extended. She fired several shots at the gill slits and eye, seeing a few resulting spurts of blood.

Scar turned back and forth, his senses overwhelmed. He couldn't smell anything but his own blood. There was movement everywhere, both by the storm and the killer whales. The constant assault made it impossible to become accustomed to the loss of vision in his left eye.

The angry whistles from the pod filled the ocean. The four orcas, led by Daisy, had regrouped and charged for another attack. The humans ceased fire as their allies of the sea took over.

Maureen grabbed the caudal fin again. Holly and Ralf took the pectoral fins, wrestling the shark into submission. With her opponent immobile, Daisy went for the head—specifically, the right eye. She extended her jaws and slammed them down on Scar's face, and tasted the blood of his exploding eye as one of her teeth punched through it.

Scar was completely blind now. With his senses overloaded, all he could do was thrash about.

Daisy's teeth raked the eye socket as she pulled away. She circled around then made another run, this time biting the dorsal fin. She tugged at the cartilage, the flesh around it peeling back from the open wound. With all of her might, she yanked up, tearing the fin clean off the shark's back. A fountain of blood sprayed like magma from a volcano.

She spat the fin from her teeth then raced at Scar again, this time going for the face. She slowed just in time to avoid his snapping jaws. Scar bit aimlessly at the water around him, desperately trying to grab ahold of one of his opponents. Daisy watched the jaw open and shut, then whistled at Ralf. The male released his grip on the pectoral fin, swam high, then slammed his jaws shut over Scar's shout. At the same time, Daisy raced forward again, positioned herself under Scar's chin, then bit down on his lower jaw.

As they pulled his mouth in separate directions, Holly rejoined Maureen at the caudal fin, eliminating any chance for Scar to whip his tail.

The flesh split at the corners of his mouth.

Still, Scar wasn't intent on losing. He twisted his body again, driving the fight back to the surface. The orcas rolled with him, still prying his mouth apart. Despite their advantage in numbers, the sheer physical strength of the shark was overwhelming. With each roll, their grip started to slip. Even blind and wounded, Scar was as ferocious an opponent as anything they'd ever met. And now, he was desperate.

A wounded animal was the worst kind, and Scar was already the worst kind to start with.

"Come on! You can do it," Lisa shouted at the orcas.

"He's too freaking strong," David said. Nick shook his head. No way was he going to see this shark escape.

"Barney, where's that Winchester of yours?" Nick said. Barney pointed at the wheelhouse. Nick rushed inside, found the weapon in a case on the righthand side, already loaded.

He stepped out, cocked the lever, and aimed it at the fish. It spun to its right, throwing the orcas about. It was facing away from the boat. Nick fired a few shots, two of which struck solid flesh, the other entering an open wound. The shark didn't even seem to register the new injury.

He needed to get a bullet through its mouth.

"Come on. Drag him this way."

The struggle continued. The orcas were quickly losing their grip. The fish was moments away from escaping. David shone the spotlight on them, helping Nick to make his aim.

Still, the shark was facing away.

Lisa felt her blood rush. An idea came to her mind. Far-fetched but worth a shot. She leaned over the gunwale as far as she could then performed the same whistle she used when getting their attention during feeding.

Water splashed as the orcas whistled back. In one unanimous move, they spun Scar to the right like a top, facing his open jaws at the ship. He whipped his head to and fro, inches away from freeing himself from their grip.

"Swallow *this*," Nick said. With a thunderous echo, he sent a round spiraling straight into the creature's mouth. With Scar's head angled up, it punched through the roof of his mouth. The fish spasmed as the bullet cut through a series of nerves leading from its brain into its tail.

Daisy and Ralf seized the moment and fixed their grips on the open mouth. They pulled back, hyperextending the jaws. The edges split further. Blood trickled out, first in small spurts, then in thick fountains.

Simultaneously, the orcas ripped back. Finally, that fountain of blood became a wall of red. Scar's mouth split apart, his lower jaw dangling by a few strands of flesh.

Lisa threw a fist in the air. "YEAH!"

The dead shark spiraled to the depths, and without the glowing red eyes, it was quickly lost to the darkness.

The orcas breached the water, victorious. Lisa cheered again, then embraced Nick in a tight hug.

Barney watched the orcas dance around his vessel. He placed the shotgun down. His attempt to look as though he didn't care failed miserably. He smiled ear-to-ear as the creatures that saved his life gazed back at him. They swam around for a few more minutes, then dove again to regroup with the youngster.

The rain intensified, as though to remind the humans that a storm was still raging.

"Don't know about you, but I've had enough shark hunting for one day," Barney said. He hurried into the pilothouse and steered toward Cross Point.

Nick remained on deck with Lisa and David. He put a hand on the young Deputy's good shoulder.

"You did good."

David smiled. "Thanks."

"I will say though, the way you throw wide, no wonder you floundered during the tryouts."

David grinned, then chuckled, which elevated into a full laugh which the three of them shared all the way back home.

CHAPTER 36

Sheriff Nick Piatt leaned back in his office chair, his eyes fixed on the article on his computer monitor.

Skomal Corp investigated for illegal animal research. Suspected involvement in tragedy near Virginia Coast.

Good thing ol' Scar didn't swallow the mercenary Heitmeyer's body, allowing it to be picked up by the Coast Guard, who linked him to Roark's group, which in turn led them to the wreckage, which they traced back to a facility near Virginia Beach. Even better, the findings allowed the Coast Guard and Navy to track the mercenaries' connection to another group suspected in the cruise liner bombings.

Once in a while, justice actually manages to get served, Nick thought.

His phone vibrated. It was Lisa.

"Hey. Wanna meet my new friends?"

Nick texted *"Be right there,"* then got up out of his chair. He left his office and immediately saw David in the lobby, slipping a piece of paper into his mailbox. Nick was surprised to see him, as he was supposed to be on leave for another two weeks to recover from his injury. Nick recognized the form he was turning in; *Time Off Request.*

"Look at you, lazy ass. Already trying to get more time off." They both smiled. "How's the arm?"

David looked down at his sling. "A little sore, but I should get full range of motion back in a few months."

"I'm glad to hear. So, what's the occasion?" Nick asked, gesturing at the form.

David smiled again. "Something important came up."

"Yeah? What?"

David pulled out his iPhone and connected to the internet. He found the article and handed it over to Nick.

"Tryouts, huh?" He looked back at the rookie. "Gonna give it another shot?"

"I think so," David said.

"Which team?"

"Detroit."

Nick laughed. "Shouldn't be too hard. All you need is to throw a ball in a general forward direction, you'll be head and shoulders above the current pitchers!" He handed the phone back, then slapped him on the uninjured shoulder. "Good for you kid. When is it?"

"Upcoming spring. Gives me plenty of time to get my arm back into shape."

"Good luck, kid. Let me know how it goes," Nick said. He started for the door.

"Busy day?" David asked.

"Lisa's got some new assistants. She wants me to meet them."

"Mind if I tag along?"

"Feel free."

****

They saw Lisa's vessel as they arrived at the pier. It was docked, with Lisa spraying down the deck with a hose. There was someone else there with her. Even as they approached, Barney Grey looked unrecognizable. Probably because he looked happy for the first time in his life.

Nick and David stepped from the truck and approached the dock. Right away, they heard the barking of seals.

Nick chuckled. All this time, he thought Lisa was joking about using seals for her research. On the deck were seal harnesses attached with underwater cameras.

"Looks like I'll be staying here longer than I anticipated," she said. "The Institution wants some underwater footage of the area."

Nick was glad to hear it.

"Any idea how long?"

"Years, it's looking like," she replied. She wiped her hands clean and approached him. "Maybe longer."

"I guess I'll have to keep my eye on you then," he joked, jabbing his thumb into his badge. He glanced at Barney, who was busy tending to the seals on deck. "The Institution approved his status as a research assistant?"

"It took a little persuading," Lisa said. Nick smiled. In all the years of seeing Barney Grey as a cantankerous fisherman who used depth charges and drift nets, it was nice to see he found a LEGAL means of income. He could hear him talking to the seals like a bunch of puppies.

"Oh, who's my buddy? Oh, you are!"

David walked up the dock and looked at the former fisherman and his new friends.

"Look at that! I can't even tell who's who," he joked.

"Watch it, kid," Barney said. "I know which shoulder hurts."

Lisa chuckled after watching their exchange. "He might need a little bit of retraining, but I think he'll be fine."

"Looks like it." Nick cleared his throat. "So? What are you doing at five?"

Lisa's eyebrows raised. "Should be wrapping up by then. You have plans?"

"Perhaps."

"Is it what I think it is?"

"Ohhhh yeah," Nick said with a wink.

"We've been doing it quite a bit. Won't you ever get enough?"

"Hell no. It'll be better this time."

"Yeah? How?"

Nick smiled, pulled out his phone, and showed her the recent order that arrived that morning.

Lisa glanced at the images, then laughed. "Killer shark targets?"

"Hey. You never know! We might need the practice!"

Lisa shook her head, laughed, then pulled him in close for a kiss.

The End

CHECK OUT OTHER GREAT DEEP SEA THRILLERS

THE BREACH
by Edward J. McFadden III

A Category 4 hurricane punched a quarter mile hole in Fire Island, exposing the Great South Bay to the ferocity of the Atlantic Ocean, and the current pulled something terrible through the new breach. A monstrosity of the past mixed with the present has been disturbed and it's found its way into the sheltered waters of Long Island's southern sea.

Nate Tanner lives in Stones Throw, Long Island. A disgraced SCPD detective lieutenant put out to pasture in the marine division because of his Navy background and experience with aquatic crime scenes, Tanner is assigned to hunt the creeper in the bay. But he and his team soon discover they're the ones being hunted.

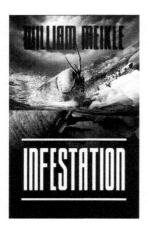

INFESTATION
by William Meikle

It was supposed to be a simple mission. A suspected Russian spy boat is in trouble in Canadian waters. Investigate and report are the orders.

But when Captain John Banks and his squad arrive, it is to find an empty vessel, and a scene of bloody mayhem.

Soon they are in a fight for their lives, for there are things in the icy seas off Baffin Island, scuttling, hungry things with a taste for human flesh.

They are swarming. And they are growing.

"Scotland's best Horror writer" - Ginger Nuts of Horror

"The premier storyteller of our time." - Famous Monsters of Filmland

CHECK OUT OTHER GREAT
DEEP SEA THRILLERS

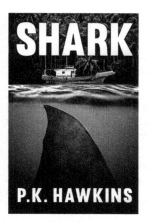

SHARK: INFESTED WATERS
by **P.K. Hawkins**

For Simon, the trip was supposed to be a once in a lifetime gift: a journey to the Amazon River Basin, the land that he had dreamed about visiting since he was a child. His enthusiasm for the trip may be tempered by the poor conditions of the boat and their captain leading the tour, but most of the tourists think they can look the other way on it. Except things go wrong quickly. After a horrific accident, Simon and the other tourists find themselves trapped on a tiny island in the middle of the river. It's the rainy season, and the river is rising. The island is surrounded by hungry bull sharks that won't let them swim away. And worst of all, the sharks might not be the only blood-thirsty killers among them. It was supposed to be the trip of a lifetime. Instead, they'll be lucky if they make it out with their lives at all.

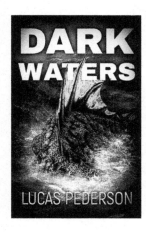

DARK WATERS
by **Lucas Pederson**

Jörmungandr is an ancient Norse sea monster. Thought to be purely a myth until a battleship is torn a part by one.

With his brother on that ship, former Navy Seal and deep-sea diver, Miles Raine, sets out on a personal vendetta against the creature and hopefully save his brother. Bringing with him his old Seal team, the Dagger Points, they embark on a mission that might very well be their last.

But what happens when the hunters become the hunted and the dark waters reveal more than a monster?

CHECK OUT OTHER GREAT
DEEP SEA THRILLERS

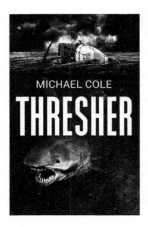

THRESHER
by Michael Cole

In the aftermath of a hurricane, a series of strange events plague the coastal waters off Florida. People go into the water and never return. Corpses of killer whales drift ashore, ravaged from enormous bite marks. A fishing trawler is found adrift, with a mysterious gash in its hull.

Transferred to the coastal town of Merit, police officer Leonard Riker uncovers the horrible reality of an enormous Thresher shark lurking off the coast. Forty feet in length, it has taken a territorial claim to the waters near the town harbor. Armed with three-inch teeth, a scythe-like caudal fin, and unmatched aggression, the beast seeks to kill anything sharing the waters.

THE GUILLOTINE
by Lucas Pederson

1,000 feet under the surface, Prehistoric Anthropologist, Ash Barrington, and his team are in the midst of a great archeological dig at the bottom of Lake Superior where they find a treasure trove of bones. Bones of dinosaurs that aren't supposed to be in this particular region. In their underwater facility, Infinity Moon, Ash and his team soon discover a series of underground tunnels. Upon exploring, they accidentally open an ice pocket, thawing the prehistoric creature trapped inside. Soon they are being attacked, the facility falling apart around them, by what Ash knows is a dunkleosteus and all those bones were from its prey. Now...Ash and his team are the prey and the creature will stop at nothing to get to them.

Made in the USA
Middletown, DE
16 December 2021

56148265R00116